I0623120

Last Line
(Book 1)

Last Line
(Book 1)

Harper Fox

FoxTales

FoxTales Publications
www.harperfox.net

Last Line (Book 1)
Copyright © 2014 by Harper Fox
ISBN 978-1-910224-25-0

Cover art by Lou Harper
All rights reserved

No part of this book may be reproduced or transmitted in any form or by any means, electronic or mechanical, including photocopying, recording, or by any information storage and retrieval system, without written permission from FoxTales.

This is a work of fiction. Any resemblance to persons living or dead is entirely coincidental.

Chapter One

The edge of the Arctic Circle, Zemelya Province
2008

The young British agent had hung on to who he was for a long time.

Lukas Oriel looked at him. He was bolt upright in his wooden chair. No need to tie him there anymore. He was physically docile, though his dark eyes blazed defiance. Candlelight flickered on his skin.

To Oriel, he was beautiful. Naked but for a torn pair of jeans. Short black hair spiked and dirty, still catching the candle-flame glow. The fire adored him. He was stripped of his spare weight and beginning to lose muscle mass under Oriel's regime of careful starvation, but still the red-gold light caressed him, picking out the crests of his collarbones, the traces of the formidable six-pack that lingered on his solar plexus.

The two men faced each other, each in his plain wooden chair. The cavernous room stretched out all round them. Deep underground, no sound reached it from the outside. Other chairs, rows and rows of them, extended into the shadows. Oriel and his prisoner were sitting in front of a huge makeshift altar, a missile crate veiled in a white cloth.

"Michael," Oriel said. "Do you know who I am?"

"You're Lukas Oriel."

Oriel nodded, impressed. The other agents he had captured had been speechless by this time. "*Father* Lukas," he corrected gently. "And have I hurt you?"

The strained figure jerked in his chair. He was tugging, Oriel knew, on invisible bonds. His hands were behind him, tendons in his shoulders standing stark. "Yes, you bastard. You've drugged me. You don't let me sleep. You've tied me in this bloody chair…"

"But you're not tied, Michael."

Dark eyes flickered wide. For a moment they fixed on Oriel, incredulous. Then the prisoner slowly drew his hands round from behind his back. He looked at his wrists. The marks of ropes were there, but they were free. A faint, rough sound escaped him— something between a sob and a groan. The prisoner sank his face into his hands. "What the fuck have you done to me?"

"I've drugged you, as you say. Deprived you of sleep and daylight. Taken everything from you that might help you remember what you are, where you come from. And why have I done these things?"

Michael raised his head. He began his recitation softly. It was rote to him by now, but still his deep voice cracked on it, as if the words hurt him, finding their way free. "Because a British fighter jet brought down a Zemel warhead on a test flight. Because the warhead landed… on Dorva, your capital."

Oriel nodded. He was rocking slightly, letting his eyes close. "Yes. Bad enough. Go on."

"The city was destroyed, the land round it radioactive and toxic for miles. The British and US governments sent aid, but that soon stopped…"

"Yes. Why?"

"Because Zemelya wasn't meant to have nuclear weapons. Banned by international law. The governments said it served them right. Taught them a lesson. Leave them to burn…" Michael shuddered. He jerked upright, as if trying to shake himself clear of mud. When he spoke again, his voice was his own, the rote's dull rhythms gone. "Oh God, Oriel! A few politicians said that, not the people! Not…" He swallowed audibly, a dry scrape. "Not me."

"Nevertheless you represent your people, Michael. You're a loyal MI5 agent. You came here to track me down. Can you still remember why?"

Oriel watched him struggle. His conditioning was grossly flawed. The fires of the man captured six months before still flared out. He was perfect.

"You're a menace," he grated out. "You call yourself the angel of these people, but you're their bloody demon. There would've been more aid, more help. But you… you set yourself up as a prophet, a priest, and they believed in you. You made them blame every outsider, every immigrant, for what's happened here. You started a genocide."

He broke off, coughing harshly. Oriel leaned toward him and, with every appearance of tenderness, pushed his hair off his brow. Michael recoiled beneath the touch. "Why?" Oriel asked him softly. "Tell me. You know well enough by now."

"To take revenge. You've got military scientists, government men, working for you. You think you can set up as God in this wasteland bloody forest of yours, in these bunkers. God with an arsenal of nukes, ready to rain down hell on the West. And for some unknowable reason… " Michael hauled in a breath and sat gasping for a moment before he could go on. "You think I'm going to help you. Be your ally, your… your right-hand man."

Oriel stirred. The thick black cloth of his cassock, its long skirts, impeded his movement. Standing, he reached to place his hands on his prisoner's shoulders. Broad shoulders, generous. Oriel's thin fingers moved over them like claws. "Don't you feel it in your*self* yet, Michael?" he hissed. "The power, the love of fire? Cold plutonium fire, the fire that comes from the earth—my earth?"

He slid one hand coldly down Michael's damp-skinned chest. Down farther—over the taut belly, down and between the strong thighs. Oriel fastened a grasp on his prisoner's cock. "Don't you feel it?"

Michael stared up at him. The bondage conditioning was strong; he had put his hands behind the back of the chair again, as if his wrists were tied. But his eyes were clear. They gleamed with deep, ineradicable amusement as Oriel stood over him. "No, you fucking nutcase," he said distinctly. "I do not."

Oriel let him go. He took one step back, far enough to get range. Then he raised his right fist, swung it to his left shoulder, and drove it down into Michael's face, a terrible slicing backhand arc that knocked him from his chair to the floor. He was helpless to save himself. His muscles were under Oriel's will, even if his mind was still free.

His mind was the only part of him Oriel wanted. He delivered a kick to his prisoner's gut. Michael took it in silence, trying to curl up against his invisible bonds. Oriel aimed the next blow at his testicles. The next and the next, and finally Michael wrenched over onto his stomach, loosing a harsh cry of pain.

It was enough. Oriel fell back, breathing hard. He ran his hands over his hair, collecting himself. After a moment, he was ice again, his passion spent.

He looked into the shadows that danced in the eastern quarter of his makeshift church. He smoothed the front of his cassock. "Anzhel," he said quietly. "Come here."

The figure that detached itself from the uneasy light would have been striking anywhere. In Criel's underground kingdom, where no daylight came, he was like a morning breeze. His grace colluded with his fine, proud build to make a music of his motions. His fair hair framed a face of easy perfection; his sweet smile kindled in eyes of summer-sky blue. He looked... ordinary, if ordinary could be the absolute daily-bread goodness of the world. He looked like someone's well-loved son.

He crouched beside Michael. The prisoner had vomited from the pain and the blows to his gut. Carefully Anzhel raised him out of the mess. He drew him into his lap. He produced a spotless white handkerchief with the gesture of unfolding a wing, and cleaned his mouth with tender care. "Poor Mikhaili," he said. Then he looked up at Oriel and smiled. "You want me to break him for you."

Oriel nodded. "The physical conditioning is there. But I can't reach inside him. And I need him, Anzhel."

"Can I do as I wish with him?"

"Oh, I understand your type of genius needs free rein." Oriel crouched too, tipping his head thoughtfully. Michael was fighting for consciousness, but Anzhel's embrace could soothe away a world of pain. "If you succeed, he's yours, once he's done his work for us. Would you like that?"

Anzhel gave him a look of melting pleasure. "I'd love it, Lukas. I've been watching this one. I almost hoped you'd fail, that you'd need me. He's so strong. The other MI5 men snapped like brittle twigs."

"Well, he's one of us, in a way. His mother was a Zemel refugee who fled to England before he was born. It's part of why he was chosen for this mission, his knowledge of our language and our ways." Oriel paused, considering. "Yes. His mother. You might use that."

"I will." Anzhel leaned over the struggling man in his arms. "They've been keeping you awake, haven't they?" he whispered, cradling him. "It's all right now, Mikhaili. You can sleep a little now."

Oriel sat back on his heels. "You're a ruthless bastard, aren't you, Anzhel?" He waited until the cornflower eyes came up to meet his, full of their own soft light. Then he nodded in satisfaction. "Yes. My left-hand man."

* * *

Michael ran through the forest. He couldn't remember beginning to, but now that he was out here, he found it hard to care. The night air was sweet in his lungs. Rain drifted down in sheets, silvered by a cloud-hidden moon.

Anzhel was running ahead of him. His skin was smudged by charcoal, and he had a black wool hat pulled down over shining hair that would otherwise capture the moonlight and glow like a beacon. He and Michael were wearing night-camouflage fatigues. They were nearly there.

Where? Michael tried to give it thought. They'd been on the run for about an hour now, he reckoned, and—yes, it was coming back—in military Jeeps for an hour before that. They'd left the vehicles hidden among the trees. Oriel's HQ must be miles behind them. But where the hell were they going?

Anzhel crouched at the top of a ridge ahead of him, gesturing for a halt. Michael dropped beside him. He must be careful to hide his confusion. If there was one clear certainty left to him, it was that he had to stick close to Anzhel Mattvei. Anzhel would lead him to Lukas Oriel, the nutcase dictator who'd taken over Zemelya in the wake of the Dorva nuclear blast. It had taken Michael nearly a year to infiltrate the paranoid religious right who followed him, three months after that to track down his bunker HQ in the forest. He couldn't recall getting there, but that didn't matter at the moment. Anzhel trusted him. Anzhel took him on missions like this one. Anzhel would lead him to Oriel, and then…

Then Michael's work would be done. He could escape. Perhaps he could go home.

"How far now?" he whispered. The scent of resin and rich earth was making his head spin a little. He was very aware of Anzhel—the warmth emanating from him, the fresh enticing tang of his sweat. Michael remembered less and less about his life prior to being sent on the Zemelya job, but he did know he'd been fighting a losing battle against his lifelong, bone-deep attraction to other men. This would be a bad place to surrender. Disastrous, he knew, with Anzhel Mattvei, but the man was so beautiful. Warm and close, calling like a siren…

"Are you all right, Mikhaili?"

He jerked back to reality. Anzhel's concerned gaze was on him, cobalt in the moonlight. "Yes. Fine."

"It's been a long run, I know. But you've done well. You move more quietly than I do now and faster than any of the others." He paused, smiling, and Michael fought a childish rush of pride. "It's not far. Look. Those are their fires over there."

Fires between the trees, like heaped rubies and gold. Michael was much closer to them now. He shuddered in disorientation, reaching into the gap. He had been up on the ridge. And now he was down here, within fifty paces of those fires. He had to be careful. The Zemel insurgents, ruthless paramilitaries who opposed Oriel's rise to power, were experts in forest warfare. Any number of snipers could be waiting, hidden among the pines. This peaceful campsite—the groups of brightly dressed women and children, clustering round the fires—could be a trap. Michael walked silently, taking his cue from Anzhel. For the first time, he was glad of the brutal Glock semi strapped to his belt.

Two men were sitting at the edge of the clearing. If they were on guard duty, it wasn't serious. Both were unarmed, chatting, faces turned to the light. They scrambled to their feet at Anzhel's approach, dropping chicken legs, raising their hands in surrender. One of them glanced over his shoulder. "Piotr!" he cried, then fell silent as the muzzle of Anzhel's rifle dug into his chest.

A hush descended on the clearing. A few women reached for their kids, and then all movement ceased. Michael wanted to close his eyes. The dawning fear in all those faces weighed on him, bruised him. He was tired. "Anzhel," he said. "These aren't soldiers. They're *Ashkeloi*—gypsies."

"That's what they'd like you to believe," Anzhel said pleasantly. "Insurgents hide out with the Ashkeloi all the time. Like baby cuckoos in other birds' nests."

"Not here, they don't!"

Anzhel and Michael both turned at the new voice. It belonged to a dark-clad man who had emerged from the crowd at his companion's summoning cry. He was striding fearlessly toward them. Michael caught Anzhel's curt nod and reluctantly raised his Glock. "These people are refugees," the newcomer continued, not slowing. "Refugees from your war, if you're Lukas Oriel's soldiers. The Ashkeloi camping grounds are clicking-hot toxic, so they've retreated here. How far would you have us go?"

"Me?" Anzhel's voice was soft as ever. Reasonable, calm. "I'd have you gone entirely. That's why we're here. Isn't it, Mikhaili?"

"What?" Michael glanced at him. Suddenly he felt as if chilly water were rising up over his chest. The world was tilting backward. "No," he rasped. "You said they were terrorists, paramilitaries."

"They're different. They don't belong to Father Lukas. That's all you need to know." Still holding his man at rifle point, Anzhel unhitched the pistol from his belt with his free hand. He gave Michael a compassionate look. "Here, it's okay. I'll show you what to do."

The pistol barked. Michael watched—though his eyes didn't feel like his own—as a hole burst open in the Ashkeloi leader's chest, and he dropped to his knees, then crashed facedown into the pine needles.

Time slowed. The cold water rose over Michael's mouth. He choked against it, snatched a breath, and felt it come again. All round him a chaotic circus was unfolding, and he was unable to account for any part of it. Couldn't account for himself. He was running in the midst of Anzhel's men. Their guns were firing and his was too, though the spasm that had closed his grip on the trigger hadn't been an effort of his will. The Ashkeloi were scattering, falling. Their shrieks ripped the night.

Except for one. One woman, still sitting calmly by the fire. Her hands were folded in her lap and she was singing—a plaintive Zemel cradle song Michael had known all his life. Her face was hidden in the shadows of a brightly patterned shawl.

Michael tripped and fell at her feet. He landed on his back somehow, and at that point the sensation of drowning became unbearable. He tried to scream, but his lungs were full and no sound came.

He was strapped to a bench in an interrogation cell. He was being waterboarded. Intellectually he knew these things, just as he knew that whenever the torture stopped, the song that filled the room came from speakers. That the melody had been forcibly dug out from among his earliest memories—his mother's lullaby, all he had left of her. These things were simple enough. He fought to the surface. "Fuck off, you bastards! Let me alone!"

The bench he was lying on dipped. Once his head was lower than his feet, someone—not Anzhel, some cold stranger with no scent at all—would pour water onto his face from a bucket or a hose. He couldn't tell which. He was blindfolded, heavy wet cloth draped from his brow to his chin. The water, when it came, was never much. It didn't have to be. Immediately it filled his nose and sinus cavities, triggering every reflex of drowning. As torture went, it was so subtle a form that the ink was still fresh on legislation classifying it as such, although the CIA agents who'd volunteered as test subjects had lasted fourteen seconds max.

Michael could do better than that. He could hold on long enough to dream a forest massacre. To believe in it too. He was breaking. The cold tide rose. His dive reflex, worn to fragments though it was, closed off his throat, hurling his whole body in bruising spasm against its restraints. This was the eighteenth time. Michael could withstand twenty or so before he lost consciousness. Not so very long to go...

He couldn't bear it. Not this time; not another vision of firelight and blood. The water battering his face became a trickle and stopped, and the cloth was snatched away, letting him suck air and desperately cough his lungs clear. "Anzhel!" he choked out. "Stop it, for Christ's sake. Please!"

The magic word. In the silence that followed, Michael almost laughed. He forgot, from session to session, that all he had to do was beg. It was equally hard for him, every single time, to get to that point. "Please, Anzhel," he repeated, loathing himself. Trying to reinforce the memory of what it took. There was a faint clatter, his unseen torturer setting down the bucket on the tiles. Footsteps retreated. A metal door clicked shut.

He was alone. And the cradle song started again.

"Oh, poor brave Mikhaili—it took you a long time today."

Anzhel was there with him. There was another gap in his head, a cold blank sea between the shore of his last memory and this beach he was washed up on now, gasping painfully, head twisting to follow the new voice. "Anzhel. Untie me."

"You know I can't do that. I'll take off your blindfold, though, if you lie still."

Fingers at the back of his neck—knifing pain as the neon contracted his pupils to pinpricks. For a while he could see nothing but white. Then Anzhel's face resolved itself out of the glare. Michael's deprived vision sucked him in, and there was nothing—nothing at all—to distinguish his smile from the real thing. The puzzled concern on his brow was as real and as sweet as if Michael were his brother. "You know you've only got to ask me nicely for the games to stop," he said. "Here. Let's sit you up a bit."

"Take these bloody straps off me. *Please.*"

Anzhel chuckled. "Ah, that doesn't work for everything." He reached to pull a lever, and the bench tipped forward, bringing Michael almost upright. His legs wouldn't bear his weight. The straps round his wrists snapped brutally tight as he slid downward. "Sorry," Anzhel said, making a face of genuine compassion. "Someone will come along and release you soon enough. Feed you too, and get you warm and dressed. I need you out with me tonight."

"Out... " Michael shivered, becoming aware of his nakedness. "Out where?"

"Another mission. Deep in the woods this time, farther than you've ever been."

"But those are just... hallucinations. I don't really go anywhere."

Anzhel looked up at him enquiringly. He had produced a big white towel and was crouched at Michael's feet, beginning a brisk rubbing motion. "Hallucinations? Why would I do that to you?"

"How the hell should I know?" Michael clenched his fists, tried to steel himself against the delicious warmth. Against the joy of being touched, after—how long alone on the bench in this desolate room? He'd lost all sense of time. "But I couldn't do those things—not the things we do when we're out in the forest. I couldn't... "

"Kill all those people?"

"I couldn't. They're dreams."

"But you're different when you're with me. Aren't you?" Anzhel stroked the towel up over Michael's knees and thighs. The movements began to restore his circulation, and he found that he could stand. "Don't you remember the Ashkeloi leader? And the woman who sang by the fire?"

Michael swallowed hard. He turned his head aside, squeezing his eyes closed. "No," he rasped, and didn't know if he was denying Anzhel's knowledge of his dreams—which meant that they weren't dreams at all—or the slow, terrible awakening of pleasure inside the curve of his tailbone. There between his balls and his anus—so deep, the fiery snake that could uncoil and blaze in spirals up and round his spine... "Stop. Get out of my head, Anzhel. Get your hands off me."

"Just drying you." Anzhel's gaze focused, a grin of innocent mischief making it gleam. "Ah. Don't tell me you don't enjoy it."

No. Mortified, Michael writhed to be away. The towel was brushing his groin now. He knew the involuntary nature of male sexual response—that, correctly handled, he could get aroused and come in almost any circumstances. *But not here.* The voice inside him howled. *God, not in the hands of this smiling monster.*

His feet slipped on the wet tiles. His wrists jerked down through the restraints, and pain like lightning bolts shot through him as the leather ripped skin off places already bleeding and bruised to the bone. He welcomed it—chased it, seeking its remedy to his helpless erection. Then Anzhel set the towel aside. "Mikhaili," he said, sliding his warm hands round behind Michael, tenderly cupping his backside. "Don't worry. It's only because you've been tormented, and mine is the only kindly touch you've known. That's all."

He opened his mouth and engulfed Michael's shaft. Shuddering, Michael pulled on his restraints, but this time the pain of it bonded to the unwanted pleasure, and he was lost. His mind closed down. For the first time since his capture he wept, thrusting into Anzhel's throat, coming almost instantly in a bitter rush that scoured him, destroyed him, wiped out the neon to black.

Chapter Two

West Kensington, London
2011

Covert Six headquarters—almost as anonymous as a bunker in the forest. Michael, half an hour early for his shift, stopped to lean on the railings of the dingy little West Ken square. Nothing much had changed since Victorian nannies had come here to wheel their charges in perambulators round the bushes. The redbrick walls of Guardian Chambers still loomed on all four sides, a pool of lingering night even at seven on a bright May morning.

A horrible place to work, really. The tide of regeneration that had swept through this part of the city had receded, leaving C6 beached, unrepentantly free of air conditioning, open plan, and natural daylight. Its corridors still smelled of dust. And, to the handful of men who worked there, it wasn't known as C6 at all. It was Last Line.

The western wall—where Sir James Webb, Michael's boss, kept his kingdom on the top three floors—was still punctuated by neon-lit windows. Sunshine seldom fought its way up there, even in the height of summer. Michael had no idea why the prospect of another day in its grim confines made him feel so bloody happy.

A window screeched—the sound of a sash being forced up past its dry rot and ancient paint. Casually Michael turned away to face the railings. He propped one trainer-clad foot on the low wall and began his stretches. His current flat was within jogging distance of Last Line, but only just. It was a hard run, and he'd need a shower—if he dared risk the clattering 1950s plumbing…

"Mike!"

Ducking his head, concealing a smile, Michael continued his little charade of oblivion. He wasn't sure why. It was part of the same impulse that had stopped him outside the building in the first place. His life in the service of Sir James was often lived at white-hot speed. He didn't often take the time to consider its miracles. Ordinary mornings. Deep dreamless sleep. His health, his sanity…

"Mike, come *on*. The sodding kettle's bust again."

John.

Michael straightened, letting the man leaning out of the window see that he could see him. Not an obvious miracle, John Griffin, with his hair still damp and his Merseyside baritone ringing off the redbrick. Impatient. Touchy as a wildcat until he got his caffeine fix, and somehow he was the kiss of death with electronics, leaving a trail of crashed computers and burned-out kitchenware behind him everywhere. He was a pain in the arse. He was also Michael's partner, and—most ordinary miracle of all—his friend.

Pressing his hands against the base of his spine, Michael stretched the moment out a few seconds longer. Then he nodded and gestured to the door. *On my way up.*

"About bloody time." John reached to grab the sash. Then he paused and flashed a grin that reached Michael through all the shadows of the square. "For the record?"

Michael thought at first he wouldn't bother. He was tired from his run, and John's childish contest over who could make it fastest up the stairs would die out sooner if Michael didn't keep encouraging him by shaving the odd second off his time. But the teasing challenge in his partner's voice suddenly grabbed him—warm and infectious as his laughter—and Michael seized the rail and took the first five steps at a bound.

He didn't stand a chance, of course. He'd turned thirty last July, and in the three years since leaving MI5 had finally put on a little weight to match his height. He was solid. It pleased him. He felt more akin to the earth now, less likely to burn up and vanish. He could outrun John on an assault course, stay staunchly ahead of him when John had worn out his sprint and fallen back. Over the short stretch, though—not a chance. John, with his dancer's frame, deceptively elegant over tempered-steel bones, would beat him every time.

But it was always worth a try. Exploding up out of the stairwell, Michael tore silently down the corridor, feet slipping on the worn linoleum. Three yards shy of the staffroom door, he put on the brakes, dropped to a nonchalant walk, and strolled in, picking invisible fluff off the front of his T-shirt. "Morning."

John turned round from the counter. The kettle was fizzing dangerously on its stand behind him. One shaft of sunlight had found its way across the rooftops, apparently just for the purpose of striking agate green flare from his eyes. "Morning." He glanced across the room. Their timing equipment was hardly Olympic standard—the second hand of a battered kitchen clock on the peeling wall. "You're way off. My old granny could get up those stairs faster than that."

"Yes," Michael returned amiably. "I suppose an orangutan could."

John stared at him, straight-faced, for almost five seconds. Then a snort of laughter escaped him. "Just fix the bloody kettle, will you?"

Michael shouldered him gently out of the way. He picked up the kettle, which promptly stopped fizzing, and settled it back on its base. "What did you do to it?"

"Nothing. Touched it. Is it okay now?"

"Fine. Sit down before you have an aneurysm. I'll fix you your jet fuel."

He was distantly grateful when John obeyed him. There were mornings—whole days, sometimes—when anything less than three feet of distance between them threatened to bring Michael's world down in flames. Mornings like this one, when John had clearly thrown himself out of bed five minutes before he had to leave his flat and was still wet from his shower, his hair in soft otter brown waves down the back of his neck, the tang of his ridiculously expensive aftershave mixing with the spice of his damp skin. Gritting his teeth, Michael concentrated on spooning instant coffee into mugs. By the time he banged them down on the stained staff room table, his heart rate was normal again—and John, feet up on a chair, apparently absorbed in that morning's *Times*, looked almost normal too, or at least sufficiently human that Michael could cope. Tousled, unshaved. His exquisite Amosu shirt badly in need of a press. "What's on the agenda today, then?"

John yawned enormously, raising a belated hand to cover the perfect tonsils exposed. "Frigging paperwork again. We don't trace back the contacts in the Irving case, Webb's gonna have the aneurysm, not me." He reached for his coffee, downed it scalding. "Mm. You're a beautiful man, Michael South."

Michael shook his head in wonder. "You're a gannet with a throat of asbestos. Seriously, desk work again? We'll both go blind at this rate."

"Be honest with you, I could use an easy day. I thought I'd call in at the Vineyard last night—just on the off chance—and I ran into this guy I'd never seen there before. Not much to look at, but the biggest bloody—"

The buzzer by the door went off. Michael met John's eyes. They shared a moment. Michael's relief at being spared the details, John's contrition for having been about to inflict them. Knocking back the rest of his coffee, John unfolded his long graceful limbs and went to lift the receiver on the wall-mounted phone. He listened for a few moments, then said, "Thank you, sir," and hung up.

Michael raised an eyebrow. "Paperwork off, then?"

"Oh yes, my son. Grab your coat. We've pulled."

Chapter Three

"So. This guy's credentials were how big exactly?"

Negotiating traffic on Holland Road, John shot Michael a sidelong glance of amusement. He sometimes suspected his quiet, clean-living partner not just of putting up with his off-duty ventures but trying to take an interest in them, like a parent tolerating a kid with a weird hobby. John was touched, if puzzled. "You don't really want to know."

"Not at all. But it takes my mind off the pileup you're about to cause. Slow down, Griff. The Met have got the place surrounded."

Griff. John smiled. He wasn't sure why that soft voice scraping over the first part of his surname was such a knee melter. "Bugger the Met," he suggested cheerfully, balancing the little Jaguar XKR deftly over chevrons and into the bus lane. The May wind was whipping his hair dry. His drop-top dream car was purring beneath him, and Mike was in the passenger seat. All was well with his world. "You know we're London's last line of defence."

"Webb said it was one guy they've got pinned down in there, not an army."

"Yeah, I know. Not sure why we got the call-out. This is small-time, isn't it?"

"Webb must reckon it's got links to something bigger. Anyway, he's keen to bring this guy in, so... " Michael leaned forward, stuck one arm out the passenger window, and gestured for permission for the move John was about to make anyway, a scything sweep across two lines of traffic and onto the Westway ramp. "So let's live long enough, eh?"

That was fair enough by John. Once out on the main road, away from the keen pleasures of carving up rush-hour traffic, he was content to let the Jag settle at a comfy eighty-five. Such mornings didn't come too often—open road and the prospect, for once, of an easy, police-assisted hunt. Usually he and Mike were hurtling into action with no other resources than their own wits and their deep-laid faith in one another. That was the point of Last Line—the freedom it granted its agents. Limitless investigative powers in return for their willingness to deny all links with government and police when things went wrong. Liberty with no safety net... A weird, heady mix, and only a handful of men could live with it.

It suited John down to the ground. He and Mike had had three years of it now, sailing through the London streets, the luck of the devil attendant on them. Serving up plausible deniability to ministers, politicians, even the MIs 5 and 6. They were the secret agents' secret agents. Even Sir James—especially Sir James— would wash his hands of them if they screwed up. John grinned, tapping a button on the XKR's stereo so that Sigur Rós swept from the high-end speakers, completing the effect of the joyride. He could cope with any amount of high-wire work if Mike's hands were ready to catch him.

"Did you hear back from Quin's school?"

John made a face. Last thing he wanted to think about on a sunny morning. But that was the downside of a perfect partner with outstretched, responsible hands. "If that *was* his school anymore. They kicked him out."

"You're kidding. Another one?"

"Yeah." John saw the exit signs for Kensal Green and shaved a little off their speed. "It's okay. With a bit of luck I can buy him into the Prince William Academy in time for summer term. They welcome gifted bloody nutcases."

"Prince William?" Michael whistled softly. "Gonna cost you, sunbeam."

"Tell me. Still, what is this grossly inflated salary for, if not to waste on my baby brother's education?"

"It's not a waste where Quin's concerned. And the salary… " John glanced across in time to see Michael's face become shadowed. "That's to make up for the fact that one day you'll be asked to do something you really, really don't want to do."

John drew a breath. He was ready to take anything Last Line dished out to him, he thought. After all, he'd signed his life away. But sometimes it seemed to him that Michael had forgotten more about life and its dark necessities than John could ever hope to know. Certainly more than he'd ever confide. Occasionally John minded it. Mike was only his own age, and they were meant to be partners. Mostly, though, he suspected he just ought to be grateful.

No time to think about it now. The exit road had taken them down into a tangle of Acton streets, and the satnav began to reel off instructions as fast as he could follow them. HQ hadn't specified a number, just a street name and postcode, but he supposed their target would be obvious enough once they came within sight of it.

Yes. The police-siege circus had come to town. Fortune Terrace was blocked at both ends and blazing with blue lights. Depressingly, broadcast news vans were gathering too. Didn't the world have anything better to watch or do? Pulling up at the barricade, instantly attracting the attention of an armed sergeant, John searched for the vortex, the eye of the storm. "Looks like that church down at the far end," he said, idly waving his ID at the officer. The gesture had its usual effect. Instant access, a respectful touching of black-brimmed hat. John supposed the novelty would one day wear off, but for now it was still fun, and he steered the Jaguar coolly through the tangle of squad cars and into a back alley. "There. Decent line of sight, and we're out of the way. Do we go straight in, or... " He fell silent. Michael was staring at the church. The healthy flush his morning run had given him had faded. "Mike? You okay?"

"What? Yeah, of course. It's just..." He shook his head. "Nothing. I'll tell control we're here."

The radio crackled before he could reach for it. Picking up, he exchanged a wry glance with John. Their boss had an uncanny gift for knowing exactly where they were at all times. He thumbed the transceiver, and Webb's uncompromising Belfast growl filled the car. "Griffin? South?"

"Yes, sir," Michael said demurely. "Both here."

"It's about damn time. Have you received a go from the Met to enter the building?"

"Not yet, sir." Michael frowned, surveying the street. "I... wasn't aware we had to wait for one."

"Well, this time you do. You'll know it when it comes. Until then, stand by and mind your own damn business."

The connection snapped shut. Michael hung up the transceiver, handling it like a tetchy snake. "Charming."

John fanned himself with one hand, brushed away an imaginary tear. "I'm so touched." Clearing his throat, he shifted his Liverpool accent a hundred and eighty miles northwest across the Irish Sea. "Morning, boys. *Tap* o' the mornin', in fact. Lovely to talk to you, boys. Lovely to know you're off on another kamikaze mission for Sir Jimmy's Last Line."

The impression was perfect. Michael broke into laughter. "Pack it in. He's probably still listening. Looks like we wait, then."

"Yeah, looks like." John sighed. Adrenaline was building in him, the sort that would only be discharged by a good fuck or a gunfight. He didn't like waiting. The bright May morning was clouding over too. As he watched, a drop of rain landed on the XKR's windshield. "Oh, upholstery. Help me put the top up."

"Oh, *upholstery*," Michael echoed, grinning. "You really are a pansy when it comes to this car, you know, Griff."

"I know." The roof mechanism was electric but needed a guiding tug to bring the catches into their slots. John caught an inviting brush of unshowered male as Michael reached up and across him. Then the top was in place, and they were sealed together in the peculiar intimacy of soft leather under the rain.

John took a deep, careful breath. His feelings for his partner didn't often give him trouble. It had been three years, plenty of time for him to accept that no meant no, and to learn to channel off his frustrations into a series of dark-eyed, lean-muscled substitutes. This morning Michael smelled so good, though, and the car was small...

"What did they expel Quin for, then?"

John blinked, then came back to surface, grabbing the question with relief. "He ran away. Again. They said they couldn't be responsible for him anymore."

"Where was he off to this time?"

"That's just it. He doesn't even bloody know. He's meant to be some kind of prodigy, but I swear the little bastard's a few bricks short."

"You're a fine one to talk."

John snorted faintly. "Ta, mate."

"Not about the bricks. You know what I mean."

John did. He stared out of the rain-streaked window. Quin, at fifteen, was barely a year younger than John had been when he had made his own blind run—away from home, school, family, into a half-legal berth with the Merchant Navy. He'd got away with it, grabbing his qualifications and a place in a private maritime-security firm, toting a gun on some of the highest-risk waterways in the world. "Least I knew where I was headed."

"Mm. Ten years overseas, with daily chance of capture by pirates. That what you want for him?"

"Of course not." John shifted uncomfortably. He hated talking about Quin. Then, Mike was the only soul in the world with whom he *could* discuss the little sod—and God knew it had the beneficial side effect of quelling his incipient close-quarters erection. Good as a cold shower. "But I don't know how to stop it. Don't know what to do for him at all."

"Well, if you ever wanted him closer to home—and I sometimes think that's all he wants, John, to have family, not a top-class boarding school—I'd give you a hand with him. You know that."

John nodded unhappily. And Michael was the only human being who could inspire Quin to good and respectful conduct. Whether it was Mike's MI5 background or quiet poise around the boy, John didn't know, but Quin adored him, and in his presence turned into something approaching a normal teenager. "It isn't that I don't want him, Mike. But it was bad enough when he was just my little brother. Now Mam and Dad are gone, I... can't be a parent to him too. Anyway," he added defensively, patting the wheel of the car which had cost more than three years at Prince William, "I like my life the way it is. Fast rides, irresponsible sex in clubs. Where does an orphan teen fit into that?"

"Not a clue, mate."

John didn't need excuses, not with Michael. He forgot that sometimes. Mike had Quin's best interests at heart, but had never judged John for not being able to provide them. John shot him a look of gratitude for the honest reply, and they fell silent. Mike knew when to let a topic go, as well.

Then, to John's dismay, he turned to him and raised a more crucial and unanswerable one still. "Speaking of irresponsible sex... God, you are *careful*, aren't you? I-I don't need to be worried about that?"

John stared at him. In part it was a desperate effort to figure him out—to read, in the beautiful midnight gaze interrogating his, where the hell the question came from. Because although John had folded up his yearning as small as it would go—taken no for his answer—when Michael quietly offered co-parenting services, followed up rapidly by concern for his sexual well-being, John couldn't help but imagine how life might have been if things were different. If *partners* meant everything, not their nine-to-five.

If Mike were hopelessly fucking well in love too.

"Yes," John grated out. "Belt and braces hygiene." *Because if, in some other bloody world, you changed your mind, I couldn't bear the thought of not being clean for you.* "For God's sake, Mike... I'm not stupid."

"No. I know." Michael was turning away. Was he blushing? John couldn't see. The morning had darkened, the rain coming down hard now. "It's just... Quin's got no one left apart from you."

Both of them jumped when one of the Met officers tapped on the windshield. John wound down his window. "What?"

The man didn't flinch at the snarl. He was a negotiator, John saw, and looked as if he'd had a hard morning. A megaphone dangled from his hand. "One of you two called Mikhaili South?"

John twisted round to look at Mike. He frowned. His pallor had turned to a shade of putty. "Yeah, but…"

"I am." Michael sounded like he'd just been punched in the gut. "I'm Michael South. Not… not Mikhaili."

"Well, whatever. Guy in there's asking for you by name. And he's strapped from top to toe with Semtex, so you might want to come and get a briefing with my chief before you decide what to do."

Chapter Four

To move in absolute silence, disturbing the air no more than a shaft of dusty light from a stained-glass window… It was its own keen pleasure, and Michael immersed himself in it, prowling down the shadowy south aisle. His Glock was in his hand, a reassuring weight. He didn't have to think of anything beyond the moment, this moment of animal functioning, of skilled predation. Of moving in silence.

You move more quietly than I do now and faster than any of the others.

Michael stilled his bone-deep flinch before it could reach the surface. There was no need for it. Anzhel Mattvei sometimes spoke inside his head. That was to be expected. They had hunted together for months in the wasteland forests of Zemelya, Michael using Anzhel to track the province's crazed religious leader, Lukas Oriel. That mission had failed. There were days when Michael could face the memories of what he had done in its name and days when he couldn't. The second type were few and far between now, three years down the line, and he took care that they occurred in his off duty. Took care that John Griffin never saw.

John. Michael sought him, located him in a pool of blue-green light in the church's west end. Relief undid locked muscle across Michael's shoulders. *And with his varying childness, cures in me thoughts that would thick my blood...* Michael smiled, beginning to make his way to him. *Varying childness* was hardly right in a hard-as-nails ex-maritime security man, but John's unhidden delight in the fat Last Line pay packet, his joyful obsession with clothes, cars, and general good living, never failed to distract and amuse his partner. Once, a long time ago—before MI5, before Zemelya—Michael had taken great pleasure in such things himself.

It was good to watch him. John had seen him now—felt his glance, as always, like a touch to his shoulder—and was coming to meet him. Once, a long time ago, Michael had fallen asleep on his sofa, woken with his head in John's lap, with John's sculpted mouth trailing kisses up the side of his face. And Michael had said no. Their partnership had been young, fluid. They had absorbed the shock. John had got over him, moving on energetically to other satisfactions.

They met by the heavy wooden doors. The church was a strange one, Gothic revival wedged into the suburbs. Leaping too high for its length, arches disappearing into raftered dusk where doves and pigeons scratched restlessly, crossing the dizzying overhead space in a pulsating flutter of wings. John stood poised, clearly listening like the good agent he was, making sure that their racket concealed nothing else. Then he turned to look at Michael. "I don't think he's in here anymore."

Michael came to stand by his shoulder. He was chilly for some reason, and John, who normally was cool as water even on the hottest summer day, seemed to be casting off delicious heat. "I don't think so either," he said. Between them they had quartered the church, every inch of it. "But I'm damned if I know how. The coppers have got every exit sealed."

"Well, we'll take another turn...." John paused, frowning. "Are you all right?"

"Fine. Why?"

"You're shivering."

"No, I... " Michael straightened away from him and made sure it was true before he finished, "No, I'm not. I just... don't like churches for some reason. And this one gives me the willies."

John chuckled softly. "The actual *willies*? I didn't think big strong MI5 men were allowed to get those."

"Oh, you'd be surprised what we get. Come on, then. Let's do another sweep so we can get out of here."

"Okay. But what was that business with your name back there? With... "

"Mikhaili!"

John and Michael jolted back into the shadows, seeking cover, automatically raising weaponry. The voice had seemed to come from everywhere, bouncing off the stained glass, making unseen bells somewhere vibrate. Back pressed to a pillar, Michael frantically scanned the shadows for the man they had missed—he and John, who missed nothing...

"Mike! Up there!"

Michael jerked his head up, following the direction of John's PPK. Automatically he had raised his own pistol too, and now had it trained on a human figure poised among the doves, high in the roof space. They'd missed him because there was nowhere to walk up there, not if you were flesh and blood. There was a single bar of wood, the top of the screen that divided the nave from the chancel. It wouldn't support a man's weight.

But this can't be a man, Michael's shocked mind told him. A ghost, a memory. Summer flu coming on, a warning mirage of fever. He had walked into a forest clearing three years ago, doing what he had to in order to maintain his cover and stay close to

Anzhel Mattvei. There had been Ashkeloi gypsies there. And this man—this man looking down on him from the rood screen now—had come toward him through the firelight, fearless, ready to defend his people.

"Piotr," he whispered.

"Mike? You know this guy?"

Michael spared John a glance. He shook his head, trying to make the face smiling down at him now something other than the relic of a nightmare. "I don't know. It can't be."

"Stay here. Keep him talking."

Michael drew breath to argue. But even an inhalation took too long when John had made his mind up, and the hand Michael threw out to stop him closed on empty air. He was gone—no more than a shadow's reflection, soundlessly climbing the stairs to the gallery.

Keep him talking. Michael had to. The man in the loft shifted, spreading his arms. The folds of his jacket—Christ, the same coat he'd worn in the forest that night—fell open, revealing the sinister bulk around his waist and chest. The streets around the church had been evacuated, but the place was half-derelict, ready to fall apart. An explosion would bring it down, and even if at this moment Michael wasn't sure he cared, John had set out fearlessly to stop it.

Yes. For John, he could still think and speak. "You were with the Ashkeloi," he rasped. "You died."

"Are you sure, Mikhaili? Those were strange nights, weren't they, when you ran with Anzhel Mattvei."

"What do you know about Anzhel?" Michael didn't register that he'd said the words in Zemel, in the language of his year-long immersion. That he'd been triggered to do so by hearing it. The foreign syllables hissed off his tongue. "He shot you. I saw it. You can't be here."

His vision fogged. He scraped a hand across his eyes to clear it, and when he looked again, it was as if Piotr had agreed with the impossibility of his presence. The space on the rood screen was empty, full of dust and sunlight, as if he'd never been.

Reality asserted itself. Whoever the hell was up there, he was twelve pounds of Semtex on the loose. "John!" Michael yelled, running for the gallery stairs. "I lost him. He's moving!"

"Got him!"

John's voice rang from the far east end of the roof space, almost over the altar. Through bloodstained sparks, Michael saw him ease lithely over the gallery rail and onto a rafter. "Griff, come back off there. It won't hold you."

"It's fine. Just don't try to follow me. It won't take both of us. What did you call him? Piotr?"

"Yes, but... " Desperately Michael followed the focus of his attention and saw the dark shape pressed into the gallery on the other side. Masonry dust was crumbling from it, small stones beginning to detach. "Jesus, get back here, Griff. That far side's about to come down."

"Piotr? Listen to me, mate. I don't know who strapped you into the gelly suit, but believe me, they don't give a damn about you. And you're not off to martyr's heaven with dancing girls and sherbet. You're just gonna die. And you're gonna take me and my partner with you, and..." John wobbled on the rafter beam, corrected himself with a cat's grace. "And we're not in the mood. So you just stay there till I can get to you and see if I can disarm all that crap or get it off you."

Christ, he sounded as calm as if he were offering to fix Piotr's car. Hands clenching tight to the stone balustrade on his own side, Michael watched, frozen. John took fearlessness to lunatic lengths. Always had. Debonair and smiling, he would walk into the fire. And it was as if nature—fate—gave his blithe courage back to him, shielding him from consequence; Michael had never known him to suffer so much as a scratch.

He was almost there. Michael, dry-mouthed, took a double-handed aim on the middle of Piotr's forehead. A misplaced shot would detonate the bastard, but a good direct hit through the skull would drop him where he stood. "Freeze," he growled. John threw him a puzzled glance, and he heard himself, but continued in Zemelyan to be sure their prey would understand. "Don't move a muscle, Piotr. Let him help you."

"Help me?" Piotr shook his head. "I don't need help, Mikhaili. I'm just a messenger—a falling star."

He stepped off the edge of the gallery. For an instant he seemed to hang in the air. Then he dropped, a flight of pigeons clattering upward as he fell.

Michael saw John duck his head and turn away. It was instinct—if pointless—to huddle from a blast. Why wasn't he doing the same? His reflexes felt dead in him. He couldn't even blink as Piotr hit the floor thirty feet below. He saw and heard everything—impact, crunch of bone—and then that was over, and like John, he stood there waiting for the flash.

It didn't come. Ten or so seconds elapsed. Then John, poised between the rafters and the gallery, lifted his head. He turned around carefully. He looked down gravely into the nave of the church, where Piotr and the twelve pounds of Semtex, which for some reason hadn't gone off, lay shattered and still. Then he broke out into his crazy, soaring, beautiful teenager's laugh.

Michael wanted to join him. But a brutal fist was twisting in his guts. He couldn't react to the cessation of threat. Instead, he shuddered with conviction of a dark wing still stretched over them. "All right," he said, shifting cautiously to extend a hand in John's direction. "Hilarious. Now get your arse back over here, quick."

"On me way." Smoothly John turned on the rafter. "What the hell was that about, though? I thought we'd had it. And I never gave you a last—" The laughter died out of his voice, leaving it flat. "Oh fuck."

"What is it?" But a heartbeat later, Michael saw. The beam's far end, fixed into the masonry, had shifted. Falling stonework from the gallery had loosened the mortar around it. As he watched, the whole structure of the rafters jolted down an inch, and then another. "Griff! Get off there. Jump!"

John tried. It was as perfect and athletic an effort as anyone could have made—valiant, hopeful, launching powerfully up and across to the gallery. His hands closed on the stone railing. And Michael knew—they both did, in the moment when their eyes met, wide sea green to depthless black—that it was not enough. John said faintly, "Mikey." Then the stonework turned to dust beneath his grasp.

* * *

Michael walked slowly through the stained-glass light. He was down in the nave of the church. He must have come back down the steps to get here, but he had no recall.

Dust was still settling. Outside in the suburban morning, the skies must have cleared, uncertain sunlight beginning to shaft and probe. The doves disturbed from the rafters were calling to one another. Michael walked. His hands were loose at his sides. Every joint in his body had turned to rusty iron. He could barely move, but still he kept walking, on and on, heavy and cold.

He stopped and looked at the space where the altar would have been. There was still a pile of packing crates there, as if whoever had cleared the place had felt that something should mark the spot. He drew a breath. His lungs were turned to iron too—or it would have been a sob. He would have expelled it in a raw howl that would bring the rest of this godforsaken hulk down on him. He wanted it to come down. He wanted it to burn. He stared blindly at the absent altar and prayed for conflagration.

Don't you feel it in yourself yet, Michael? The power, the love of fire?

Frantically he shook his head. Another voice spoke there sometimes as well as Anzhel Mattvei's. A deeper and older one, older than sin. He didn't know whose it was. There had been another church too, and in it something dreadful had happened. The memories moved in him, slow dark shapes under ice.

Something dreadful. The sun found its way to the low step three yards in front of him. It coalesced, a red-gold nimbus in the dust. It lit up the man lying there, dragging Michael's attention to him at last.

John had landed on his back. He was sprawled across the altar step in a scatter of broken stone. Dust coated every inch of him, turning him into a serene plaster saint, the only holy presence left in this deconsecrated place. He looked as if he had stretched out on his bed and fallen asleep. Michael had seen him like this a dozen times, when they'd had to share quarters on one op or another. He slept with a child's abandonment, a cat's enjoyment and concentration. Michael, who couldn't sleep at all without a wall at his back and a gun under his pillow, had envied him.

He dropped to his knees beside him. He brushed back the tangle of soft hair from his face. "John," he whispered and slipped an arm under his head, raising him. *Don't move a fall victim,* his training echoed, but nothing could hurt John now—nothing ever again. Disbelief rose in Michael—panic and a loneliness deeper and blacker than space. "John," he choked, cradling him, leaning close over him. "Oh God! Oh no. No!"

Movement rippled in the body he held. Michael started back with a faint cry and almost dropped him. Tears had splashed into the dust on John's face—Michael's own, falling still as he sat up. "J-John? Griff?"

The green eyes opened. After a long, long moment when they seemed to be watching an unseen sky, they focused on Michael's. "Christ," he rasped. "What the hell's the matter with you?"

Michael stared down at him. He took him in—the wide, startled gaze. The fine dust-caked skin with blood running palpably under it—blood pulsing, beating, driven by his living heart. The lovely mouth, half-open in shock... Suddenly everything in Michael's world boiled down to a wild desire to kiss that mouth, and he bent over John, whispering his name.

He couldn't. He froze. John had raised a hand, reached round him and clasped the back of his neck. His face was still a blank of astonishment, but in it Michael could somehow read his absolute acceptance, a silent yes that reverberated in the air around them. "No," Michael told it desperately, recoiling. *No. I am corrupt, untouchable.* "No, I can't... John! Jesus, how the fuck... How the fuck are you alive?"

Blinking, John looked past him and up into the void through which he'd fallen. "I dunno. I... No idea." Abruptly his face contorted. He clamped his other hand to Michael's shoulder. "Oh Mike. It hurts!"

"Fuck. Let go of me. Let me lay you flat."

"Nn-nn. Please don't let go."

"I have to. God knows what damage I've already done you."

"I'm not damaged. I..." He shuddered, gritting his teeth. "There's just so much *pain*."

"I know. Okay, okay, let me call help for you." Propping him against one knee, Michael scrabbled in his jacket pocket for his radio and phone, dropped both, and was stilled in his dive after them by the death grip of John's hand around his wrist. "Griff, let me go!"

"No. Listen to me for a moment." Against his will Michael stopped. John's eyes were burning. "I don't *get* you, Mike. We share everything. Every day, every…" He broke off, coughing. "It's not like there's anyone else. I can see in your face how bad you want me sometimes, and I…"

"John. Please."

"And I'm all fucking yours. You know that. I don't get you…"

The great wooden doors burst open. Michael jumped hard, moving to shelter John, but suddenly outlined in the light from outdoors he could see the wide bulk of Sir James Webb. He was flanked by policemen, paramedics, officers with rifles running to cover all points of the derelict church. Michael wanted to tell them to stand down; the game was over, played out. He found he couldn't speak at all.

Webb limped slowly toward them. A massive bull of a man who hadn't changed his lifestyle or food intake since having one kneecap torn off him by a bomb in County Armagh, he blocked out the light. He had been a major in the British army then, and his much-decorated retirement and knighthood hadn't consoled him one bit. He looked down on his men. "Still alive, then, Griffin?"

"I… Yes, sir."

"You too, Agent South?"

Michael drew a breath. He would have used it first to demand paramedics, and second to tell his boss what he thought of him for not bringing them down in a storm—but suddenly they were there, surrounding him, green uniforms and competent hands, carefully lifting his partner from his arms. "Yes. Yes, sir."

"Good. In that case one of you can tell me why the bloody hell you killed my witness."

"Killed him…" Michael's head was spinning. He could scarcely remember the fight that had led up to the shift of woodwork and stone and what he thought had been the end of his world. "We didn't. He jumped. He—"

"If anyone's interested, he's still alive too."

Webb jerked up his head. Michael, still holding tight to John's outflung hand, picked out through staticky clouds the voice of Last Line's chief physician. A formidable woman and the only one of Webb's employees who didn't give a toss about his temper or his war wounds, she was kneeling with a group of other medics on the far side of the church. "Only he's doing what Griffin should—dying of internal injuries, fast. You better get over here, Webb, if you want any moving last words."

Michael felt a tug as John withdrew his hand. His reactions were delayed. For a moment, he couldn't look away from the lumbering hulk of his boss, heaving off to inspect this new phenomenon. Then he blinked and frowned, reaching to steady himself on the floor. John, surrounded by bewildered paramedics, was getting to his feet. He was making use of their support, and he was white as a cod, but he was standing. "Something must have broken his fall," one of the paramedics said wonderingly, whether to himself or his colleagues, Michael wasn't sure. "I'll… I'll go get an ambulance pulled right up to the doors."

John detached himself from their grip. He swayed a bit, then steadied. "I don't need an ambulance," he said. "I just want to get out of here. Please, Mike."

* * *

Michael led him to the car. He had agreed to go to hospital but objected to doing so flat on his back.

"I, er, might need you to drive. I'm a little bit stiff."

Michael came to a halt. He had had his arm around John's waist. Now he let go of him, except for a steadying grip on his shoulders. He eased him back, examining his face in the sunlight. The fire engines and police cars were on the retreat, an ordinary morning beginning to unfold in the streets around them. He could hear planes overhead and the shout of kids on their way to school. "John," he said. "That was a thirty-foot fall."

"Well, like they said, something must have broken it." John put a tentative hand behind him and winced. "My arse, I think."

Michael swallowed. If he laughed, it would tip into hysteria. "All right," he said. "Yes. I'll drive."

"Speaking of the fucking incomprehensible... Why didn't your mate Piotr blow up like Nagasaki when he fell?"

"Don't know. Webb'll tell us, no doubt. Maybe the explosives were fakes or duds." He looked down. "He wasn't my mate, John."

"Then who the hell was he? He knew you. Why—"

"For God's sake." Reaching around him, Michael pulled open the Jaguar's passenger door. "Okay, so you're Lazarus, and you're walking around now like nothing happened. But you scared the shit out of me, sunbeam, and there's no way you've got away with it. Get into the damn car—if you can—and—"

"All right, all right." John was smiling, his face lit up with surrender. If he remembered his outcry on the floor of the church, there was no sign of it now. He put out his hand to the car door.

A fat blue spark leapt from the metal to his fingertips. Michael saw it—heard the crack. He grabbed John, steadying him against his recoil. "Ow, you *bastard*!" John commented feelingly.

"How the fuck can that happen? It's static buildup, isn't it? I haven't even been near her!"

Michael didn't know. He clamped a hand to his mouth. This happened to John all the time. He couldn't touch a car—or a metal stair rail, or the barriers on the Tube—with impunity. To Michael's shame, he always found it funny. But now, juxtaposed to his near-death plunge, the relative stoicism with which he'd handled that—to see him wince and suck his finger like a kid at this tiny injury… Events caught up with Michael, and he sat down on the Jag's bonnet, tears of laughter welling in his eyes.

Chapter Five

Low, insistent bass; a rattle of glassware. Sweeping lights, although Webb had ordered a retirement party, not a bloody disco, and was at this moment stumping around behind the scenes looking for someone to shout at. The peculiar clatter of tight-wound men and women finally letting off steam.

It took time and a hell of a lot of alcohol. Michael caught the barman's eye and silently requested a fourth refill for his vodka. The first three hadn't done the trick at all. He was as painfully tense now, as twitchy and restless as when he had arrived an hour ago.

He didn't want to be here at all. John was fine—somehow a battery of X-rays and an MRI showing his spine intact—but the hospital wanted him kept overnight for observation, and it was Michael's instinct not to be far from him. He might not have slept on a chair in the corridor exactly, but nor would he have gone off partying if Jeffrey Hall's partner hadn't intercepted him back at HQ, reminding him that Jeff, an unlikely survivor of fifteen years at Last Line, was due to get turned out to grass at the Dog &

Duck that night. And Jeff was a good friend. Distractedly Michael had promised an hour or so later.

And here he was. He leaned his elbows on the sticky bar top. John would have pulled a face and mopped the surface down with napkins, not wanting to spoil his Armani jacket. Michael's wasn't exactly Primark, but he didn't honestly care. He just wanted to do his duty here and get out.

And go where, he didn't know. He wouldn't be able to sleep. He felt as if the marrow of his bones was on fire. The events of the day flashed across his vision in time with the strobes, but out of sequence, ragged, too bright. John starting to attention in the church. An impossible face—Piotr, for God's sake, a long-dead Ashkeloi gypsy—appearing like biblical vengeance in the shadows far above. And John falling. Again and again Michael's flashbacks reverted to that, played it out as a backdrop to everything else, until he was seeing it constantly. He had looked into Michael's eyes. *Mikey.*

Michael put his face into his hands. Part of him had died when he'd seen his partner start to fall. The rest of him would have followed soon enough if John had been lost to him. He knew that. And yet, down in the dust, when John had opened his eyes and lain there like a miracle, ready to accept his kiss, Michael had denied him. Again. One more time and Michael was fairly sure he would hear cockerels crowing before sunrise.

"Penny for 'em, Agent South."

Michael jumped. He turned on the uncomfortable barstool and saw Diane Shaw, Last Line's longest-serving female agent, clambering onto the seat next door. He gave her a reluctant smile. The night had washed a fair amount of traffic his way, most conspicuously Jeffrey Hall, who had popped up several times now, on each occasion assuring Michael more fervently than the last that he loved him—no, *really* loved him, and he wasn't just saying that. Michael had grinned, hugged him, posed for photos. He was fond of Jeff too, and anyone who had survived this racket long enough to retire certainly deserved his wild night. Diane, however, was definitely a more attractive prospect. Her hair was down around her shoulders, and she'd left her professional deportment somewhere on the barroom floor. "They're not worth it, Di. How about you? Enjoying the party?"

"It's like watching bears at the zoo. How's John?"

"Still in hospital. But they think he'll be okay."

"Thank fuck for that. I heard he nearly joined Webb's beloved dead this morning." She gave the bartender a beaming smile and accepted the Budweiser he handed her as her royal due. "So, he's all tucked up for the night. Which leaves you…free, I suppose?"

Michael looked at her with some affection. She was laid-back, sweet natured and brave, and it wouldn't be the first time he had taken her up on the offer. The fact was that an occasional girlfriend made life simpler. He could tell John he was straight and have it be true, if just barely. It kept his other colleagues off his back. Diane took her pleasures as they came and pursued her own business when they were over. She was a friend.

He would hurt her if he slept with her tonight. His hands would close too hard on her soft skin. Or he would bank down his fires as fiercely as he could and yearn in silence for an answering flame… No. Not fair on her, and about as far from what he really wanted as…

"Am I interrupting, then?"

Michael knocked over his glass. Diane, who had a cat's reflexes even when drunk, caught it and set it down safely on the bar. "John!" she said, her lovely smile betraying only the faintest disappointment. "I'm so pleased you're okay. No, darlin'. Safe to say you're not interrupting anything at all."

She slithered off her stool and disappeared into the crowd. For one second Michael looked after her—then had no eyes for anything but the apparition of his partner, pale and smiling, hands in the pockets of his jeans. "Christ almighty, Griff! You're meant to be in hospital."

"I know." John shrugged, the movement displaying his broad shoulders, their contrast to the graceful lightness of his hips. Helplessly Michael held up Diane's template against him, all her gentle beauties, and watched them crumble to ash. "But I got bored, and… worried about you, to be honest."

"Did they discharge you?"

"Nn-nn. I did a flit."

"Oh. John, for God's sake." A passing drunk buffeted him. John smiled, caught the offender and set him back on his feet, but Michael saw that he'd paled still further. He put out a protective arm. "Come here." Installing him on Diane's vacated stool, he mimed to the bartender for two more vodkas. "What were you worried about me for? I didn't drop off a thirty-foot balcony today."

"No, you didn't. But I've never seen any man more… entirely freaked out than you were by the time we got done in there." John frowned, his gaze becoming diagnostic. "Than you still are."

Michael looked away. "Are you surprised?" he asked uncomfortably. "I thought you were dead."

"Not about me. I mean—yes, about me, and thank you. But about that guy in the church. That was your mum's language you were speaking to him, wasn't it? That dialect?"

"Yeah. I knew him, that was all. I knew where he came from."

John picked up his glass. "Ugh. What's that? You drink like a bloody Russian peasant, you know. Do you want to tell me about him?"

I met him in a clearing in the woods. I stood by and watched my comrade shoot him; then I ran in and murdered the people he was trying to protect. "No. There's nothing to tell."

He watched John settle back on his stool. He understood, with plunging relief, that he wasn't going to push it. Michael could rely on his discretion in such matters. Christ, he could rely on him for everything. Heat flickered through him. The fifth vodka had made a difference, finally. "John," he began, then had no idea where to take the sentence and fell silent, clenching his hands on the bar.

"You can't come down, can you?"

Michael shivered. It was so quietly observed. John hadn't moved or taken his eyes off him. Michael couldn't meet his gaze, but it felt like green-gold seawater around him. "What... what do you mean?"

"It's all still banging round inside you. Everything that happened today. You feel... hot on the inside, like your skin's a few sizes too small. You'd rip it off if you could."

Michael lowered his head. He ran his fingers into his hair. "What the hell do you know about it?"

"Everything, mate. I'm the only one who *can* know."

"Stop it."

"I will. Listen to me for one moment; then I'll get up and walk out of here, and if you don't follow—everything's the same, okay? You're my partner. My best friend."

"John..."

"Or come home and sleep it off with me. You can fuck me through the mattress and into the bloody basement, or I can do the same for you, or we can do both. It's safe. I can bring you down."

Michael didn't move. For almost thirty seconds he sat where he was, fingertips pressing painfully tight into his scalp. The air became empty around him. When he finally looked up, John was gone.

He got to his feet. He had to keep one hand on the edge of the bar while he did so; the room was lurching around him. Then he sat down again—long enough to grab his jacket and drape it over his arm, a frail concealment but the only one available. He was an aching mass of need from the waist down. Away on the far side of the crowded bar, the door to the outside was closing. Swallowing, the breath beginning to rasp in his throat, Michael followed.

* * *

"My place, not yours. Okay?"

John glanced out of the window. The purr of Michael's BMW had soothed him. He hadn't noticed that they'd gone past the turning for Islington and were heading into Highgate. It was fine with John. He'd never got far enough in his fantasies of this night to endow them with a location. "Okay."

"Too many windows. And no walls."

John smiled. He hadn't been about to ask. He could see how a stylish open-plan loft apartment might not suit their purposes. Only the loft-dwellers next door and passing jets could see in, but they could see everything. He inched down the BMW's passenger window and took deep breaths of the warm, petrol-laced London night as his dreams acquired their backdrop. Michael's white-facade Regency terrace, where you could murder someone or shout yourself mute with orgasmic yelling, and no one would be any the wiser. Thick walls, high ceilings. A place built for human habitation, not—as Mike had observed of the Islington loft—the packaging of meat. Not looking, he reached across and laid a hand on Michael's thigh. "*Okay.* Jesus, pull off behind the bus depot and we'll do it there if you like. I just want you."

He waited for Michael's laughter or his groan of disgust. But all he felt was a flicker of tension in the muscle where his palm was resting. Helplessly he thought of a caged, restless lion flicking a fly off its skin, and he withdrew his hand, wondering at the image. Cautiously he observed his partner. His hands were quiet on the wheel, but their knuckles were white. His profile was set. A trickle of unease went down the back of John's neck. It hardly stood a chance against the cauldron of arousal further south, but it was unexpected. He hadn't painted for himself the prelude to this encounter any more than he'd bothered with where it would go down. If asked, though, he would have sworn that he and Mike would have tumbled into bed in the same spirit that informed all their days out of it. Laughing, ripping the piss. John swallowed drily. He'd have banked on affection. "Are you all right?"

Mike's dark gaze didn't leave the road. "Fine."

"Because… this can just be John getting drunk and hitting on you again. Nothing has to happen."

"But you're sober, aren't you?"

John thought about it. The rough Russian vodka was dancing with his painkillers, but he'd only had the one. One more than Michael would normally let him combine with medication, he reflected. They were pulling up in Kingsborough Crescent, an elegant urban backwater quiet at this time of night, empty but for parked cars and leaf-dappled streetlight. Whatever they were discussing—and John was no longer sure—it would have to reach conclusion soon. "Yeah," he said. "Sober enough."

Michael stopped the BMW outside an elegant three-floor terrace whose steps led to a pillared doorway. The building was very *him*, John had always thought. Little by way of decoration but lovely lines. He had often experienced a frisson of excitement just from running up the steps to meet him on a Monday morning.

The hand brake ratcheted up, breaking his contemplation. Michael was staring grimly at the dash. "Well, I'm not," he announced. "In fact I… had four of those filthy peasant vodkas before you even arrived. Then I bought you one—on top of what I imagine is a skinful of meds—jumped into a car and drove you home."

This recitation very nearly struck John as funny. He bit the reaction back. "Okay," he said cautiously. "Put like that, it's… out of character for you, yeah."

"Out of character? It's fucking unforgivable."

"You didn't force the drink down my throat. And I'm not condoning drunk driving, mate, but today was a bit of a one-off, wasn't it?"

"Don't make excuses for me. I should call a taxi for you, send you home out of my way."

John inhaled softly. He put his hand back where it had been, on the powerful curve of Michael's thigh. A little higher this time, to leave no room for doubt. This time the muscle remained firm and still under his palm. He said, "Yes. You could do that. If you want."

* * *

His spine impacted hard against the wall. The blow drove breath from his lungs. He was glad, because if he had developed some kind of immortality when it came to falling off buildings, he was still human enough to bruise, and he was sore as hell. Being winded meant he couldn't yell in pain. If he did, Michael would stop. John knew—he was completely certain—that Michael would crash to a halt at his least sound of discomfort.

The last thing John wanted. He had got him here, the beast unleashed and in his arms at last. He gritted his teeth and hauled him tight for his next urgent thrust. He'd already torn him out of his jacket. The shirt could go next. Ripping at the buttons, John lifted his face to intercept the hot mouth exploring the side of his neck. The pleasure of that—kissing Michael, though right now it felt more like a mutual devouring—wiped out even the memory of pain. "Mikey, yeah," he grunted when he could. "Getting so hard."

"Shut up."

John gasped. Something in him was shocked, but his cock had leaped at the growled command, and if Michael wanted to play it strong and silent, that was fine with him. Had he spoken at all since their collision over the BMW's hand brake ten minutes before? John wasn't sure. The time was a blur to him. They must have made it up the steps and to the top floor somehow. Cameras in the foyer and the lift must have restrained them. Yes, he vaguely recalled standing waiting by the old wrought iron doors for the cage, Michael beside him. Both of them burningly silent.

There was no need now. The new recruits' flats were bugged, but not, Sir James had assured them, those of trusted senior agents. John threw his arms round Michael's neck and groaned as strong hands closed on his backside, lifting him, grinding their stiff shafts together in the prison of their clothes. Weird. He'd have pegged Mike as a talker in the sack, or a listener anyway, wanting to hear his lover's response.

The wall behind him changed to thin air. John fought dizzily for balance. Michael had swung him around, barely set him on his feet again before beginning to back him up, step by step, through the nearest doorway. The bedroom? Passion had fogged the familiar geography, and the place was in darkness, only picked out by alarm-pad lights, TV stand-by, the phone, a spinning constellation of weird stars. Clinging to him, John let himself be borne into unknown space. The fact was that this treatment, brusque and painful as it was, was going to make him come like helpless Armageddon very soon. "Mike, slow up. At least get my pants off."

"Oh, I will. Wait there."

Something banged into John's back. Not the bed or any of the furniture in Michael's room… He was suddenly released, grabbing at the object's cold edge to stay upright.

The kitchen table. Breathing hard, John watched his partner turn and stride calmly off into the hallway. He heard the sound of a drawer opening and closing somewhere in the flat, and then Michael was back, a panther-like darkness cut out of the doorway. John could see only the glimmer of his eyes, catching amber from the streetlights. "This gonna be it, then?" he asked hoarsely. "Here in the kitchen?"

"Yes," Michael said. His voice was bleak. "Right here."

John could have stopped him. A word would have done it. Less—this was Michael, who knew John had an itch before he reached to scratch it. Michael of a thousand dangerous city days. He could have read a muscle twitch in John that said he wasn't ready to be fucked facedown across his kitchen table.

John knew this. And yet for a few bitter seconds he also knew he would regret trying him—knew he had better keep any protests or twitches to himself. Pain lanced through him, even while he squirmed out of his jeans, letting those and his briefs be roughly yanked down round his thighs. What had he expected—hearts and flowers?

Yes. At least those. This was Michael, who had wept to think that he was dead.

Michael's fingers, lube-soaked, found the entrance to his body. John's mind went gloriously blank. "Oh *yes*," he whispered. Two fingers, hot and strong, broached his rim, and he stretched out on the table's cool oak surface, groaning. The pressure inside him mounted, then withdrew a little. Knuckles caressed his anus from the inside in a circling motion that pulled a wail of pleasure from him. He clenched on the intrusion, writhing. "Mike, you bastard..." More lube, a third finger, and a reach inside that woke his prostate.

He shoved up onto his elbows. His body was beginning preorgasmic cramps, hot contractions in his balls and the root of his cock where it was painfully trapped. He could resist them for a while, but once the deeper rhythm started, he would be lost. In another world, he'd have Michael do him like this, put his hand up there and fist him unconscious, but now he knew he'd better court his fate before it overtook him uninvited. He could feel Michael's shaft pushing hard against his arse. "Don't make me come like this. Fuck me."

Rubber. Flinging a hand back to welcome and guide him— Christ, not that he needed either—John's fingers brushed the steel-cold buttons of Michael's open fly and then a length of condom-sheathed cock. Already it was burrowing into his body. Snatching his hand away, he slammed it to the table's surface. God, he was big! Shuddering, fists clenching and flattening, John heaved back against him. He wouldn't have asked him to wear a condom. Somehow, stupidly, hadn't expected him to put one on unasked. Why? Michael wasn't a saint. And if things had been the other way round, John might have wanted—Michael thrust hard, and the thought disintegrated in John's mind, patching itself back together in rags—he'd have wanted to wear three of the damn things, with his track record...

Another thrust, this one big enough to slam John flat, impaled. He felt a new depth in him open. His mouth stretched soundlessly. To his ecstasy and desolation, Mike clenched a fist in his hair, yanking his head back, and without another second's warning, John came, shooting his load violently against the table's edge.

He hadn't meant to. It had felt like detonation, not a climax. Sucking breath back into his lungs, he fought to brace up, not to melt into inertia as Michael took serious hold of him and began to fuck him hard. He didn't know John had gone over, did he? And John couldn't tell him—for want of breath, partly, and out of shame too, for bursting like a randy kid so soon. At least Michael's arms were around him now, the cable-cord muscle tight across his belly and over his chest. The shove of his hips, the hot tight friction of his body, sent flowers of pain blooming up and down John's bruised spine, but to be held like this—yes, that was some part of how he'd dreamed it. The embrace would carry him through being screwed this hard on the wrong side of climax.

No. Not the wrong side. John cried out, a wild, incredulous moan. Almost a protest, as against all odds and all his experience of what his flesh could do, excitement rose in him again. *"Jesus,"* he rasped. He spread his feet, got a grip on the floor and fought back hard enough to free his cock. Felt it leap, still semen-soaked, rising stiff into his hand. The savage motion of Michael's hips, the twisting bloody earthquake it was causing inside, became too much. He bore down, a terrible involuntary spasm as if he would thrust him out, and he came again, convulsing in Mike's embrace.

"Mike," he pleaded when he could. His voice was worn to a threadbare croak. Michael had slowed his pace, his breath rasping against John's ear, but he was still buried deep. "Lover, I'm done. Please… Let go or you're gonna kill me."

To his horror, Michael sobbed. He crashed to a halt. "I can't."

"What?" John could feel every inch of him, taut and hard, holding him wide open. Ready. "Yeah, you can. Give it to me." Propping himself shakily on his arms, he ground back against him. "Just let go."

"No."

A huge inner movement. Never great to be pulled out of, but not too bad with a spent, satisfied cock. Just a slither, not this sense of being brusquely gutted… Grunting, John braced and got through it as best he could. "Mikey, what the hell's the matter?" He turned. His vision had adapted to the dark, but sparks were dancing across it now. Through them he saw that Michael had fallen back against the wall. Lifted his hands to shield his face. "Jesus. Mike?"

John hauled up his jeans. He discovered that he still could walk—just about—and he limped over to his partner. He took him in his arms. The still-sheathed, still-rigid cock pushed hotly against his thigh. He kissed Michael's feverish cheek. "All right," he told him. "Bed."

Where they should have started off. For all John's fantasies about the backseats of cars and dark alleyways, that had been his deeper thought. One day, if the impossible happened, he and Mike would fall into bed together. They did so now, like an avalanche, John landing on top but almost too tired to push home his advantage. The corridor that led from the kitchen to the bedroom had been a long walk, steering Michael passively in front of him.

He pinned Michael down. He was breathing hard, a tremor of exhaustion in his limbs. "Okay, handsome. What's it take?"

Michael looked up at him. "It would take," he said distinctly, "for you to tie me up." The instant the words were out, his eyes and voice became hollow with shame. "Leave it, John. I'm a freak."

John sat back. It came as a surprise, he'd give Mike that. Doing it with the lights on was about as kinky as he'd ever have imagined his straightforward partner got. But as for *freak*... Mike should have been with him on a few of the wilder Soho nights. He'd have seen things in the back rooms of the bars that might have restored his perspective. "Tie you up, eh?" he echoed, straddling him, not hiding the dawn of a smile. "Sounds reasonable to me. My set of cuffs is in your car, or—"

"No." Michael shifted restlessly under him, trying to pull his wrists from John's imprisoning grip. "I can't wait. Your belt and mine."

"Oh." John swallowed, a dry spasm that hurt his throat. His cock couldn't rise to the occasion again, but a pang of excitement, dark as blood, passed through him. *I can't wait.* Mike was deadly serious. His face was flushed and wild in the lamplight, his shaft stiff and urgent, swelling the tip of the condom with precome. Fingers unsteady, John drew his belt out from the loops of his jeans. Michael was arching beneath him, lifting his hips. It was the work of a second to slide his belt free too.

And it was sexy as hell, but something inside John ached and cringed as he took the strong, fine-made wrist Michael was offering up to him. He'd played bondage games in the clubs. He didn't mind tying—or being tied, for that matter. It was fun.

But Mike was crying.

"John," he rasped. "Go home. I'm not fit for you."

"What?" Quickly John leaned in, kissed the salt off his cheeks. "Jesus, lover. Don't make a big deal. This is fine, okay? Nothing wrong with it." Before Michael could pull away, John drew his arm up and out, slipped one belt round a hoop of the wrought-iron headboard and fastened the leather tight round his wrist. "Not sure how to keep it there. I'll knot it if you—"

"Nn-nn. I'll hold the end."

"Okay." That was better—Mike's choice, not his. Mike, at least, regulating this impossible scenario. John reached and attended to the other outstretched hand. And there he was—laid out beneath John, tendons standing, exposed. He was so bloody lovely. It should have been the stuff of pornographic dreams. "It's fine," John told him. "It's hot, okay? Sexy for me too."

Michael turned his head to one side. He closed his eyes. "Now I need you to hurt me."

John sat back on his heels. Suddenly he felt cold and tired as he never had been in his life. What the hell was going on here? Wanting Michael had been like a meteor, flashing across John's inner sky, blinding in its beauty. Getting him—Christ, the meteor had hit the gravity well and was breaking up, fragments dropping in fiery chaos all around. "You need what?"

"You heard me. I keep a knife—back of the drawer there, wrapped in a shirt. I can't get off otherwise. Please!"

"You want me to..." John couldn't get his mouth round the words, much less his head round the concept. He wouldn't have batted an eyelid anywhere else but here. Men needed what they needed—didn't they?—though he stopped short of such games himself. This flesh, though, the beautiful skin he would have laid down his life to keep intact on the street... "You want me to cut you?"

"I warned you. I'm a freak. Now do it, or—"

"Shut up." John couldn't bear to hear the end of the command. *Do it or forget it. Do it or leave me alone.* Part of him wanted to bail. He felt sick and utterly lost, glad of his shagged-out excuse for not getting it up.

Couldn't leave Michael like this, though. They were partners; they saw to one another. And as for *I can't get off otherwise*, John hadn't spent three years on the London scene without learning some quick, efficient methods of release. Michael was holding on to the ends of both belts, pinning his wrists into position. John kissed his damp brow, one last effort of benediction on this bizarre scene. Then he eased down the bed. He was too tired and sore to take him into his body again, but he had it on good authority that he gave the best head this side of Soho.

Michael flinched as he peeled the condom off his straining cock. Murmuring vague reassurance, John knelt between his thighs. He leaned over him, trying not to set this experience against his dreams of it, and drew him into his mouth.

Briefly he thought it wouldn't work. Michael bucked underneath him, muscles of his backside and thighs locking in resistance wherever John tried to place a soothing hold. What the hell was holding him back? He was ready—desperate, if his bitten-back moans were anything to go by—and yet he felt to John like some beautiful car revving against an intractable hand brake. John rippled his tongue up and down the length of him, circled the head in a motion that had driven past lovers wild. He opened his throat, stilled his gag reflex, and let him slide all the way down, squeezing; reached strong fingertips into the crease of his backside and massaged hard around his opening.

Oh yes. There—a giant, speared-fish convulsion in the body he held. A spurt deep in his throat that made him forget his technique and choke before he got control and began to swallow, carefully, methodically. Two, three more of the huge whole-body spasms, as if Michael were dragging down on his restraints with all his strength. John grabbed him, hearing his climaxing shout with wonder at the fear and pain in it. Oh, he'd get it right next time with him—whatever his demons, chase them off or learn to love the bastards. Hanging on, John drank him down, forbidding himself to let go until the last drop was expended and Michael's cock was softening, freeing John's airway at last.

He sat up. Already Michael was struggling away from him. "Hang on," John rasped, then broke off, coughing. "I'll undo those."

"No. I've got them." Twisting, Michael freed one hand, then curled up on the bed, turning his back on John to reach across and untie the other. He was breathing hard and unsteadily, as if he were only just holding back sobs. Tenderly, frightened, John said his name, and ignored his evasive flinch, taking hold of the other wrist to help him.

The skin was wet. Sweat-soaked, yes, like the rest of him, but sticky too. Dark streaks painted his arms.

Blood went black in streetlight.

"Shit," John whispered and snapped on the bedside lamp. Mike tried to haul away from him, but he'd yanked the belt too tight through its buckle and the leather had turned sideways and caught. Had cut so deep, John saw, snatching the other hand—the one doing its best to shove him away—that its edge had ground into and then torn the flesh. Michael was bleeding. "Mikey, what the fuck...?"

"Let me go."

"Okay. Let me unfasten that and—"

"No. Back the fuck off. Now!"

The free hand landed hard on John's sternum, and he fell back, too sick and bewildered to resist. He watched with a sense of nightmare as his partner and best friend tore his bloodied wrist free of the restraint. The belt—John's, of course—was a fashion accessory, not needed to hold his trousers up, and just as well; he'd never be wearing it again. "Michael..."

"What?" Michael turned on him. "I asked you to cut me. You wouldn't give me the pain, so I had to find it for myself. You happy?"

John scrambled back to him. He put both hands on his chilly, rigid shoulders. Michael tried to jerk away, but he was backed against the headboard. "Listen," John whispered, resting his brow on top of the bowed skull. "You listen. I'll tie you up if you want. I'll tie you up, tie you down, fuck you seven ways to sunset. But don't ever ask me to hurt you again. Not like that."

"Again?" Michael choked. He raised his head, and just for a moment his eyes met John's with such an abyss of pain in them that John almost cried out. "There's not gonna be an *again* for this. And—I could never let another man fuck me. Let me go, Griff."

John, on his hands and knees on the bed, watched him stumble out of the room. It was his instinct to go after him. Get the first-aid kit out, wash the grazing and weals—which, now John came to think about it, were new wounds on old, faded scarring he had often wondered about but never dared ask—and bandage them up.

There's not gonna be an again for this.

He had sounded disgusted. Miserable. And what did he think of men like John, who did let themselves be fucked?

Exhaustion caught up with him, a merciful wave. He subsided onto the bed, flat on his stomach, burying his face in the quilt. The house remained silent. After a brief struggle against exhaustion, he slept.

Chapter Six

The surface under him was his own sofa, not a bunk in a cell. Michael sat up. The sun had laid a fiery sword into the room. He squinted into the light, shielding his eyes. Why the hell had he slept here? Courting nightmares, apparently. Sometimes he would have the cell dream anyway, but sleeping elsewhere than his bed, in narrow, uncomfortable places, was a good way to wake up screaming.

He got to his feet. His mouth was dry, his limbs heavy and stiff. He'd made a job of it, hadn't he—facedown on the couch, not bothering with a rug or duvet, naked from the waist up. He was still in his trousers from yesterday, and these were unfastened, barely pulled up over his hips, as if he'd staggered off to lie down after...

His wrists were sore. Michael looked down at them, at the grazing, the deep-scored weals—and his heart tried to stop.

He knew that his mind, although still efficient, didn't work in the way it had before his mission to Zemelya. He thought he remembered his time there, but, joining event to event, it didn't add up. His memory was full of dark matter, lost weeks and months, a terrifying failure to account. His dreams tried to fill in the blanks. And his waking mind was sluggish, often substituting dreamtime for reality until he had a shower and woke up. He would forget what had happened the night before.

He tried to say his partner's name, but no sound came. Slowly he made his way across the living room. As always he felt pleasure in the press of his bare feet to the silky Afghan carpets he'd put down. The flat smelled agreeably of coffee and leather, the sofa warming fragrantly in the sun. He loved his home. He'd bought good things on his MI5 wage and installed them here, when Last Line security had passed the place suitable, with desperate energy. He needed the link between the past and now, needed a refuge. He took his bearings from his own four walls when all else failed—and all else had. Without the familiar textures and scents, he would dissolve into nothing this morning, blend into the sunlight and be gone.

What the fuck had he done?

He eased open his bedroom door. The back of the flat overlooked an alley, and sunlight didn't make it until late afternoon. The curtains were wide open. He hadn't even done that much to protect John's privacy and the thing that had happened between them. He flashed back to the kitchen and what he had done there, and he had to bite back a moan. The bedroom was shadowy. John was an abstract pattern on the duvet, his long loose limbs hard to pick out. He'd fallen asleep where weariness had dropped him, one hand hanging limply off the bed. His T-shirt had ridden up, exposing the stretch of his spine.

He'd fallen nearly to his death the day before. Michael therefore wasn't responsible for the dreadful bruising, black as grapes, marking the tawny skin that kept its golden warmth all through London's darkest winters. Nevertheless he had forgotten about it—obliterated his memory of the damage in lust, banging

John up against the wall, pinning him to the kitchen table. Unsteadily Michael went to crouch by the bed. Fuck, how did he even dare touch him? For a moment he couldn't, only extending one finger to the waistband of his jeans, drawing it a little lower. Remorse and mortification tore through him. Whispering his name, he put out a shaking hand and stroked his hair.

John lifted his head. Briefly he stared straight ahead, his eyes dark and blank. Then he rolled stiffly onto his side. "Mike?"

"Yeah. Jesus, you really did break your fall with your arse."

"You haven't even seen my—" He shut up, meeting Michael's eyes in consternation, memory impacting on him in visible shocks. "Oh God."

Michael swallowed. "It was dark. I couldn't see, or I'd have never…" *Thrown you down and screwed you. In my right mind I wouldn't have done that, or ordered you to hurt me, then for want of your compliance pulled on my restraints until at last the pain and the pleasure met hard enough inside me to let me come.* "I'd never have done any of that."

"Well…" John shoved cautiously up onto his elbows. His expression was apprehensive, but a faint smile was lighting it— achingly familiar to Michael, full of mischief and affection. "Some of it was… unexpected. And you are—oh, so much kinkier than I'd have given you credit for in a million years, but… it wasn't all bad. As you must have been able to tell."

Involuntarily Michael flashed back to the feel of John hitting climax in his arms. Christ, he'd hardly noticed at the time, his own cock like a spear in pursuit of its demands. How could he have been so lost—blind and deaf to the best part of it? "I made you come," he said softly, almost in a tone of confession.

"Twice. In the space of about two minutes, which is some kind of land-speed record. Mikey. Look… I know it got out of control, and somebody said *never again*, but we can deal with it. If you want to. Let me see your wrists."

Michael had no choice. He could hardly stick them behind his back like an unwilling child. He bore John's inspection as best he could, feeling a painful blush invading his neck and his face. "You don't understand," he said hoarsely. "Sometimes it's the only way for me."

"Sometimes? Or always?"

Not with a woman. Michael couldn't say it. He hadn't hidden his occasional flings from John, but the thought of throwing them into his tired, pale face now was repellent to him. Being with a woman, even the redoubtable Diane, meant nothing. The scratching of an itch. And last night, fuckup though it had been, had meant the world. John was caressing his wrists, frowning over the wounds as if they had been legitimate, acquired in the line of duty. "I don't know. Maybe. That's too screwed up, John."

"There's more than one way to skin a cat. If pain's what it takes, I mean." He leaned on one elbow and gave Michael a look of kindly penetration. "Doesn't have to end in knives and bloodshed. And"—his thumb gently skimmed the old marks—"it sure as hell shouldn't leave scars."

"Oh, I didn't get those doing that. I got them—" He crashed to a halt, the last word dying in his throat. He knew, didn't he? The memory had been there. Now there was only a cold weight, as if someone had put a stone in its place.

Fear swept through him. He felt sick. John was watching him, brow creased in concern, and Michael could read him like a book, ready to offer him any damn thing he wanted. To wash the darkness off all his desires. But John didn't know the half of it. Michael didn't know himself. God alone knew what he'd done in his memory's gaps. What he recalled was bad enough.

"Mike? Where'd you get them?"

"Doesn't matter." He tried for a smile and began to get up, but John's hand closed on his shoulder. His palm was starfish cool, soothing to fretted skin. "Don't. We'd better go."

"Was it while you were with MI5?"

He froze. John never asked him. Michael had made it clear during the first days of their partnership that MI5 was a no-go zone for small talk or even the large kind they'd soon started to enjoy over a pint in the evening, and John had left well alone. It wouldn't have mattered now, except that everything bad in Michael's life—the memory gaps, the need to be hurt, the sense of his own soiled worthlessness—dated from his time in MI5.

No. From his time in Zemelya. And, since setting eyes on the Ashkeloi the day before, Zemelya had rushed back into the world all around him, the world he'd struggled so hard to make safe. The buildings beyond his bedroom window would turn into impenetrable ranks of pine if he didn't concentrate. He would smell resin and frost... "John," he said urgently, easing out from under the restraining hand. "We're due on shift. If you're okay..."

"Yeah." John scrambled upright. Shadows of pain clouded the bright compassion in his eyes. "Feel like I got fucked by some big ex-secret service bloke, but I must just be imagining that."

Michael swallowed. When he found a voice, it didn't sound like his own. "You wanted us to have sex. That's what sex with me is gonna be like." Anger flickered in John's eyes. It was better than hurt, but still Michael couldn't hold his gaze. He turned away and pulled a fresh shirt from his wardrobe. "You might want to think better of it. Christ, we haven't even got time for a shower. You bring your gun back from the hospital last night?"

"What do you think?"

"Then grab it and let's go."

* * *

An hour later they were on the steps outside HQ, looking at one another in the light of a brilliant May morning. Folding his arms, leaning on the railing, John asked cautiously, "D'you think we screwed up?"

"I don't think so. He seemed to be in a good mood. If I seem unsure, it's just that it's the first time I've seen it."

"I've never known him to offer us leave before."

"I can understand it for you. You should probably be on sick leave anyway."

"Mikey, you look worse than I do."

Michael blinked. The old rough trace of tenderness was back in his partner's voice, and how he had deserved it he couldn't imagine. Their silent drive in had been a torture. Webb had summoned them at once on their arrival, and they'd gone into his office shoulder to shoulder as always, and a million miles apart. "Ta," he said. "Okay, maybe we both need some time off."

"Yeah. We had the Vauxhall business before this one, and that was a ballbreaker. Still, I thought he'd be too pissed off about his witness to offer us anything but paperwork."

"That guy couldn't have given us much anyway. He was bit-part."

"In whose play? I know you don't want to talk about him, but…"

"No. It's okay." Michael had done some fast thinking in Webb's office. The witness had died almost instantly, the old man had informed them brusquely. The explosives he was carrying were duds. The whole thing was a mystery, a waste of Last Line's valuable resources. Michael had drawn a deep breath as Webb had closed up the file. With Piotr gone, what did it matter that Michael's memories of him didn't match up? If Webb wasn't inclined to pursue it, the matter could drop into darkness, and Michael could give John a half-truth to settle his fears too. "I don't mean to be a clam about MI5. I did a mission to northern Russia—to Zemelya Province, where my mother came from. You were right about the language. That guy in the church was an insurgent I was meant to be tracking. I thought he was dead, so seeing him again was a shock. That was all."

John shrugged. When was the last time that Michael had tried to slide a fiction past him? Usually he didn't bother. The look in those green eyes would tell him exactly how far he was getting. "Okay," John said. "Look, I don't care, mate—long as you're all right."

A silence fell. They stood facing one another on the steps. In a way it felt so ordinary—to be here within arm's reach of one another, catching a breath of air between tasks—and in another way, Michael knew, it was fucking outrageous. He might be able to drop Piotr back into oblivion, but he couldn't drop John there. He had to say something that would acknowledge the night they'd just spent. "I'm fine," he began, then shoved a foot toward his partner in an echo of their old camaraderie. "But I am tired. I might head down to Glastonbury, if the old sod's really giving us this week off. Do you fancy a few days on the farm?"

John snorted faintly. "You just want a brickie."

"Well, where would I find a better one?" Michael smiled. John had put in so much work with him over the years on the derelict farmhouse Michael's grandfather had left him, together with its six acres of rich green Somerset land, that the place should belong to him as much as to Michael. So much so that Michael had often thought about putting it into both their names, a task he had somehow never got around to. Given their sudden-death line of trade, the omission had been stupid. "Come on, Griff. Let's just go and kick back for a bit. I feel like we... walked into some kind of bloody explosion last night. Maybe we can—"

John's phone buzzed. For a long moment, he didn't move to answer. His gaze was locked seriously to Michael's. Then he glanced down at the screen. "Oh shit. I have to take this."

"Who is it?"

"Quin's bloody school again. I swear…"

He turned away and jogged down the rest of the steps to the pavement. Michael watched him go. How easy it was to push a whole world off its axis. Only yesterday, John would have stayed within earshot, would have put his hand across the phone's pickup and mouthed obscenities at Michael while the conversation went on.

He went to lean on the roof of the Jag. Michael had driven it carefully back from the hospital for him, minding its tricky gears. After a minute or so, he straightened up, running a hand through his hair. All his movements, Michael saw, were slower than usual, tired and stiff. He tucked the phone back into his pocket.

"Everything all right?"

John tried for a grin and managed the ghost of one. "No. Little fucker's in trouble again. I've got to go and sort it out."

"I'll come with you if you—"

"Nn-nn. Time I learned to kick his arse myself. I'll come down to Glasto in a couple of days, if that's okay. I…" The smile amped up, became genuine, if laced with regret and irony. "I don't think a bit of time apart will do us any harm at the moment, will it? I'll see you soon."

Chapter Seven

The river Teal was sparkling seductively in the hot May sun. John pulled the XKR into the familiar lay-by and switched the engine off. For a moment he just sat, leaning his head back, grateful for the leaf-stirred silence. Dealing with Quin had been a three-day job this time, and a joyless one: meetings with staff and advisers at one school, a dreadful hostile overnight with the brat in a hotel near the next one, then a round of interviews during which he had persuaded more staff and advisers that Quin's genius, and a full year's fees paid in advance, more than made up for the fact that the genius was disturbed, destructive, and an incorrigible runaway.

John rubbed a hand over his eyes. He knew he wasn't doing the right thing by his brother, but unless he could turn back the clock and stop the lorry that had broadsided his parents into oblivion during a run to the local supermarket, he didn't know what else to do. He hadn't even been in England at the time. The news had hauled him back from a stint on a Merchant Navy ship in the Gulf of Aden. He had landed at Harwich an unskilled, unwilling guardian to a bereaved thirteen-year-old, and things had gone downhill from there.

The river looked tempting. John clambered out of the car, tugging at his sweat-dampened shirt. He could see Michael's house high on the hillside—or the promise of a house that was beginning to rise from the masonry scattered around it. No car was parked outside, and the garden was empty. For a moment he wondered if Michael hadn't come down after all, then remembered it was Thursday. He shook his head, smiling. On holiday or not, Mike never missed his drill with the local volunteer fire brigade when he was in Somerset. He would be out, tearing around the country lanes in a seven-ton truck, causing—John always told him—far more danger to life and limb than he and his colleagues could ever hope to avert. John had met him head-to-head on a curve once or twice, poised behind the wheel, face a pure mask of concentration, all the lovely musculature of his arms exposed in his uniform tee.

Damn. John had set himself carefully not to think about Michael in any sexual context at all. Easy enough until now, despite their recent clash. The last three days had been among the least arousing of John's life. Here, though, in the lazy sunshine, lush green meadows rolling and dreaming all around...

He locked the car and shinned over the roadside fence. The water was calling to him strongly. No matter how bad he felt, a dip would usually help fix him up, even if it was only half an hour in the training pool at HQ. The Teal curved round Mike's land in a sheltering half circle here, an embracing arm. The banks were deserted and tree lined. He wouldn't frighten anyone. He made his way through waist-high goldenrod to the water's edge. Late willow-fluff or early dandelion was floating on the surface. John knew that the leisurely motion concealed a strong, deep current, and having skinned out of his shirt, jeans, and boxers, he went in cautiously, gasping at the cold.

He let the current carry him downriver for almost half a mile, then turned, set his muscle against the great brown-gold liquid one surrounding him, and began to swim for all he was worth. He was more keenly aware of his strength in the water than anywhere else. It was one of the few areas in which he could outstrip Mike when it came to a physical contest between them. Patiently, arms and legs tingling then slowly numbing out, he worked back upstream to his starting point, turned, and repeated the exercise.

He found his depth and stood, waist high, water sheeting off his shoulders. He squeezed his hair back from his brow. He was trembling slightly with exhaustion, and that was good. He had wanted to take the edge off before seeing Michael again. If he closed his eyes, he was back in Michael's kitchen—in his bedroom, caught up again in everything that had gone so shatteringly wrong and right on his table and then in his bed. In a red-hot fuck without a trace of tenderness—about the last thing John would ever have predicted from his partner, unless it was the bondage, pain, and blood.

Tiredly he sank down on the water-rippled sand. It was deliciously warm. His limbs still held the river's chill, and he stretched out on his back, idly drying himself with the bunched fabric of his shirt. A faint moan of pleasure escaped him, audible only to the drifting willows and the birds. His bruises had healed with weird rapidity. He was almost all better, no aches or pains left to distract him from dangerous thoughts. Nothing but the cold in his marrow, and that was melting fast. He had to accept that he and Mike might have taken their swing at passion and failed.

So John needed to stop replaying the tape. Instead he turned his mind to his own warm skin. Letting go of his shirt, he idly ran a hand down his chest. His palm brushed a nipple, which promptly tightened, raising a corresponding twitch near his groin.

"Oh fuck," he whispered to the cloud-chased sky. He was horny as hell. He couldn't stop remembering.

He let go a shuddering breath. Well, there was more than one way to grind off an edge, and there was nobody around. Tipping back his head, he stroked a hand across his cock, and arched hungrily as it leaped. Shame and bottled-up laughter shook him. He was screwed if the Somerset Anglers' Club chose this bend of the river for an afternoon jaunt. Not that this would take long. He was hard, throbbing in his own grasp. Driving his heels into the wet sand, he stroked his chest and belly again, opened his eyes wide to the sapphire sky, and began to jerk off.

It was sweeter, more intense than he could have anticipated. He'd always enjoyed his own touch, but it was for lean times, dry spells between boyfriends—purely practical. Water-scented breeze lifted his fringe off his brow. He drew a deep breath. Nothing practical about this, and to all intents and purposes, he wasn't even alone. His starved imagination had material now, memories… A bare five more strokes did it for him. Hitting the crest, he rolled onto his stomach, words shuddering helplessly out of him. "Mike! God, I love you!"

He lay for a long while in the sun, feeling his shattered breathing steady. Maybe that had been the problem. Michael knew his habits. How was the poor bastard supposed to know he was anything more than the next notch on John's bedpost? Maybe a quick, hands-off fuck had been all he'd dared risk. Easing his come-soaked hand out from under, John tried to imagine the scene where he put Mike right on that. *I've been looking for you all my life. You don't have to hit-and-run. I love you.*

Well, it might not be the end of the world. John sat up, reaching for his shirt. In the distance, he could hear the purr of an engine. A few moments later, a car broached the hill to the north of the farmhouse and swept down the single-track road. Mike's

BMW, as powerful and understated as the man himself. Desire swept through John, marrow-deep, entirely divorced from sex. What had he said to him: *time apart might do us good?* Who the hell was he trying to kid? Three days and he was parched half to death just for the sight of him. *Love* barely covered the feeling. He got up, shaking sand out of his hair.

It had to be worth a try.

* * *

He left the car where it was and followed the track up through the fields. He would go and collect his holdall later. For now all he wanted was to close the gap between himself and the tumbledown farmhouse, and the most direct route was across the meadow, where the grass was knee-high, swaying in the wind like pods of silver-backed dolphins riding the wake of a ship. He strode through it as if spellbound, damp skin drying under his shirt and jeans.

The land crested a few hundred yards from the house, concealing it briefly, opening up a vista to the west. Warmed through now, breath catching slightly in the heat, John paused at the top of the hill. Nothing in his Mersey-suburb childhood or his years in the capital could have prepared him for the sight of Glastonbury Tor across a sweep of summer countryside. He had crashed to a halt to stare the first time Mike had brought him up here, and it still stole the breath from him now. A sudden leap of land, nothing more than a teardrop-shaped hill but somehow profoundly startling, mysterious. Trackways—explained as everything from agricultural terraces to ancient ceremonial paths winding up around its flanks—attracted every ufologist, crop-circle maker, and general cuckoo for hundreds of miles around. Michael refused to go anywhere near Glasto town at any of the eight points on the wheel of the ritual year. If his mother had been a crazy Russian refugee, he had pointed out to John, his granddad had been a plain farmer, growing his crops without benefit of fertility rites or alien intervention. John had thought it best not to confide in him that he too had seen weird lights gleaming over the Tor on certain summer nights.

Scrambling over a stile, he let his attention refocus from the enigmatic distance to the small world spread out at his feet. He wasn't sure why he had spent so many weekends down here over the past couple of years reconstructing a moss-covered ruin, except that it felt good to spend time with Mike away from the job. No harm in picking up a few of his partner's construction skills, either. If things went tits-up at Last Line, they'd agreed, they could always set up as builders. And the nights had been pleasant too, sprawled on a sofa in the recently finished living room, talking or reading, looking at a wall he'd helped put together with his own hands. He had his own bedroom—like Michael's, currently a wooden prefab, soon to be properly walled and roofed—and his own set of drawers. He and Michael slept, chaste as priests, each on his own side of the thin partition wall.

Setting aside speculation as to where he might sleep tonight, John slithered down the last steep bank and vaulted the fence into the lane. A wave of honeysuckle assailed him, sparking one city-boy sneeze before his lungs adjusted. The gate was open into the wide sweep of turf they'd optimistically started calling a garden. The back door too. Michael, in the city cautious as a cat, left security concerns behind him there, something John was not sure he approved. "Mike?" he called, padding over the daisy-starred lawn. No response came, and John paused to glance in admiration at the courses of unmortared drystone that had risen on the back barn's foundations. His strange, half-Russian sheep farmer must have been working his arse off all week. "Hoi! It's just me. Got any beer cooling?"

He wandered through the open door into the kitchen. At the moment, this consisted of some battered stone flags and a loose collection of dark oak cabinets and worktops. Standing in its cool shadows, John found himself hoping it would never change too much. He and Mike had spent a day in the Shepton Mallet kitchen showrooms—feeling and, John suspected, looking queer as fuck—but hadn't found any modern units that seemed right for the rough-plastered old walls, for the building's solemn but somehow benign atmosphere. Mike, who loved to cook, had invested in a good gas oven—the tank was discreetly buried under the turf outside—but that was all.

No, wait. The shadows had acquired a new, unobtrusive hum. Turning round, John saw gleaming in the corner a charcoal-metal fridge as tall as he was. He grinned. Last time down he'd had to tell Mike that *good enough for my grandfather* didn't really cut it when it came to chilling beer and keeping gorgonzola fresh, great though the stone pantry was. He hadn't thought Mike had taken any notice. The door opened with a rich, sticky resistance, and there on the top shelf, quite respectfully laid out, were half a dozen bottles of the locally brewed Ringwood John liked.

Footsteps scraped on the path. Michael appeared in the doorway, looking fresh as new butter in a light cotton-knit jersey. "Ah," he said, eyes kindling with laughter. "I see you found it."

"You bought a new fridge without me?"

"I didn't think you'd disapprove."

"Not a bit of it." John snagged a beer from the shelf and waved it at his partner, who nodded, then got another for himself. He watched Michael dump a shopping bag onto the worktop and begin to unload it: a cylinder of asparagus spears neatly tied in twine, lemons, eggs, a beautiful fat half salmon. "That looks a lot like my ideal dinner."

"Mm," Michael agreed. He took the beer John had uncapped and offered him, tipped the bottle in casual salute. "Might be."

"You gonna make the hollandaise yourself?"

"Naturally."

"I'll stay, then." John reviewed the array of good things on the counter. He said, puzzled, "Nice timing, by the way. I tried to call you to tell you I was on my way, but—"

"The signal's as bad as ever." Gently edging him out of the way, Michael brought the salmon over to the fridge and tucked it in. Then he gave his partner what John could only think of as an exotic Russian look and added pensively, "I just had a feeling you were coming."

"Really?"

"No, you moron. I saw your car parked by the river, and I doubled back to Linda's farm shop. Why didn't you drive up?"

"Bastard," John remarked without anger. This was a different man from the tense, hollow-eyed one he'd left behind in London. Relaxed enough to tease him. Maybe everything would be fine. "It was too hot. I stopped off for a swim, and I couldn't bear to get back into the car after that, so I walked up through the fields."

"The sheep fields? In your bare feet?"

There had been a few sheep scattered about, now John came to think of it. His shoes, which he'd absently carried up with him then left outside the door, were a bit of a giveaway, he supposed. "Yeah, I…" A cold chill went through him. "Oh."

Michael sighed. "All right, go sit down. Let's have a look."

John obeyed him, repressing shudders. He'd done quite well as a holiday landsman here on the farm with Mike, digging manure and planting veg as if it came naturally, but he still occasionally betrayed himself for the townie he was. A dreamy barefoot stroll through long grass in this season meant not so much freedom and sensual pleasure as sheep ticks. He half fell into the kitchen chair Mike had pulled out for him. "Ugh, I hate the little fuckers."

Michael crouched in front of him. He pushed John's clumsy hands aside and neatly pushed up the hems of his jeans for himself. "Well, you might've been lucky... Nope. You've got a passenger or two."

"Oh *shit*." Peering at his ankles, John saw the three or four little black dots that would, unattended, swell up to blood-gorged balloons. He twitched irrepressibly. "Jesus. Get 'em off me, Mike."

"Hold still." Michael got up and went to lift a well-stocked first-aid kit out from under the sink. He stopped at the dresser too, and John heard a clink of glass and a brief splash. Returning, he held out a tumbler to John with an inch of tawny liquid inside it. "Here you go."

"What's this? Antiseptic?"

"No. A shot of brandy for you, you absolute pussy. You've gone green."

John closed his eyes in embarrassment. That felt good, he decided, and he kept them closed, downing the brandy by feel, while Michael went to work. He kept a special little tool for the purpose, John remembered, and he didn't want to watch his parasites being grabbed round the neck and twisted deftly out of his flesh. He gagged faintly, almost losing the brandy, and opened his eyes in time to see Mike glancing up at him in alarm. "God. Sorry."

"All done." Michael uncapped a bottle of TCP, soaked a wad of cotton wool, and began to apply it to the bites. "Sheesh, John. You really are a big girl's blouse."

"I know. Ta. What was God thinking when he made those?"

"He was probably thinking you'd have the sense to wear socks, like I keep telling you. It's okay, Lazarus. You may rise now and walk."

But neither of them moved. Michael stayed on his knees, and John, once his stomach had stopped lurching, leaned an elbow on the table and gazed down at him. A silence fell in the cool, sunlit room, broken only by the chitter of house martins feeding their chicks in the eaves of the old barn. "How are you, Mikey?" John asked at length. "I love that jersey. But those are long sleeves for this weather."

"Don't." Michael looked down at the stone flags. "I'm fine. Just didn't want to scare the village shopkeepers."

"What about your fire crew? Didn't you have to get changed?"

"Oh, I skipped a shift for once."

"Still pretty bad, then." It wasn't a question. John reached out a hand, and after a long moment's hesitation, Michael surrendered one of his. John rolled back the fine, close-fitting sleeve far enough. "Jesus, sunbeam. We can't ever fall down that rabbit hole again."

"I know."

"You had to do that to yourself because I wouldn't hurt you."

"Yes. No. I…" Michael pulled down his sleeve to cover the damage. He didn't withdraw his hand, though, and his voice was soft as he went on. "To tell you the truth, I can hardly remember. Th-the first bit with you, yes."

"The first bit with me was fine. A bit startling, I'll grant you, but…"

"But we can't do it again if I'm gonna freak out and turn into some kind of bondage sub."

"Well… I told you I'm not about to carve you up, but that's not a problem either, if we go about it right."

"It is a problem." Michael lifted his head and looked at him square-on. His eyes were very black, but lit once more with the strange fires that had scared John and aroused him in equal measure three nights before. "It's a huge fucking problem for me, because that's not who I am. I don't know where all that crap came from, and I don't feel like I can risk it again, and that's…" He trailed off, voice scraping a little. "That's a tragedy in a way, because…"

John swallowed. His ticks and his apprehensions were forgotten. His good intentions too. When Michael looked at him like that, he felt the pit of his gut turn to liquid gold, his bones to meltwater. "Why?" he whispered, locking a grip to the edge of his chair.

"Because you look so good. And you smell of the river and brandy, and…" He sat up a little, inhaling. A small, wicked smile, surmise and astonishment combined, began to tuck itself into the corner of his mouth. "And something else. My God! What did you get up to on the way here?"

"Oh—*Christ*," John burst out, blushing painfully hard. "You can *smell* that? I-I did it for you, Mike. I didn't want to come blazing in here with my cock pushing the bloody doors open, so after my swim, I stopped on the riverbank for five minutes and…" He shut up. He eyed Michael narrowly. He had seen him make suspects babble and incriminate themselves like this. "And it's none of your business," he finished calmly, returning him sardonic smile for sardonic smile.

"Oh, don't stop," Michael said innocently. "I was getting such a nice picture in my head."

"Screw you," John returned—or tried. Somehow Michael was kneeling between his thighs. Somehow, without an instant's warning, they were in each other's arms. Which was fine—beautiful—but instantly they were locked into a kiss just as merciless and bruising as the one that had opened their scene at Michael's flat. Not something Mike was doing to him. It was mutual, John's fingers driving into the short silky hair at Mike's nape, imprisoning, just as fierce as Mike's grip on his shoulders. Why the fuck couldn't they be gentle with one another?

It was all out of balance, too hot. Mike had lurched from *I can't risk it* to *I can't stop* in less than a minute—and so had he. John transferred his grasp to the sides of Michael's face. Slowly, carefully he forced him back. "No. Stop a second."

"Christ, John. I... didn't even mean to start."

"I know. Me neither." Unsteadily John smoothed the rumpled black hair, planted a kiss more fraternal than sexual onto the top of his skull. "So here's what we're going to do. You're gonna make dinner for us; then we'll sit around and have the... nice, boring, no-brainer night we usually do have when I come down here. I'll moan at you about Quin, and you can tell me one of your interesting stories about what type of sheep your granddad kept." He waited until Michael registered the insult, reddened lips parting in silent protest. "Then if anything happens—and I'm not saying it won't—maybe it can happen a bit slower and less like we're trying to kill one another. Okay?"

"Okay. I... thought you liked my sheep stories."

"I do, but they're passion killers. Maybe no bad thing."

"Maybe not." Still breathing quickly, Michael sat back on his heels. He looked like himself again. Handsome but ordinary. John's partner and friend. John couldn't bear to lose that—not even for the best shag in the world. "Still, I wouldn't rely on it. I'd have thought picking ticks off you would've killed the romance."

* * *

Michael poached the salmon, steamed new potatoes to a state of heartbreaking tenderness. He sent John off into the garden to pick chives. He let John watch while he brought an alchemist's concentration to the hollandaise, which would separate out if left unstirred for so much as a second. John, whose notions of cooking began and ended with the microwave instructions on a ready meal, allowed himself to be chivied round the kitchen with a good heart. He liked these rituals. In London, dinner was often a sandwich washed down with a flask coffee in the back of a surveillance van. He liked to set the massive kitchen table with linen and silverware which, though spotless, looked as if they belonged to the house from its earliest foundations.

John grabbed a bottle of crisp cold Pinot from the fridge, uncorked it, and was in time to draw the chef's chair back for Michael in a half-mocking, half-serious gesture that made Michael grin and shake his head. "Pack it in, you clown."

"Least I can do. This looks bloody gorgeous."

"Sit down and eat it, then."

John complied willingly. He wanted to ask why all his best-loved foods were on the table—and a summer pudding gently chilling in the fridge—but suspected he knew. It was on his lips to tell Michael there was no need, that their collision of three nights before had been entirely mutual, a shared if unexpected violence. No call for him to do anything to make it up. That would put the whole thing on the table, though, huge and inappropriate among the old crystal glasses and the handful of eglantine roses John had awkwardly borne in from the garden. Better not to look it in the mouth. Instead he said, reaching for more hollandaise, "One day you're gonna tell me who taught you to cook like this."

"Yes, all right. My mum did."

John almost dropped the jug. Michael had turned that question aside with a joke for the best part of three years. He never volunteered a word about his family. John had gathered, in scraps and with painful slowness, that his father had died in the far-flung Russian province where he'd gone out on business and met his mother. That his mother had fled Russia for reasons unknown with her five-year-old son, and on motives equally mysterious taken refuge with her father-in-law, the dour old sheep farmer who'd lived here until the house fell into dereliction around him. Learning that much had been a major victory. "Your mum?" he echoed, trying not to sound too astonished. Michael was continuing calmly with his meal. "This is top-notch English cuisine for a Russian refugee, isn't it?"

"Well, these were the raw materials she had to hand." Michael topped off John's glass with the straw-pale Pinot. "She adapted. I kept her recipe book after she died. I could do you kvashenaya kapusta and borscht with pelmeni if you wanted."

"That would be interesting sometime." John let a minute or so elapse, watching his partner as subtly as he could. He knew every flicker of tension in him, as well as all his measures for trying to hide them. Just now he seemed absolutely relaxed. A good time or a bad one to push it? He decided to take the risk. "What happened to her, Mike?"

Michael looked up, wineglass gently cupped in one palm. His eyes were dark but untroubled. "You've been very good about not asking."

"Oh fuck." John shivered in dismay. Had he managed to bugger things up already? "I've got a big mouth. Forget it."

"No, it's okay. I only haven't told you because—there aren't any answers, not really. I came back from school one day and found her in bed. There wasn't a mark on her. The coroner recorded death by natural causes, though neither he nor any of the doctors who carried out the inquest could tell what those were."

"Oh—Jesus, Mike."

"Look, I was seven. It all went straight over my head. I don't even really remember any of it, not properly. So take a deep breath and finish your dinner." Michael picked up the vegetable dish and served him more potatoes, then helped himself by way of example. "Now, tell me what happened with Quin."

Are you kidding me? Reflexively swallowing half a glassful of wine, John stared at him. *You tell me you found your mother dead when you were seven years old, and now we just... politely turn the conversation?* "Quin? Bugger him. Mike, why—"

"Hush. I've no idea why I told you that. My brain feels full of all sorts of weird flotsam at the moment. Can we leave it?"

"God, yes, of course." John shook himself. "Right. Quin... This time the police retrieved him from the Forest of Dean. He'd built and equipped a fully operational survival shelter using an SAS handbook he'd nicked from Waterstones." He waited until Michael had recovered from a half-choked burst of laughter. "When they asked him why he'd stolen the book—he's got plenty of pocket money—he said it was part of the game. He's not of this bloody earth, Mike."

"Did he tell *you* why he'd done it?"

"Fat chance. He hates me. We had to stay in a hotel when I took him up for the interviews at Prince William, and he wouldn't even sit at the same table with me for breakfast."

"Ouch," Michael said, pulling a face of wry sympathy. "What pissed him off so much this time?"

"Oh, I dunno. The fact that I exist, maybe. Every time I tell him to do something, he just reminds me I'm not his dad." Leaning back from the table, John shrugged. "And he's right; I'm not. Why should he listen?"

"Have you tried asking?"

"What?"

"Asking him, not telling. He's sixteen and apparently ready to join the paras. He's not thick."

"What? *Quin, would you mind staying at your expensive new school for more than a couple of weeks this time?*"

"Start lower. Ask him down here for the weekend."

John felt his mouth fall open. "Mate, you've got a radically different idea of a peaceful few days than I have."

"Well—maybe not *this* weekend." Michael paused long enough to let John see the teasing glimmer in his eyes: a brief, veiled promise, reasons why this particular weekend might be best left to the two of them alone. "But sometime. He'd be very welcome, and you know he loves it here."

Making sure the acceleration in his pulse didn't reach surface, John shook his head. "He loves *you*. He'd probably move in, follow you back to London and ask Webb for a job."

Michael chuckled. "He'd be less bloody trouble than you. Did the academy accept him, then?"

"Yes, on production of fees up front. Look, I take your point. I'll try requests instead of orders."

"For that noble intention, you get dessert."

Michael stretched out a hand for John's main course plate. John noticed that his palm was grazed, the pad of his thumb scraped and blistered. He'd been too busy looking at his wrists to notice before. He was moving stiffly too. "You all right? You should've waited till I got here to finish off that barn wall."

"Yeah, I probably should. Felt like a week where punishing hard work was the best thing for me, though."

"Mm." John held his gaze for a few seconds. His pulse notched up again, feeding hotly to nerves all down his spine. He felt for the first time as if Michael had stopped running from him. The dark eyes were unfathomable as ever but keeping no deliberate secrets. "Tell you what," he said. "I like my summer pudding well chilled. I'll wash this lot up, and you can go and have a hot bath."

He thought he would meet with resistance. But after a moment, Michael gave him an odd little half smile—acceptance? surrender?—and took the dishes through to the kitchen. He set them down and disappeared without another word into the shadows of the corridor that led to the old farm's bathroom.

John watched him go. He pressed his wineglass gently to his lower lip and considered following him. But he'd meant it about the washing up. Events, if any, needed longer to unfold of their own accord. Like paper flowers in water, he thought irresistibly, though when he closed his eyes, the flowers blazed up and transformed in fire.

Chapter Eight

Michael closed the bathroom door behind him. He sat on the edge of the bath and listened for a moment, wondering if John would follow him.

No, he decided. John was giving him large and conscientious amounts of space, even if that was so much against his natural inclination that the poor sod had arrived here fresh from a stopgap session on the riverbank. Michael appreciated it, though if the bathroom door had clicked and opened now, he would have taken what the hour had to give. He felt different. Maybe he'd worked out his demons on the drystone wall. Maybe the appearance of Piotr in the church had been a good thing, shaking up the deep layers of his memory. He'd never have been able to tell John about his mother until now. Maybe the silt would clear from his mission to Zemelya too.

He heard the clatter of silverware and crockery in the kitchen and turned, smiling, to switch on the hot tap. A good lad, his John. He thought himself wicked, with his voracious trawling of the clubs, his flash cars and unwillingness to sacrifice his carefree youth to play dad to his little brother. But Michael knew that in every way that counted, he was as innocent as day. Incorruptible. Michael, allowed to walk in the aura of that innocence for the last three years, had been happier than he could have imagined.

The ancient hot water tank groaned and rattled but began to produce its usual thunderous stream. Michael put the plug in and ran the cold tap too. He'd parboil himself otherwise. This was the next part of the house that could really use a refit, but he and John had kept putting it off. They wouldn't soon find a replacement for the deep ceramic tub, which had been built for washing dirty shepherds and was delicious to stretch out in.

Not that Michael could remember the last time he'd done it. He frowned, thoughtfully swirling the water with one hand. He'd got into hurried city habits, he supposed, and even here, with time on his hands, had stuck with the efficient but soulless electric shower unit. Stupid, really. The last few nights, grazed and aching, he could really have used a deep hot bath.

He'd make up for it now. The water was halfway up the sides of the tub and steaming temptingly. Did he have any bath salts? Getting up, he glanced in the cabinet, but he hadn't used the Radox in so long that it had solidified to a brick inside its box. There was, however, a gleaming bottle of John's ridiculously expensive bath foam, in the same range as his aftershave. Michael was pretty sure he wouldn't mind. Uncapping the bottle and pouring a little in, he smiled at the exactitude with which the scent conjured the man. Michael teased the crap out of him for his addiction to such things—a ruthless little Merseyside scrapper, standing for ages in the perfume hall at Liberty's trying to decide between the cologne and the aftershave—but he had to admit that it was very nice, and quite unmistakably him.

To bathe in his scent would be pleasant. Michael switched off the taps and pulled his jumper over his head. Immediately the godawful, nightmarish bruising and cuts round his wrists leaped out at him, but he pushed them aside. He didn't know what that had been, but surely it was gone now. If John was still willing to let him anywhere near him, Michael would show him how it could really be, in his arms, in his bed—as hot and sweet as sinking into water. He peeled off the rest of his clothes and cautiously lowered himself into the fragrant bath. He could salvage things still. It would be fine.

He stretched out. The water eased gravity's grip off him, undoing the knots in his muscles. He was more tired than he'd thought. He'd better be careful not to fall asleep in here. Drifting thoughts tugged at his mind. He wished he could have been the sun or the wind-stirred trees down at the riverbank, to look down on John, laid out and pleasuring himself there. What the hell had he been thinking, telling him he couldn't let another man fuck him? Right now Michael couldn't think of anything better than surrender, a slow luxurious opening to John's fingers and his big urgent cock.

He drew a shivery breath. All these things were much more likely to happen, weren't they, if he was clean and didn't smell of mortar dust and sweat. His hair was sticky. Sliding down in the bath, he submerged.

Water flooded his sinuses. For a second it was only a nuisance. He should've held his nose.

He should close his eyes. But he couldn't. They had snapped wide open. Through burning pain he stared straight up and into neon glare. He couldn't move.

Drowning.

A huge spasm seized him. He heaved upright, a howl ripping out of his lungs. He could hear water all around him, splashing, churning, but all he could feel was the cold choking cupful—all it took—that had entered his mouth and his nose. He lurched against his bonds and found they weren't there. Terror blazed through him. In the church, in the candlelit underground church, Lukas Oriel had made him believe he was tied when he wasn't. Now his tormentors didn't even have to strap him down.

The cell door banged. The sound came from nearby, as if the room were far smaller than he remembered. He didn't have to endure this. If he wasn't bound, he could and he would struggle off the waterboarding bench and defend himself. He twisted and encountered something slippery and cold, like a low ceramic wall.

"Michael! Jesus Christ! Mike!"

The wall bruised his chest and stomach as he tried to launch himself over it. Hands closed on him. He tore free, but all that did was dump him back in the water again. Fear reached its pitch. This was the end, in a white ceramic coffin. He loosed a roar of denial and rage, lashing out blindly at his captor. "Fuck you, Anzhel! I'll come back from hell for you!"

"Mikey, for God's sake! Hold still."

A grip went into his armpits, lifting. It was warmer and stronger than Michael remembered, but that could be part of the torture as well: to be held, caressed, and then let go. He flung himself at the side of the tank again, succeeding this time because of the assisting grasp—an arm round his waist, hauling him out onto the floor. He landed with a crash on wet tiles. Oh God, he was free, but it would do no good. He was too weak to follow his advantage. Anzhel would only summon faceless men with rubber-gloved hands to put him back. The torture would go on, unless...

He remembered what he had to do. It broke him every time, but he remembered. He pushed up onto his arms, lifting one hand to shield himself from the glaring light. "Anzhel, please," he rasped. *"Please."*

"In English, sweetheart. English, or I won't understand."

English? Michael retracted his hand. He pressed the back of it to his lips, feeling the shape they were forming again and again. *Please...* No. *"Pazhaluysta. Pazhaluysta. Anzhel, pazhaluysta."*

He shut up. Not Anzhel in front of him. John Griffin. His own Griff. Captured and imprisoned here too? The flashback dissolving, Michael told himself this wasn't true. He told himself that he was in his own bathroom at home, on his hands and knees in a flood of cooling bathwater. Everything was very real: John, wet to the skin, holding out a trembling hand toward him, his face a blank of shock, the scent of coffee drifting through the open door.

But so had the cell been real—clearly, absolutely. More so than this. Caught between the worlds, he subsided onto his backside, lifting both hands to hide his face. "Oh fuck. John..."

"Yes." The outstretched hand descended gently on his soaking hair. "Christ, mate. You scared the living shit out of me."

"What did I..."

"You screamed. I was making coffee. I... I'm sorry, I dropped your percolator jug. Are you all right?"

Michael couldn't tell him. He didn't know. He wasn't really interested anymore—cell and bathroom, life and death, were falling away from him. Neither was real, he concluded. He didn't care. "I dunno."

"Stay there. Don't move, okay? I'll be back in a second."

It could have been a week or a millisecond. The airing-cupboard door creaked. John reappeared with an armful of dry towels and a blanket. In sheer weary indifference, Michael allowed himself to be hoisted up to sit on the edge of the bath. The towels went around him. From a long distance out, he could appreciate that their friction on his skin was pleasant—that John was efficient in his ministrations, and kind too. Anzhel had sometimes used to be kind. He didn't come and sit beside him, wrap both arms around him suddenly tight and ask him in a rough, frightened whisper how the fuck he had got so cold—didn't softly beg him to say what was wrong—but the difference felt irrelevant, meaningless, even when John kissed his brow and the side of his face and called him *sweetheart* for the second time. His mind darkened, and he lost the contrast, the memory, the whole chain of horrors that had dragged him here. "John. What happened?"

"That's what I'm dearly hoping you're gonna tell me. Got to get you warmed up, though. Can you walk?"

"'Course. Don't be stupid."

"Good. Then walk it through here."

They were in the living room. Michael looked around it—a big, pleasant room that belonged to someone else. New, although constructed from the original stone. John and a laughing stranger wearing Michael's skin had finished tiling the roof on their last visit. The stranger had lit a fire in the open hearth earlier in the day even though it had been so hot, just a handful of flame to tick over and help dry the mortar and timbers and freshly plastered walls. There were books scattered on the chairs and sofa. No carpet down yet but a rug borrowed from the stranger's flat in London, bright and clean in front of the fire.

"Can you hang on here a second?"

Michael nodded. John had eased him down to sit on the arm of a chair. Detachedly he watched while John pulled the dampers open on the fire, chucked on three logs and the remains of a bucket of coal, then applied himself vigorously to shoving the heavy sofa to within five feet of the blaze. "Okay," he said, holding out a hand. "C'mere."

Michael subsided onto the sofa. He wasn't aware of being particularly cold—or particularly anything else. He was floating. He felt vague irritation as John insisted he clamber into a thick jumper, then a pair of jersey-cotton running pants; vague relief when this was accomplished and he was being pushed down to lie flat, a cushion going under his head, a duvet descending over his numb limbs. Habits of courtesy stirred in him. Someone was going to a lot of trouble. He ought to say thanks. *"Spasiba."*

"Oh shit."

Someone—it was hard to tell in the soft golden light—sat down hard on the sofa beside him. His jaw was taken in a careful but very firm grip. "Michael, you speak English to me—and make it make sense—or I'm going to have to get help."

"Shto praiskhodit?"

"Oh *shit*."

* * *

"Well? How is he?"

"Not too bad, as far as I can see. More sleepy than anything now."

"Thank Christ. I thought he'd had some kind of stroke."

"There's no sign of that. His pupils and his responses are normal. But he must have given you a fright."

"What? The screaming flip out and the lapse into Russian? Just a bit."

A faint chuckle. Michael, lying on his side, sleepily watching the flames, thought he knew the second speaker—Dr. Anselm, the village GP. If he made an effort—the mental equivalent of squinting round a corner—he could just recall the doctor here in the firelight with him, shining a beam into his eyes, making him lift and bend various bits of himself. A pressure cuff tightening, then easing off. A routine exam, and the old man's face too familiar to be of much interest. Who was he talking to? There were two candidates in Michael's bruised mind: John Griffin and Anzhel Mattvei. He didn't know why he couldn't work it out.

They were different as water and air. But he was tired now, something pulling at him, weighing him sensuously down. He listened to the doctor's low voice, losing interest. "His mother was Russian, wasn't she? A nice lady. I'd just come to Somerset when she... Well. Never mind. Did he say anything else you could understand, anything to give an idea what was going on in his head?"

"Not really. I think once or twice he said the word *angel.*"

"Hmm. Not terribly helpful. Does he ever use drugs?"

A faint snort. "Michael? He'd sooner eat dog food."

"I didn't think so. You're his partner, Mr. Griffin. I should think you know more about his past, what he's been through, than anyone else. I know he was doing something very hush-hush for a while. In my opinion, he's had some kind of flashback, and it's disoriented him. I've seen it lots of times in lads returning from the Gulf."

"Will he be okay?"

"Well, he was fairly coherent—and English—with me. I've given him a shot to make him sleep. If he's still distressed or confused in the morning, call me, and we'll get him to Yeovil for some checks. You should probably have your people in London look him over anyway."

"I will. Thanks, doc. Thanks for coming out."

A shot to make me sleep. Shifting, frowning, Michael remembered the sting in his arm. He tried to lift his head. "No," he tried to say, but the figures outlined in the brightly lit hallway were oblivious, deaf to him. *No, you mustn't sedate me. I won't remember who I am, or who I love or hate. Please...*

* * *

Quarter past four. This close to midsummer, light like pearls was already finding its way over the hills to the east. It gathered, cool and spectral, in the farmhouse living room, slowly winning out over the fire's rosy glow. Michael stood looking down at his partner, who had fallen asleep in an armchair. He was pale in the dawn light, his expression undefended, long limbs in an abandoned sprawl.

The effects of the sedation weren't as bad as Michael had feared. He had woken with his mind clear enough, although his memory gaped vacantly over a stretch between running a bath the night before and being bundled onto the sofa like a sack of potatoes, then wrapped up in clothes and duvets despite the mild May night. The clothes were on him still—restrictive, too hot. Impatiently he stripped and let them fall.

He was okay. He must have had a blackout. God knew what he had done to scare John into calling the doctor, but it didn't seem to matter now. Nothing did. No, Michael knew who he was, and who he was meant to love and hate. He just didn't care. The cold John had fought to claw off him last night had moved inside.

"John, wake up."

He did so instantly, eyes flicking wide. His sprawl became a stillness, a readiness to jump. Michael observed how his right hand twitched toward a gun holster that wasn't there. Neither of them ever brought weapons to Glastonbury, but Last Line habits died hard. His gaze swept the room behind Michael, looking for threat, then focused. "Mike? What's wrong?"

"Nothing."

"Are you okay? What time is it?"

"Early. I woke up, and…" He frowned. He couldn't recall the train of thought that had brought him from the sofa to here… wasn't sure how long he had stood in silence, watching John sleep. But his reasons were simple enough now. He stood naked in front of his partner, his cock growing heavy, beginning to rise. "And I wanted you."

John's lips parted. His eyes, more slate than green in this light, kindled with amusement. "So I see," he said, stretching out a hand. "Come here, then, morning glory."

Michael straddled him on the chair. John's arms went round him, and for a moment, all he wanted to do was bury his face in John's shoulder, fall into the embrace he knew would catch him, and weep. But the coldness moved inside him—glacial, ruthless—and instead he grasped John's shirt in his fists. "I want you."

"Well...*have* me, sweetheart, as long as—" John arched up, needing no encouragement to meet Michael's kiss, meeting the thrust of his tongue with open-mouthed willingness and a strong push of his own. "God, that's nice," he said when he could. "As long as you're properly with me, and we can do it in English."

"What?"

"You don't remember? You weren't well last night." He put his hands on Michael's shoulders and surveyed him anxiously, stilling his dive for the next kiss. "I should probably put you to bed, not—"

"No!" Michael strained against the halfhearted barricade, transferred one fist from John's shirt to the hair at his nape, and captured his mouth again. He wanted its fullness, its beautiful shape. Wanted to silence all the words that might come out of it. Wanted—and deliciously suddenly got—the fearless ingress of John's tongue, a hot penetration all the way to the back of his throat, a promise of how it would be if... "Nn-nn." He grunted the refusal against the sweet obstruction in his mouth, then tore back. "No. Don't."

"What? You don't like me to kiss you like that?"

Michael couldn't have told him what he didn't like or what was the source of the icy denial rising inside him. He pushed John to arm's length, then got up clumsily, still holding the front of his shirt. John rose with him, grabbing at his shoulders for balance. He was laughing, but there was a note of fear in it. "Mike, go easy. How do you want this?"

"You know how."

"I'm not...*one hundred* percent sure, no, but—"

Michael swept his feet out from under him, an easy judo move he'd never have pulled off if John had been on his guard. He heard without compassion John's scared gasp and followed through, dropping him to his knees on the fireside rug. Renewing the grip in his hair, he bore down on top of him, using all his weight to drive him down flat on his belly. "Lie still."

"Mike, I don't think—"

"Quiet."

The body under his went rigid. "Listen, Casanova. I'm not up for it again, not like this—and not without lube; you're too bloody big." John's voice softened, as if despite all appearances he could salvage this, make it into something good. "You know, you could...let me do you for a change. I'm told I'm very good."

Michael slid an arm under his throat. He didn't tighten it—not yet. He buried his face in the soft hair just behind John's ear. He forced his free hand under John's body, feeling with satisfaction how he'd hardened. Every hurt Michael had ever received, he could turn outward and exorcise upon this willing man. For every time he'd been pinned down and raped... "You want to fuck me?"

"Crossed my mind. This isn't gonna be a one-way street, you know."

"Let me tell you something. Slaves get fucked, John. Prisoners."

"Mike, you—you *bastard*!"

The protest was rough with astonishment. Michael ignored it. Awkwardly in the cramped space, he unbuttoned and unzipped John's jeans. He pressed a hard kiss to the side of his face and ignored the salt of his tears.

"Michael! Jesus Christ! Stop!"

"Be quiet." Michael got a hand inside his pants. One good jerk down and he would be there, driving deep and hot into his flesh. Escaping, leaving all the pain behind...

The air left his lungs. His ribs contracted as if he'd been kicked in them, and he fell back. It took him a second to associate the sensation with the man on the hearth rug—on his hands and knees now, then his feet, quick and lithe as a cat, his face purged of everything but rage. That was the trouble with John's combat moves. You never saw them coming. Michael had sparred with him in gym and dojo for years and never got the measure of him.

Nor had he ever been on the receiving end of his uncensored fury. Michael had accused him of holding back in their training fights, something he'd angrily denied. Just for an instant, Michael saw murder in his eyes, and a fear went through him—sweet, real, the cleanest thing he'd experienced in years. He balled up on instinct, just in time to avoid his pounce, choking and retching as his lungs tried to reinflate. He grabbed the arm of the sofa and hauled himself upright. "John—"

"Don't you fucking *John* me. Stand up and look at me."

Michael obeyed. He wanted to ask why but couldn't get the word out. Then he didn't have to. John would never hit a man when he was down, that was all. John was drawing back, not for a subtle piece of martial art but a roundhouse punch. His face was still immobile, but tears were streaming down it. Michael heard him sob before he swung. He didn't flinch or try to block the blow—felt its impact with a wild relief, knocking him down onto the hearth.

Not quite hard enough to lay him out cold. *See, mate—you do hold back*, was the thought that made its way through the sparkling fog all around him as he pushed up onto his arms. He wished to God the punch had brought down the dark. He was waking now, the fugue of the night—which had wrapped him round like polythene, invisible, suffocating—falling away. He was beginning to feel. To be aware of what he'd done. "Oh God…"

John was lifting him by the armpits, helping him sit up. Michael had a moment of hope, but his partner was only checking him over, his touch impersonal as a medic's. A touch to the head, looking for skull injuries. Chilly fingers under his jaw, lifting his face to the light to examine the side of his mouth. *Bleeding*, Michael wanted to tell him, *but no real damage done*. There was no need. John was clearly drawing the same conclusion, letting him go.

Michael curled up, bare backside going numb on the hearthstones. He lowered his brow to his knees. He felt the rough warmth of a blanket round his shoulders, curtly dropped there. Then the living room door slammed with a violence that brought plaster dust pattering down from the new-made ceiling, and the house fell silent.

* * *

Daylight. Bright and vivid now, filling the room without mercy. Groggily Michael lifted his head. Had he slept there, in his naked curl by the fire?

He wasn't alone. Swiping a hand over his eyes, cautiously shifting his jaw to see if it still worked, he looked through the open kitchen door. His partner was moving briskly about in the sunlight. He was dressed in fresh clothes, barefoot, his hair damp from the shower. Michael heard the tap running, then saw John put the kettle on its stand and promptly snatch his hand back, swearing. Michael almost smiled. "John? There's rubber gloves under the sink if that's electrocuting you."

John came to stand in the doorway. He looked at Michael coldly, as if he'd never seen him before. "It's all right," he said. "I'm getting used to it."

The rowan tree that grew outside the kitchen window shifted in the breeze. In the altering light, Michael noticed a dusting of glass on the flagstones, and remembered. He had been sitting by the bath, John crouching anxiously beside him. *I broke your percolator jug.* He must have swept up and missed a few bits in the dark. "Mind your feet."

"What?"

"There's still some broken glass on the floor. There's another coffee jug somewhere on top of those cupboards."

"Oh. Right. I'm just making instant. There's no time for fresh."

"Why?" It occurred to Michael that he should be doing more than huddling like a refugee in his blanket, but he was too chilly and stiff to move. "What's the hurry?"

"Webb wants us back in London."

"You're kidding."

"No. I found a voice mail from him at six o'clock."

"Christ, does he never sleep?"

"Well, he called at five, so maybe not. My phone only picked it up in that clear patch halfway down the hall." John turned away and went to take mugs out of the dresser. If he cared about broken glass, he gave no sign. Brusquely he spooned instant coffee into both mugs and sloshed the contents of the just-boiled kettle in on top. "Right," he said, padding into the living room. He offered Michael one of the mugs at arm's length, like a zookeeper charged with feeding a cranky tiger. "Drink that. I'm having mine, and then I'm off. I'll field whatever it is he's after until you catch me up."

"Griff—"

John winced. "Just be quiet and listen. Make yourself another two or three of those once you're done. Have a cold shower. Don't go near your car until you're properly awake."

"I am awake. Why—"

"Are you?" John took a careful step back and sat on the arm of the sofa. He looked exhausted. "Awake enough to remember last night?"

Michael swallowed what felt like a rock. "Parts," he admitted miserably.

"Parts. Okay. What about the part where you tried to shag me down on that rug?"

Oh Jesus. Michael lowered his head. He raked his fingertips back through his hair as if he could reach through his skull and rip the memory out. It was one thing to flip out and lose a chunk of time, though that was frightening enough. He couldn't bear the thought of these waking fugues—where he spoke, heard, and kept total recall, and was able to hurt his partner. He thought about lying, but the truth boiled up in him, burning like acid. "Yeah," he said raggedly. "I remember."

"You know what kills me about it? You could have had me, Mike—any time these last three years. With a word. With a *look*, for Christ's sake. You didn't need to—"

"Don't!" Shuddering, Michael cupped a hand around the back of his skull. "We can't do this anymore, Griff. I... I'm not fit to touch you. I can't be with another man."

He was distantly aware that John got to his feet. That John was standing over him. The morning sun was harsh. He cast a cool shadow, even at the height of his anger and disgust, like water on parched skin. "Last night I told you to stop," he said bitterly. "And you fucking ignored me. You're not fit to be with anyone."

Chapter Nine

The rush hour was beginning by the time John hit the M3. After an hour or so of lane-swapping, tailgating, and short illegal dashes along the hard shoulder, the boiling anger in him began to abate. He wasn't built to sustain much rage. A glance in the rearview revealed Mike's BMW negotiating traffic behind him—a long way back but catching up fast, headlights on full beam. Either he'd skipped the coffees and the shower or, more likely, driven like a devil from hell through the narrow lanes to the motorway.

John almost smiled. Mike was so sedate within city limits when the trip wasn't urgent. Such a nag as a passenger too, glancing across at John's speedometer. *We're still in a thirty zone, mate.* Watching him carve up a school bus now, John felt the familiar surge of amusement and affection.

Slaves get fucked, John. Prisoners. John's hands clamped tight on the wheel. He almost went into the back of a taxi and frantically slewed round. He couldn't hang on to the anger, but pain could stay with him indefinitely, lodged like a thorn under his heart. His memory tried to replay for him the moment of terror and betrayal when he had said *stop*, and…

No. Whatever the fuck had happened back on the hearth rug in this day's first light, John couldn't think about it now. It was alien, impossible. The traffic began to thin as he passed the sticky Andover junction, and he got the Jag into a clear lane and up into fifth. After a minute he saw Mike gun the BMW into the fast lane beside him, and they flew toward the city wing to wing.

* * *

Shoulder to shoulder in James Webb's office. The underground car park had been full, and they'd had to park up at different ends, had taken separate stairways to the top floor. But they'd met in the corridor with outward calm—not meeting one another's eyes—and entered the dragon's lair as they always did. Taken their usual seats when Webb, nose in a file, had distractedly waved at them to sit.

Webb put the file down. He rested his meaty fists on the surface of the desk. Hands like butcher's blocks. John wondered how he managed to clutch a pen, let alone produce the small and elegant script that covered their fitness reports and tersely refused their expenses claims. Webb swung his head in Michael's direction, a bull looking for its next matador. "What the devil," he rumbled, Belfast brogue in full ascendant, "happened to you?"

John flinched. He hadn't taken a good look at his partner's face yet this morning. He'd remembered to pull his punch a bit at the very last instant, but...

"Some moron of a townie was letting his dog chase sheep," Michael said smoothly. His shoulder was almost touching John's. Those were the seats they took, the ones that let them imperceptibly touch, bracing one another no matter what the old man dished out. The half-inch gap between them felt to John like an abyss. "He didn't like it when I stopped him."

"You let a civilian bust your lip, Agent South?"

"You always tell us not to use our combat skills on civilians, sir."

John repressed a snort. Webb gave a kind of growl that could indicate anything from amusement to disgust. "Well, you're a disgrace. You too, Griffin, by the way. You look as if you haven't slept in a week. Are you fit to be back at work?"

"What?"

"After your fall, man!"

"Oh." John hadn't given that a thought since the Glastonbury river bank. There were, as he'd discovered, far worse heights through which he could plummet. "Yes, sir. I'm fine."

"You damned well oughtn't be. That drop turned Piotr Milosz into raw steak."

From the corner of his eye, John saw Michael give a galvanic twitch—saw him absorb it, not quite seamlessly, into an interested forward movement in his chair. "You got a name from him?" he asked. "I thought he died before he could talk."

"No. He talked first."

Webb's words dropped into the morning sunlight like stones. In the silence that followed, John found himself listening to tiny, irrelevant stitches in its tapestry: phones ringing off down the corridor, the regular warning beep of a lorry reversing in an alleyway outside. He was sitting at Michael's left hand. He thought he could hear the anguished thud of his heart. "Why didn't you tell us?" he asked when it became clear that Michael wasn't going to.

Webb didn't glance at him. He kept his gaze fixed steadily on Michael. "Because what he gave me might not have been good," he said. "No point in stirring up mud until I knew."

"So…it *was* good," Michael said drily, not as a question.

"It may be. He had links to a man named Lukas Oriel. Your target in Russia, Agent South, during the Zemel civil war."

"That's classified."

John drew a quiet breath. No one snapped at James Webb. To his surprise, the old man only sat back a little, drumming his fingers on the file. "Spoken like a true spook," he rumbled. "Believe it or not, MI5 did declassify *some* information when they handed you over."

"Handed me... I left!"

"They let you go."

John cleared his throat. His boss and his partner both turned to glare at him, their confrontation breaking. He inquired innocently, "Would you like me to leave the two of you alone?"

"No!"

A simultaneous bark from both of them. Webb's was a command. In Michael's there was a shadow of a plea that reached John's heart despite everything. He tried to flicker him a reassuring smile. "Okay," he said. "Who's Lukas Oriel, and why do we care about him?"

Webb grunted. He waited until Michael had relaxed his combative tension and fixed his gaze at some point beyond the office window. "Oriel is a war criminal. After the nuclear... incident in the city of Dorva, he gathered together scientists and weapons men with a view to launching a vengeance attack on the West. He got quite a long way with his plans. When US and British forces invaded his stronghold in Zemelya, they found weapons of mass destruction in a state of advanced preparation."

"Must've been a relief to Tony to find some somewhere. Wasn't it a British jet that detonated the Dorva warhead?"

"Is that a particular concern of yours, Griffin?"

"No. I'm interested in the application of the term *war criminal*, that's all."

"Don't be naive," Webb snared. "Or facetious, for that matter. Oriel set out to destroy everyone in Zemelya who didn't share his point of view. He's culpable of genocide. Further, when the coalition forces invaded, he was nowhere to be found. Intelligence told us he'd fled to the West, but all trails went cold." He shifted his bulk in the chair, transferring the weight of his attention to Michael once more. "Until Piotr Milosz dropped out of the church rafters four days ago. He believed Oriel's in London. Where, he didn't have time to tell us."

Michael left off his study of the rooftops opposite. When he responded, he sounded to John more like his old self than he had in days. Since before their call out to the bloody church, in fact. Cheerful and pragmatic, as if he'd made a decision. "Somewhere in London? That's the best we've got?"

"Better than *somewhere in the West*, I'd have thought. You and Griffin have tracked men down on less."

"Not this time, sir. I don't know what line MI5 fed you, but I failed in my mission to Zemelya. I never found Oriel. Never got near him, in fact. I don't know what he looks like, what his habits are, or—"

"No. I... I know all that, son."

John stiffened. Webb had said it almost gently. If John didn't know better, he'd have thought that some kindly impulse had passed through the old bastard's stony heart. In John's experience, that could only mean trouble.

"Which is why I've drafted some help for you." Webb reached for his desk phone and stabbed the keypad with a thick forefinger. "Ms. Pearce? Is the Russian transfer here yet?"

The arid tones of Georgina Pearce, Webb's longtime secretary, hissed back through the speaker. Last Line legend had it that she was a former mistress of Webb's, put out to dignified grass in his employ, but John dismissed the idea. You couldn't mate a bull with a spitting cobra, and even the old man could never have been that brave. "Yes, sir. He's waiting."

"Be so good as to send him in."

A door creaked in the corridor. Michael turned a little and shot John one of their old *what the fuck now* looks, as if everything was just as it had been between them. John returned it on reflex. Christ, *could* he just forgive it, let it all go? He would never have believed it, but even a morning spent at odds with Michael had exhausted him, set a weary pain in his chest. If Mike wanted to pretend nothing had happened...

The door opened. John had a half-second's vision of the most beautiful man he had ever set eyes on, and then his view was blocked. He blinked. Michael was standing in his way, for some reason on his feet and shielding him. John hadn't even seen him move. "Mike...?"

Michael was reaching for a gun that wasn't there. They hadn't had time yet to check their weapons out of the arsenal. "Hold it!" he barked with the same snap of authority as if he'd been holding his Glock. "*Astanavaityes!* Don't you move another step."

"Agent South!" Webb was surging to his feet. John, automatically doing the same, noted that Michael was trying to keep his boss in cover too. "Stand down, man! What the devil is wrong with you?"

Michael glanced over his shoulder. He was ashen, but his voice was steady. "I don't know who you think this clown is, sir. The last time I saw him, he was leading a pack of Lukas Oriel's foot soldiers. His name is Anzhel Mattvei. He's a known associate of Oriel's, one of MI5's most wanted."

The man in the doorway took one step forward. John could see him now. His impression of his beauty didn't diminish. Six feet tall, eyes bluer than the sunlit morning sky, he looked as if he should be struggling to fit great white wings through the door behind him. His hands were up, the gesture gently mocking. "And, since Oriel's fortress fell three years ago, a loyal servant of the Zemel government's secret police," he said in accented but polished English. He took Michael in—slowly, appreciatively, from his shoes to the top of his skull. "Your information's out of date, Mikhaili. I changed sides—as did you, when it was expedient."

Webb stumped round to the front of his desk. He laid a hand on Michael's shoulder, and once more John noted the kindly gesture with profound unease. Michael didn't react, stood rigid and motionless, his eyes fixed on the newcomer. "You heard him, Agent South. Our sources in Russia confirm this. Stand down."

Anzhel. John took up position at Michael's other side. *He didn't say* angel *when I was fishing him out of the bath. He said* Anzhel. "I don't care who he is, sir. If Mike's unhappy about him, I am too."

The sapphire eyes fastened on him. John had never encountered a gaze at once so exquisite and so clinical. It sized him up like so much horseflesh. Then the wide, full mouth—the only mar to his perfection, and that only in motion, revealing a cruelly sensuous curve—broke into a smile. "*Bozhe moi*, Mikhaili! Is this your *zaichik*?"

"What the fuck did you just call me?"

"Enough!" Webb let Michael go. He stepped into the middle of the crackling three-cornered field of static that had sprung up in his office. "I called Agent Mattvei here in order to brief you all as to the details of your assignment. However, there seems little point in that until you've all got this infantile pissing match out of your systems." He turned round slowly, facing each one of them in turn. "South, since you and Agent Mattvei already know one another, you may escort him to his accommodation. Safe house five. Get the keys from Ms. Pearce."

Anzhel shrugged. "Very well, Sir James. I appreciate the courtesy. Mikhaili, shall we?"

"His name is Michael," John growled. "And he's not going anywhere without—"

"It's all right, Griff."

John started. He had almost forgotten that his partner had a voice in this.

But Michael had finally let go his frozen stance in front of Anzhel. He threw John a bright, desperate smile. "Calm down, okay? I'll talk to you later."

"Mike, who the bloody hell is this guy?"

"Later."

Anzhel had turned in the doorway. The sunlight caught his fall of pale hair, so bright it almost took a reflection. Michael, going after him, looked like a shadow. Instinctively John moved to follow but found Webb's solid arm blocking his route. "Not you, Agent Griffin. I want a word with you."

"Won't it wait?"

"Possibly, but I don't choose that it should. Your last expenses claim redefined the word *exorbitant.* You've got some explaining to do. South, Mattvei—back here in two hours for full briefing. Griffin, close that door and come and sit down."

John obeyed him as far as closing the door. Then he leaned his back on it and folded his arms across his chest. He waited until Webb had resumed his seat behind the desk. "This isn't about my bloody expenses."

Webb sighed. He looked weary, as if the confrontation that had just taken place had drained something out of him. "No, it isn't," he said. "Though it damn well ought to be. You can't put in a claim every time that ridiculous car of yours develops a rattle."

"Main work vehicle, sir. And if this is about Mike, he should be here."

Webb looked at him consideringly. "You're very loyal, aren't you, Griffin?" he asked, as if that were somehow a bad thing. "I should warn you now: if your relationship with Agent South has gone beyond the wishing-and-hoping stage, I may have to think about reteaming you."

"What? Why?"

"Same reason I'd separate a husband and wife. Same reason I reteamed Lucy Davis and Sandra Watts last year."

John found himself momentarily distracted. "Really?"

"Yes. Not that it's any business of yours. Couples can't work together, Agent Griffin, not for Last Line. What are you smiling about?"

"Didn't even know you knew we called it that, sir." John gave up his watchful posture by the door and moved to sit down. He felt his smile become bitter. "Anyway, I wouldn't worry. We're nowhere near wishing and hoping now. Not that it's any business of yours. What did you want to tell me about Mike?"

"Insolent, Agent Griffin," Webb said in evident approval. John sometimes thought that the only time he really pleased the old sod was when he was cheeking him. "How much has Agent South told you about his stint with MI5? His undercover op in Zemel Province in particular?"

John shrugged. "Next to nothing. Just that he was there."

"He never mentioned Lukas Orel to you?"

"Never heard his name until today."

"You shouldn't take that as a sign of lack of trust, you know."

John looked up in surprise. Since when had Webb been concerned about his feelings? "I don't," he said. "Just of having signed the Official Secrets Act. I know he can't just…chat to me about it."

"Well, no. But there may be more to it than that in South's case. His debrief on return from that mission is more or less a confession—of having infiltrated Oriel's paramilitaries and run with them in the Zemel forests, hunting down opposing insurgents and anyone else who hadn't espoused Oriel's cause. Particularly groups of wanderers, Russian gypsies called Ashkeloi. South did what he had to do to keep his cover—which included taking part in several massacres."

"Jesus." John felt the floor shift under him. Nausea coiled in his gut.

"Does it change your opinion of him, Griffin?"

"No. Because I don't bloody believe it." He didn't, did he? A week ago, he'd have thrust the idea away from him—maybe slammed out of Webb's office in disgust. He wished to God he could lose the image of Michael standing over him—expressionless, inexorable—in the farmhouse living room. Wished he couldn't feel the tightening grip of his choke hold in the instant before *no* had somehow failed to mean *no*. "He couldn't have. He must have been under duress."

"Very possibly. But it's his own report. Would you implicate yourself in a genocide, Griffin, unless you absolutely had to?" Webb leaned his elbows heavily on the desk. "Anyway. The important thing that you should know is this: Agent South named the leader of Oriel's soldiers—the man who headed up the forest massacres—in that report too."

An icy chill went down John's spine. He pressed his fingers to his lips for a moment. "Please tell me not Anzhel Mattvei."

"The same, I'm afraid."

"You're *afraid?* You knew all that, and you sprang the bastard on him anyway?"

Webb sighed. "That's exactly why I did it. I had to see how he'd react."

"I think you nearly gave him a bloody heart attack. Was that satisfactory?"

"What? To frighten and grieve one of my own men? One of my best, at that? No, Agent Griffin. It wasn't satisfactory to me at all. If I could leave South to make his own peace with his past, I would."

Webb's regrets meant nothing to John, not unless they were backed up by action. "Why the hell can't you?"

"Because I need Oriel. I've been tasked to find him by a higher authority than I'm at liberty to reveal to you. And to get him, I need Mattvei. I have to know South is stable enough to work with him, and to be sure of that"—Webb paused, and looked at John assessingly—"I need you."

John shook his head. "Not a chance. I'll watch his back, but any monitoring or spying… no way."

"Watching his back will suffice. You may not find that such an easy task, however." Webb flipped open the file on his desk, and John saw a flash of solemn MI5 letterhead. "The report Agent South gave on his return doesn't tally at some points with that of other witnesses, among them the British soldiers who eventually stormed Lukas Oriel's headquarters building. Your partner didn't make his escape from Mattvei's paramilitary group, and despite what he says, he did succeed in tracking his target—or at any rate, his target found him. South was liberated from a cell in Oriel's fortress."

"Liberated…" John sat forward in his seat, trying to ignore a wash of fear. "He was being held there?"

"That's right. We don't know how long for."

Prisoners get fucked, John. "Was he all right?"

"Bruised and half starved. Beyond that, not much obvious physical damage, though investigating officers found equipment used in… Do you know what waterboarding is, Agent Griffin?"

"Of course I bloody do!" John lurched to his feet. It was that or jump out of his skin. He took three tense strides to the window and stood staring blindly out. "It kills people. They can dry-drown. The trauma lasts for… Did he get treatment?"

"In order for any treatment or therapy to be effective, Agent South would have to remember and accept the torture. And as far as he's concerned, he was picked up by British forces in the Zemel forest. No amount of MI5 deprogramming served to shift that belief."

"But this Mattvei bloke, this Anzhel…" John paused, then spun back to face Webb. "He knows better, right? He knows what happened to Mike."

"Maybe. Mattvei claims he worked closely with Oriel. But he may have been, as Agent South believes, no more than a foot soldier, an extremely blunt instrument. When Oriel's kingdom fell, the Zemel government cut Mattvei a deal: his freedom and a place within their secret service in return for the location of Oriel's WMDs. It's no use looking at me like that, Griffin. It's not my fault if the Zemel SS is less particular in its choice of employees than I am."

Are you so particular? You hired a shell-shocked amnesiac. "Did you know?"

"Did I know what?"

"That this Oriel would rear his ugly head one day. That Mike might have connections to him."

"Oriel is wanted by law enforcement agencies all over the US and Europe. It wasn't beyond the bounds of possibility that—"

"Did you plan to use Michael?"

Webb raised his brows. To John's surprise, he looked less annoyed than pleased with the question, as if his employee had finally worked something out for himself. "Use him?" he echoed. "I *plan* to use you all. You know the terms of your employment,

Agent Griffin. Whether there's anything left when I'm done using you is entirely up to your own endurance and resourcefulness."

Don't mince words, now. John sat in silence for a moment, giving the old man's straightness its due of reluctant respect. "Fair enough," he said. "But there's a difference between that and screwing with someone. Mike's been off-kilter since we ran into Piotr Milosz. I think he's having flashbacks. He needs taking off this case, not…winding up to see what he'll do next."

"Your opinion is noted."

"Or being left alone with side-swapping bastards like Anzhel Mattvei."

"But he won't be alone, will he? He'll have you to keep an eye on him. I'll expect you to do so assiduously." Webb reached for the next file on his desk. It was a gesture John had learned to read as a dismissal, but this time he stood his ground. He needed to tell Webb, without betraying Mike's confidence, that flashbacks were the tip of the iceberg.

An instant later he regretted it. Webb looked up. "Still here, Griffin? I was going to suggest you took a break for lunch, but since we have a little time, we might as well look at those expenses of yours in good earnest."

* * *

Three-quarters of an hour later, philosophically tucking into a cheese and Marmite sandwich in the corner café instead of the fresh deli salad he normally enjoyed—best let the boss simmer down for a few days—John watched Michael carefully reverse his BMW into a tight space across the street. He set down his newspaper. He wasn't about to spy on his partner, but he was hungry for the sight of him, even after so short a separation. Even after last night.

The driver door swung open. Michael got out slowly, as if aching. The bruise on his lip stood out lividly in the sunlight. How the hell had they got themselves to the brink of rape? Because that was how Mike would look at it, John knew, in a cooler moment, once whatever madness it had been had worked its way out of his blood.

Mike leaned his hands tiredly on the car roof. For a moment John thought he would look up and see him. If he did, John would waggle his fingers at him, beckon him over. Buy him a sandwich and try to make him laugh with the story of the bollocking he'd just had off the old man. Or—better yet—John would get up, run across the street to him, enfold him in a hug and tell him it didn't matter, to forget the sodding disastrous sex and just be his friend again.

John thought he might do that anyway. They didn't indulge in public displays of affection, but to hell with that. His heart felt swollen and sore with the need to put things right between them. God knew what Michael had been through in Zemelya. Halfway to forgiving him anyway, John had felt the rest of his anger drain as he had listened to Webb. No wonder the poor bastard was screwed up. It half killed John to think of him trapped, imprisoned at the mercy of creatures like...

The BMW's passenger door swung wide. The car was too small and low-slung to accommodate a man of Anzhel's size comfortably, but he got out with easy grace and stood looking up and down the street as if he owned it. The breeze caught his hair and turned it into an aureole, then a silk flag. Heads turned on the street. John couldn't look away either. He watched unwillingly as Anzhel went to stand by Michael on the pavement.

Whatever they were discussing, Michael wasn't enjoying it. He stood passively for a while, hands still resting on the car roof, head down. Then he straightened up and made a gesture of warding off, of passionate denial.

John had seen enough. Abandoning his paper and sandwich, he got up and edged his way out of the noisy, crowded café. But by the time he'd crossed the street, Michael had reached the top of the HQ building's steps and was pushing open the door, Anzhel following after with long, loping strides.

Chapter Ten

To capture Lukas Oriel wouldn't be enough. John, perched on the edge of the briefing room table, watched the door through which Webb had just limped out. "Let me get this straight," he said. "He just asked us to make a hit, right?"

Five people had sat through Webb's briefing. All apart from Anzhel were among Last Line's longest serving agents: Michael, Diane Shaw and her partner Nick Skelton, a grizzled army veteran who set off Shaw's beauty picturesquely. All three sat in silence for a moment. The question hung in the air. Then Diane shrugged. "Problem for you, Griffin?"

"Isn't it one for you?"

Diane made a wry face. She shot a sidelong glance at Skelton. "If it was, we'd have been out of here years ago."

Not a first for you, then. Automatically John looked at Michael—to share the moment, gauge it by the expression in his eyes—but Mike's attention was fixed on Anzhel, who had casually set a vicious-looking semiautomatic on the table and begun to break it down into parts. Anzhel smiled at Diane in approval. "You have to see your superior's point," Anzhel said. "Your government's too. Dress it up how you will, a British finger pushed the button when the bomb dropped on my city. Oriel knows whose. Knows which US interests controlled that finger. He's too inconvenient—on both sides of the Atlantic—to be allowed to live."

John glanced around at his colleagues. "Or look at it another way. He's a freedom fighter, a man who tried to rebuild his nation and take revenge—with good reason—on the people who destroyed it."

At last Michael turned to him. There were shadows under his eyes. He hadn't taken time to shave before leaving the house—Christ, had it only been that morning?—and his hands were knotted tight on the surface of the table. "You wouldn't be concerned," he said hoarsely, "if you knew the half of what he's done."

"And you do, right? You do know what he's done, Michael?"

Michael swallowed. He opened his mouth as if to reply, but Anzhel cut across him smoothly. "We're wasting time," he said. "If Oriel is here, I assure you *he* won't. If you want your first clue to his presence to be a dirty bomb in the middle of London, you go ahead and sit here wringing your hands, Agent Griffin."

"So we're going to track down Oriel and kill him? I'm not questioning the necessity. I just want to be clear on what that old sod just told us to do."

Nick Skelton, who until now had sat in thoughtful silence, looked at him levelly. "The old sod pays for the privilege," he said. "Did you think it was all for nothing, John? You must've known that one day he was gonna ask you to leave your conscience behind in your locker."

John ran a hand into his hair. "Jesus. I feel like I'm trapped in a bad modern version of *Faust*. No, I understand, Nick. I've done dirty work for him before. Just—"

"Just not an assassination," Anzhel Mattvei finished for him, completing his inspection of the gun and snapping a clip into its chamber. He smiled up at John with a brilliance that, if he didn't know better, would have made him believe all was right with the world, and Mattvei the very angel his name echoed. "Don't worry, zaichik. The first is the worst. After that you'll hardly feel it at all."

* * *

"Michael. Mike!" John, following his partner down the corridor, forbade himself to break into a jog to catch up. But Michael was ignoring him—or oblivious—his attention fixed on Mattvei a few strides ahead. Ashamed of himself, John shot out a hand and grabbed the back of his jacket. "Mike, for God's sake."

Michael stopped. He turned to John without irritation, only a look of mild surprise to find him there. "What is it?"

"Where are you going?"

"I'm taking Mattvei to the gun room."

"It looks to me like he's already been."

A flicker of amusement touched Michael's face. "To turn that cannon in and get him something more in line with the Geneva Convention."

"Okay. But I need to talk to you for a second, without"— John directed a hard stare down the corridor at Anzhel, who had stopped and was regarding them with interest—"without our new colleague."

"All right. Mattvei, it's in the basement. I'll catch up with you there in a minute."

Michael allowed himself to be steered into the nearest empty office. John closed the door behind him and leaned on it as if warding off evil. "You want to tell me what's going on?"

"What—in general, or…"

"No. Pretty specific, actually." John watched Michael settle on the edge of the desk and tried not to be distracted by the easy grace of the movement. "Why are you running round with that gun-toting Calvin Klein model out there? Do you trust him?"

"Of course not."

That took the wind from John's sails a bit. "Oh," he said, then added lamely, "Good. Look, Mike, don't... don't you think we need to talk?"

Michael was nodding. "Definitely. Not now, though, mate. I've got to—"

"Yes, now." Leaving his post by the door, John moved to stand in front of him. "Not about anything that happened last night. Forget that if you want. Listen, Webb talked to me after you left, and not just about my extravagant lifestyle. He told me what happened to you in Zemel Province."

"He doesn't know what happened to me there."

"He does know some of it, Mike. It was in that file he had. He said you were caught up in some... bad shit, and Anzhel Mattvei was closely involved in it too. He said you were taken prisoner and tortured, though you don't remember that part." Michael made a faint sound in his throat. He tried to get up, but John put both hands on his shoulders. "No. Don't run away from me. It feels like you're a thousand miles off anyway. I don't want you on this case, not while you're so upset."

Michael shook his head. "Upset..."

"Or not well, or whatever the hell this is."

"I can't believe he told you. I can't believe I'm having to hear this crap again. John, when I came back from Russia, I gave MI5 a full and honest debrief. They didn't like it, and they... practically dissected me to get at a truth that wasn't there. That's the only fucking torture I've undergone."

"I'm sorry. But what if it *did* happen?"

"No! I won't bloody hear it from you!"

This time John couldn't restrain Michael's surge to his feet. He stepped aside. Michael got as far as the door, then turned like a hunted animal and said, "Did he tell you the rest, then?"

"What?"

"The *bad shit*. Did he tell you what that entailed?"

"Yes. I didn't believe it. I don't."

Michael stared at him. John saw all the anger suddenly drain from him, leaving him pale, looking ready to drop. "Oh, Griff," Michael said unsteadily. He put out a hand.

John went to him in silence. He took the hand, pulled Michael close, and put both arms around him. "All right," he murmured, feeling Michael resist him, then give it up and lean into the embrace, wearily returning it. "Whatever's best for you."

"God, I wish we could... leave all this. Go down to Glasto, lock all the doors and..."

"Is that what you want?" John stroked his hair. Footsteps came and went in the corridor outside. They were going to get interrupted any second, but he would sooner have died than let go. The feel of Michael's grip on him now—formidable but passionate, fiercely tender—was the first point at which John's fantasy of touching him had met with truth. "Let's do it, then. Screw Lukas Oriel. Screw Last Line, for that matter. We can go."

"You'd do that?"

"Say the word."

Michael lifted his head. He met John's eyes with a kind of yearning wonder. "Jesus, Griff. You'd pack it in? What about Quin's school fees, and... and the car? Why?"

Tell him, a voice screamed in John's head. *This moment will never come back. Tell the man you love him.*

But the words dried to dust in his throat. He had been able to bear—just about—the demolition of his dreams concerning sex with him. He had even found a place inside himself where he could lock up the memory of *no* not meaning *no*. If he gave up this last secret of his heart, though, and saw it fall on stony ground…

"Ah, screw the car," he said. He smiled. "Screw Quin, for that matter. He can go to the local comp.'

"Might be better for him." Michael returned the smile, but in it John thought he saw the ghost of a sorrow, a disappointment, a closing door. Michael eased back a bit, not letting him go. Gently he rested his brow against John's. "No, mate. We can't run away. We've got to find Oriel, and…"

"And kill him?"

"I don't know. That'll depend on the moment, the way it always does."

"What about Anzhel? Mike, I don't want you mixed up with him. I—"

"*Ssh*. Let me deal with Mattvei Seriously, Griff. Stay out of his way." Briefly Michael caressed his face. "I'd better go. He's probably testing out sniper rifles from the roof by now."

"Okay." Reluctantly John released him. "Look, the old man reminded me, I've got another checkup for my back this afternoon, not that I need it. Will I see you later?"

"Yeah. I'll be around. Listen, I'm gonna hold you to that promise one day."

"What? Sheep farming in Glastonbury, Quin in the spare room, and a thirdhand Fiat Panda in the garage?"

"The very one. Does it sound so horrendous to you?"

No. At the moment it sounds like bloody paradise. John shook his head. He couldn't speak. He folded his arms and looked at the floor until the door's faint click told him Michael had gone.

* * *

Michael was nowhere around HQ when John came back from his appointment. Neither was Anzhel. Webb's office was closed and locked. He was at a meeting elsewhere, Ms. Pearce told John, as if he'd asked her to strip and dance a hula for him.

John had paperwork to do. About a month's worth, if he thought about it, and he supposed he should be grateful for a few quiet hours. He went downstairs to the big shabby room where he and his colleagues kept informal desks and did their admin. It had once felt odd to John to spend an afternoon being shot at, then come back and fill in a form about it, but he'd got used to that.

He'd got used to a lot of things, he reflected, slumping down behind his half of the desk he shared with Michael. These days he didn't blink when asked to burgle someone's house for disks or documents or festoon it with invisible surveillance gear. He knew how to scare the crap out of a suspect without leaving marks. He had been shot twice and had himself shot dead eight men and one grenade-toting woman. On reflection, he couldn't think why he had balked at the idea of an assassination.

Fuck it, why should he care? John had come to love the hunt. Tracking down and killing a man who had been instrumental in Michael's torture would probably be enjoyable. Grabbing the nearest file, John went to work. If he kept himself occupied, he might be able to stop his abstract concept of *waterboarding* from becoming a practical demo in his head, with Mike strapped to the board.

When he next looked up, the patch of sky he could see from the office window had changed from cerulean to an ominous coppery pink. It was later than he'd thought and the weather was about to break, from the look of things. An oppressive heat had gathered in the room. Diane came in yawning. John asked her if she'd seen Mike anywhere about in the building and tried not to notice her look of penetrative sympathy as she said no.

No need for sympathy. No need for John to be suddenly prickled all over with foreboding, either, but he was. He didn't need to ask Diane if she'd seen Anzhel Mattvei.

Michael wasn't answering his landline or his mobile. John, taking the stairs to the car park three at a time, told himself sharply not to be so paranoid. Why shouldn't Mike have taken Anzhel out to the pub, or whatever you did with visiting ghosts from your past? Somehow John couldn't see the two of them together at a table in Pizza Express. He gunned the Jaguar out from the underground and into the traffic stream. It was raining heavily now. Holland Park was predictably snarled up. Lightning flickered as John executed a U-turn to get out of it, the thunder that followed partially drowning the outraged chorus of horns. Rattling the Jag down a cobbled alleyway that would get him onto the West Cross Route, he tried Mike's numbers again, cutting the connection impatiently when he got his voice mail again.

The windows were dark in the Highgate flat. Nothing odd in that. Michael liked the evening sky and would often delay switching on the lights well past dusk. John couldn't account for the sense of desolation that touched him as he got out of the car and stood looking up at the building. The last time he had been here, he supposed, he'd been high on the anticipation of fucking his beautiful, hard-to-get partner. On the way in, anyway. The differences since then might account for his feeling like lonely, exhausted crap now. He couldn't believe only four days had gone by. It felt like bloody weeks.

He jogged up the stairs, absurdly reluctant to face the lift in whose antique Victorian cage he had stood, hands wedged in his pockets, cock beginning to strain at the fabric of his jeans, Michael at his side, just as conscientiously casual. He stood for a moment outside Michael's flat. The door had a look of particular closure—

of sealing up secrets, though how the plain oblong of wood managed that, John couldn't have said. He rang the bell.

Nothing. He tried both of Mike's numbers again, willing the dial-out screen of his phone to change to a pickup. He didn't want to do this.

But they both kept keys to one another's flats, and it was Last Line policy to make the check. *One last chance, mate.* He raised a fist and banged on the door as hard as he could. He knew that if he'd only thought that Mike was sick or hurt, he'd have been through the door in a flash—forgotten he had a spare key and kicked it down in his haste, more than likely.

There was more to it than fear. Quietly letting himself in, pausing in the corridor to listen, John accepted the nature of the gnawing, circling beast making itself at home in his innards. He accepted that his instant, bristling dislike of Anzhel Mattvei had been less to do with Anzhel's national affiliations than the look in his eyes when he had seen Michael. Amused. Familiar. Intimate.

The flat was occupied. No one in the living room or kitchen, but light was spilling out from under the bathroom door. John's foot caught on something. Reaching down, his fingers closed on Michael's leather jacket, crumpled there as if dumped. John could hear the shower running at full blast—loud enough, he supposed, to drown out a phone ringing or even a pounding at the door if you were preoccupied enough to *want* to ignore it...

Oh, Mike, please just be in there having a wank. Dry-mouthed, John hung up the jacket, gently smoothing its folds.

He took a breath. He had no bloody business here. The beast in his guts was jealousy, pure and simple. Turning away, John started back the way he had come. He could wait in the car if he was so sodding worried—give it half an hour or until the appearance of lights in the flat indicated the end of whatever performance was being played out in the bathroom. Then he would call again and—

A howl ripped through the flat. John stopped dead, frozen. It was worse than the cry that had made him drop and shatter the coffeepot back in the farmhouse kitchen, and that had been enough to congeal the blood in his veins. The worst sound he'd ever heard, a strong, stoic man's raw scream of terror. "Mike," he whispered, and the howl came again. There was nothing of pleasure in it. Uncomprehending desolation, the roar of a lion with a spear in its side. John drew his PPK, glad he'd taken time to check it out again. There'd been nothing for him to shoot and kill in the bathroom at Glastonbury. Maybe this time Michael's nightmares were flesh and blood enough to die. Maybe they were manifest as Anzhel bloody Mattvei. John strode down the corridor and shoved open the bathroom door.

Through the half-drawn shower curtain, he had time to count two thrashing, struggling bodies, not one. All right. Enough. He took a step backward, meaning just to get out as fast as he'd arrived. But pain had made him blind and stupid, and he dropped the pistol with a clatter on the floor. "Fuck," he choked out, crouching to grab it, peripherally seeing the shower curtain jerk back. Then Michael cried out again, and somehow when John surged upright, he found the gun cocked and steady in his best two-handed grip.

The curtain was semitransparent. There were bright red stains across it, blurring and washing out to pink. John saw that Michael's arms were up, his wrists awkwardly caught above his head. What the hell had Anzhel tied him to? The fittings were solid, like everything else in the flat, but wouldn't withstand the kind of fight Michael was putting up. The water thundered on the sides of the bath. Through plastic and steam, John slowly became aware that Anzhel had stopped the motions of a violent fuck and was staring at him—calmly, without anger, as if he had arrived right on cue. In his right fist he held a knife. Its blade was short and businesslike, the tip buried in Michael's skin, just below his sternum. Not deep, but enough to make him bleed freely in the hot water. His flanks were already marked with narrow, deliberate cuts. Behind the curtain Michael struggled for a few seconds longer, then went passively still, his head down.

"Mattvei, you bastard. Let him go!" John heard how the command cracked down the middle, broken by the sob he couldn't repress. Mortified, he tried again. "Untie him. Put that goddamn knife down. *Michael*"

"He can't hear you." Anzhel, one snake-muscled arm tight round Michael's waist, studied John with interest. His sculpted face was flushed, his hair soaked but still in rich gold waves, as if he could never be anything other than beautiful. He grinned at him, panting. "Hello, Griff."

"Don't you fucking call me that. Mike!" John jerked the PPK's muzzle up. "Tell me this is…" Rage briefly stole his words. "Tell me this is *consensual*, Mikey, or I'm gonna shoot this fucker, I swear!"

"He won't hear you. Only me for now."

"Why the fuck can't he hear me?" John took one nervous diagonal step, keeping the muzzle at a point between Anzhel's eyes. From here he could see that Anzhel had stopped at the pitch of a thrust. That his thighs were corded, tense, clamped hard to Michael's backside. "What have you done to him?"

"What he wants. What he has to have from time to time, if you don't want him to do worse to himself…" Anzhel tailed off. His eyes became abstracted, their light turning inward. He turned his face away from John and stood for a moment trembling, muscles flickering in tiny, strained movements under his flawless skin. To John's disbelief, he tipped his head back, eyes closing.

His hand closed tight on the haft of the knife, and he jerked the blade downward with terrible, exquisite precision. "Oh, Griff, you came at the wrong moment. Or the right one. Mikhaili, wake up, *moy lyubovnik*! Show John how we come... how we *come*..."

Michael reanimated. He hauled with all his strength on his restraints. He groaned as if his soul was leaving him. Anzhel gave a kind of bark of atavistic triumph, grabbed the shower curtain and ripped it down off its rings so that John could see everything. Rigid, the gun still clenched in his hands, John stood helpless and transfixed while Anzhel thrust to wild-eyed climax, and Michael, after a shuddering moment, convulsed and sent a hard white jet from the tip of his belly-flat cock, washed away an instant later in the shower's downpour.

Anzhel pulled out of him. John noted—as if from five miles out, as if he were watching this scene from a satellite in low orbit—that his long, lax cock was naked. *Couldn't even put a condom on for him.* He holstered the gun. To his bewilderment Michael subsided onto his knees. John looked in vain for the handcuffs or belt that had been holding him.

Anzhel turned the shower off and stepped unconcernedly out of the bath. He laid the knife down by the washbasin, pulled a towel off the rail, and dumped it over Michael's shoulders. He smiled at John, who had involuntarily backed away until stopped by the wall. "And that," he said, picking up a towel for himself, "is how you fuck the daylights out of—what do you call him?—*Mikey* South. For future reference, you don't even have to tie him up, though he told me you'd had a go. You just need to make him think you have." He turned and caressed Michael's bowed head. "Hey, Mikhaili. John's here."

John stood rooted—long enough to see Michael look up with perfect horror dawning on his face, long enough to see and understand for himself that his wrists were free. Then he turned and stumbled out.

John felt sick, and that was bad—the bathroom was spectacularly occupied. The kitchen sink would have to do. When he got there, though, his stomach locked tight and all he could do was cough and choke miserably. The dark room spun around him, floor heaving under his feet. He had to get out.

A padding of bare feet on tiles. A touch to his shoulder. John jerked out from under it, dragging a hand across his mouth. He checked the sink to see he hadn't made a mess and quickly ran the taps.

"John."

"I'm all right. Leave me be."

"Why did you come here?"

"Because of..." His throat was raw. He coughed again and reluctantly took the pieces of kitchen roll Michael was holding out to him. John could barely look at him. He'd put on a dressing gown, and he looked like the man John knew, but everything had changed. "I came because of code seven."

"Code..."

"Seven. If an agent fails to answer his door or his phone. That's all. Will he see to you?"

"What do you mean?"

"To your cuts. You're—you're still bleeding. It's coming through your robe."

Michael glanced down at himself. "Oh God. No. I can do it for myself."

"All right. I'm going. I'll see you tomorrow."

Michael caught him up in the hall. Again John evaded his hand. He let himself out into the corridor and started walking.

"Griff, wait."

"No!" John barked, whether in denial of the request or the name he didn't know. He stopped and swung round. Michael was out in the corridor, dripping wet and pale. Having started shouting, John found he couldn't stop. Were there cameras in this section? He couldn't remember, didn't care. "What happened to *I could never let another man fuck me*, Mike? What happened to *only slaves and prisoners get fucked?*"

It wasn't the kind of building where people had public arguments. A door clicked in the ringing silence that followed. Glancing down the stairwell, John saw a wedge of light as the lady downstairs stuck her head out. *Great.* He could round off his evening by exposing himself as a hysterical queer. He threw Michael one last uncomprehending look, then turned and began to take the stairs four at a time.

Chapter Eleven

"Why didn't you tell me there was someone else in your life?"

Michael started. He and John were leaning with their elbows on the South Bank rail, a fanciful medieval dolphin grinning down at them. For the past quarter hour they had been watching the Thames in silence. Outside of business and civilities, these were the first words John had addressed to him in the three days of their undercover. And Michael couldn't for the life of him think of an answer.

"If you had, I'd never have chased you round the way I did. I must've been a real pain in the arse."

John hadn't taken his eyes off the water. Michael turned and glanced around them, making sure he did so with the weary stiffness of the hungry down-and-out he was meant to be. There was no one within earshot. "He wasn't in my life," he said grimly. "It was a long time ago."

"Three years. Or quite a bit less than that, if we're counting from Thursday."

Thursday. Michael's shoulders sagged. He was cold beneath his duffle coat in spite of the warm June sun. He'd wondered if

John would consign *Thursday* to the same pit of oblivion he himself had tried to prepare for it. Shouldn't have underestimated him. Michael remembered it in scraps. A fast ride home in the BMW, then arrival at the flat. Arguing with Anzhel in fierce muted Russian, telling him—begging him—to go back to the safe house and let him alone. That whatever there had been between them was over, long dead and buried. He had given up and gone to take a shower, feeling filthy from the marrow out.

The door had clicked. There had been a weird, sweet music. Then he had been burning up into violent orgasm, with someone—Christ, with Anzhel—fucking him hard. Blood all over the place, his skin striped by shallow cuts. And somehow John had been in the room.

Wake up, Mikhaili. John's here.

"Did you see much of that?" Mike asked miserably.

"Enough to get the gist."

"It wasn't…"

"If you tell me it wasn't what it looked like, I think I'll chuck one of us into the river."

"No. It was what it looked like. It's just not what you… I can't explain."

John gave up his perusal of the river and turned to face him. "Mikey, I love you, but he had his cock up your arse. He wasn't in there looking for the soap."

Michael's mouth opened. For a long moment, he and John stared at one another. Then pained, involuntary laughter tore from both of them. "Don't," Michael said "It's not bloody funny."

"No, I know it isn't. Is he coercing you? Forcing you?"

Yes. Yes, surely. But when Michael had checked himself over on Thursday night, apart from the cuts there hadn't been a mark on him to excuse what he had done. And then there had been the times since… "No."

"Are you still fucking him?"

A silence, too deep for the purr of passing pleasure boats and the splash of the Thames to penetrate. At last John said, with difficulty, "All right. Like I say, I just wish—I just wish you'd told me."

Michael studied him. Three days into their undercover, John looked the part with startling thoroughness. There was more to it than stubble and Salvation Army coat. Webb tended to send John on ops that needed dash and verve. He made a good expensive rent boy or con man, a bad down-and-out. It was hard for him to conceal his lights. Now it seemed to Michael that they had gone out of their own accord. "Griff…"

"Don't. Here he comes."

"Dobroye utro."

Michael concealed a twitch. He needed to pull it together: the op they had set up was a delicate one, requiring all his attention, and he had just let a six-foot Russian stroll up to him unnoticed. Anzhel was resplendent in the kind of suit a low-level *Russkaya mafiya* man would wear, heavy gold chains at his throat and wrists. Hard to miss as Michael and John were hard to spot. Michael asked flatly, "Did you get us an in?"

As arranged, Anzhel opened his jacket in a none too subtle display of the cash swelling its inner pocket. "Are you two hobos ready to do anything for money, then?"

"Any time," John returned cheerfully, making a convincing grab for payment in advance: a junkie needing his next fix, an alcoholic desperate for the next drink.

Anzhel knocked his hand away. "Nice," he said. "You look it too. The thug who thinks he can't be seen behind the pillar over there is my tail. I finally caught up with Dmitri Sergeyev. He was high up in Lukas Oriel's chain of command. Now he's dealing crack in the Zemel immigrant ghetto in Kennington." Anzhel smiled. "He seemed quite pleased to see me."

"An old soldier's reunion. How touching," John said, with every appearance of sincerity. "How does that help us?"

"He's expecting a massive delivery tonight. Big enough to pull in Zemel illegals from all over London and the poor street scum they use as their runners. They all knew Oriel. He'll be a major topic of discussion—in Zemel-dialect Russian, of course. Don't worry, John. I'm sure Mikey will translate for you. Be in the Black Bear pub at seven tonight. Someone will come and get you."

He was gone. Michael watched him merge his height and his vibrant beauty seamlessly into the crowd on the South Bank esplanade and disappear. Glancing to one side, he saw that John was watching too. "You all right?"

"Yeah," John said. They both enjoyed the spectacle of the thug who'd been sent to tail Anzhel darting frantically after him. "He's good."

Michael nodded. Personal differences aside, they both could appreciate the sight of a fellow professional at work. And, other than a little verbal sparring, Anzhel hadn't given John much obvious cause for complaint over the last few days. Hadn't flaunted his intimacy with Michael—had even kept undemonstrative distance when they had been alone together. If Anzhel had had a point he'd wished to make to John, Michael supposed he had already done so with unforgettable force. "You okay with this setup?" Michael asked awkwardly, turning back toward the river, resuming his role of a man with nothing to do and all day to do it in.

John followed his movement. They were elbow to elbow on the rail again. The medieval dolphin was still grinning. "Yeah, fine. Why not?"

"It'll be dangerous. Oriel's operatives were ruthless back then. I don't suppose they've improved morally since."

"Well, it's two birds with one stone, isn't it? We'll get a lead on Oriel tonight, then go back and bust the drug ring some other time."

"Yeah. After we've assisted them by acting as errand boys for a week."

"At least we'll get paid."

Michael nodded. "Pity it all goes into Webb's Christmas charity box, but yeah. Our cover will probably stretch to a B&B tonight, if it's cash in hand. You can get cleaned up."

"You know, I'm not all that bothered." John pulled off his black wool hat long enough to scratch at tangled curls. He yawned. "Life seems simpler like this sometimes."

Michael looked at him in alarm. John never minded getting dirty in the course of an op, but he would wash like a cat when conditions improved. The sun struck ripples of light off the surface of the water. In their shifting, scalloping patterns, Michael saw that his partner was ashen with weariness, his eyes hollow. Had he even lost some weight in the last three days?

In another world, a world where Michael hadn't placed their partnership on a knife's edge, he would have put an arm around him, and to hell with passing tourists who wanted to stare at their first gay English tramp. He would have asked him if he was all right. But even that question—the ordinary commerce of their shared days—seemed wrong now, as if he'd sacrificed the right. Sorrow, keen as a spear, passed through him.

What could he do? Anzhel possessed him, body and soul. They had run like wolves together, touched the same pitch, and been forever tarred. If Michael wanted that darkness contained, he had better make sure Anzhel's attentions were focused solely on him. He looked across the river, blindly taking in the familiar skyline: the immortal elegance of St Paul's, as outrageous in its day as the St. Mary Axe tower—the Gherkin—which had controversially risen to the east of it. His elbow brushed John's, and they waited in the floating river light like strangers.

* * *

Michael had to admit, there was more of a party atmosphere in the warehouse than when the English equivalent of all these drug lords and their sidekicks got together. No one had gone so far as to lay on a buffet, but unmarked bottles had appeared and were getting passed around among the cold-eyed, watchful men. If Michael closed his eyes, the scent of it would put him back into a frosty forest night. Pine resin, breath rising visibly on the air, the stolen contents of someone's backwoods still going from hand to hand...

He kept his eyes open. This place had been well chosen. Semiderelict but not so abandoned that the scattered arrival of cars in the surrounding alleys would draw attention. Anzhel's contact had led them down from the Bear to the dockside until they were in sight of the river—the same Thames whose progress they had watched that afternoon. But this stretch of it, a mile to the east, was a different world, smelling of darkness, moss, and decay, not expensive perfume trailed by tourists leaving the Festival Hall. They had been inconspicuous. Plenty of men just like them shuffling about the alleyways. Michael had found himself wondering, as he often did, where the hell these people went when each successive tide of docklands regeneration swept through their former refuge.

A few of them found jobs with entrepreneurs like Dmitri Sergeyev.

Only one end of the warehouse was lit up, flickering neon casting a surreal glow over the crates on which Dmitri was conducting his business. Packet after plastic-wrapped packet of what looked like pure Afghani heroin appeared on the makeshift table, was weighed, tasted for purity by each customer's hollow-eyed connoisseur, and paid for in inch-thick wads of cash. Michael dared a glance at his partner. Good as John was undercover, the sight of a deal like this going down under his nose would normally affect him like a shark encountering a fat baby seal.

It didn't seem to bother him tonight. He leaned just outside the circle of light, his back to the wall, one foot hitched up. The other runners were good cover for him, just as they were for Michael, waiting in the shadows opposite. His eyes were downcast, his whole air passive. His odd beauty was eclipsed. No one would have looked at him twice.

Not so Anzhel. He was made to shine by unnatural light. Leaning almost over Dmitri's shoulder, he laughed and gibed fearlessly at the other dealers, his flashy suit and jewels only striking sparks off him. Listening, Michael reflected that the Zemel SS must have cut him a good deal in return for his information. Some of the petty gang lords here tonight knew him, but only as a confederate of Oriel's, a refugee like them. Oriel had by now achieved near-legendary status among them. A vanished hero, a symbol of the motherland left far behind.

Anzhel was playing on that expertly. He was bloody good. Michael could see that. For a while he forgot the razor wire tangle that bound them and detachedly watched him at work. Funded by Last Line to be the wealthiest of the assembled dealers, his place at the table was secure, even the normally irascible Dmitri tolerating his proximity and smiling at his jokes. He didn't ask questions—hinted, rather, that he had half the answers already. Oriel might have confided in Anzhel alone where he intended to go if he had to flee to the West. Anzhel threw out theories and locations casually. Oriel would be a rich prize to whoever did track him down. He had resources and power beyond imagination.

Michael watched and knew that Anzhel was subtly watching too, the changes in one inconspicuous face at the end of the table: a little, ferret-eyed man, dried up by who knew what dissipations. Boredom on his hardened features changed to disbelief and then disgust, and when Anzhel next fell silent—as if giving him his cue—he leaned forward. "You talk horseshit, Mattvei," he grated in a gutter-level Zemel even Michael was pushed to understand. "You always were a boastful fool. Oriel has nothing. He's hiding like a rat in a church in Hounslow, only alive because some sap of a priest took him in—"

"Silence!" Dmitri Sergeyev's big fist banged down on the crates, making the drugs and the piles of bank notes bounce. The other dealers looked likewise outraged—Anzhel most of all, Michael noted with bitter amusement. He had allowed a painful flush to darken his fine skin. There were actually tears in his eyes. "Who says these things of Oriel says them of all of us," Dmitri snarled, and the little dark man shrank back into the shadows. "Your words will be stones in your pockets, Yuri."

"It is… It is only what I hear, *gospadin*."

"You hear lies of envy and spite," Anzhel said hoarsely. He was bolt upright beside Sergeyev. He was a hell of an actor, Michael thought, watching how the stone-faced villain next to him gave a fervent, respectful nod and reached to clasp his shoulder.

A tiny movement in the darkness opposite. Michael glanced across to John and forgot about Anzhel completely. He repressed his reaction as thoroughly, as instantly, as John had done, but it didn't change the fact that they were both quite suddenly screwed nine ways to hell. Leaning on the wall beside his partner, whispering in his ear, was a snitch they had used two years before in a drugs op. Used, paid well, then left to take the fall. The little bastard had done time.

Not enough. And John's time was up. Michael saw it in the resignation with which he got to his feet. Heart heaving, Michael eased back. They'd been frisked on their way in here. No shoulder holster and no way he could get to the weapon strapped just inside his calf without alerting the entire room. But if it came to that, so be it. Better to pick the little fucker off right now and pass it off as a spat between low-level runners than have him expose John and let the whole gang get the drop on them. All attention was still on Anzhel and Dmitri. Carefully, holding his breath, Michael began his move.

But the snitch had a game of his own. He made a tiny gesture at John. *Move. That way.* The shadows swallowed them, and they were gone.

No way Michael could cross the neon-lit space to follow them. Instead he retreated, holding out a hand behind him till he felt a concrete block wall. The door they'd been brought in through had creaked—no good, though it was the nearest one on this side of the warehouse. Silently, not taking his eyes off the group round Dmitri, he felt his way in the other direction. Each step took him deeper into the dark. When the dealers and the crates were a distant tableau, lit up by the neon like some appalling Russian gang lord's Last Supper, he turned and just as silently ran.

He found himself in a corridor, a narrow tunnel leading to disused workshops. The door at the end of it was padlocked and chained. Spinning round, Michael surveyed the rooms that opened off the corridor. Most were pitch black, but one must have connected to the outside world. There was a hatch at shoulder height, maybe for forklift deliveries. The gap was narrow and covered now with chicken wire, but it would do.

He made short work of the wire, clipping it with the cutters on the handyman's Swiss Army knife John had bought him the Christmas before, smilingly informing him that a part-time bumpkin like Michael was bound to need to take stones from horses' hooves at some point. Trying not to think about the gift or the giver, he tore the wire back and got a handhold. An easy scramble, though John would have made a more graceful job of it, and then he was poised in the hatchway, unable to tell from the uneasy remains of sunset light beyond it how deep a drop lay on the other side.

Well, no help for that. He swung out and let himself fall— just far enough to grab and lose a breath before his feet hit concrete. Instinctively he let the muscles of his thighs absorb the impact, powering down into a crouch, steadying himself with one hand. He took a moment to let his eyes adjust. He was in a narrow access way between one warehouse and the next, and neither the glow from the western sky nor the faint orange flicker of the single streetlight he could see had made it this far. He listened. Nothing but London's ceaseless traffic purr and the distant slap of water on the wharfside piers. Of course the snitch—Michael struggled for a name and plucked *Eddie* from his mind, *Eddie Harvey*—might not have brought John outside; might have dealt with him—a hand across the mouth, a swift-moving blade—in a private corner of the warehouse.

John could defend himself, of course. But straightening up, beginning to make his way along the narrow defile, Michael fought a cold conviction that he wouldn't bother. He prayed that Eddie had some business to transact. A deal to cut, maybe—a slice of whatever Anzhel would buy and give him to trade on in return for his intact cover. Or just a chance to play with him, to scare and humiliate the copper who had helped put him away.

Yes. Voices. Michael swore silently as he saw that the alleyway terminated five yards ahead of him in a sheer brick wall. Beyond it he could hear Eddie Harvey's hectoring tones. Occasional replies from John too, though if Eddie had brought him here to be frightened, that wasn't working out. John sounded more bored than anything. Relief swept through Michael, pins and needles in a limb he'd unconsciously cramped. He glanced around him. No way out of here except back the way he'd come, unless...

A rusted metal drainpipe, twenty feet or so up the side of the warehouse next door. The worst that could happen to him was that he fell and broke his neck, a matter of indifference to him right now. He shed his heavy coat, gave the pipe one diagnostic tug, and began to climb. At the top was a flat roof. Hoisting himself noiselessly onto it, he ducked low. From here he could see everything he needed to.

For all the good it did him. Harvey was holding John at gunpoint at the end of the alley on the wall's far side. Michael slipped his lightweight Colt from the leg holster, but he knew he didn't have a shot. No chance of getting one either, unless John shifted, somehow understood that he was there, and moved through 180 degrees out of the line of fire.

Michael thought about that. It wouldn't be the first time, would it? If he were to let the name form in his mind—*John*, or better still *Griff*—and simply and unquestioningly push it out toward him... Wouldn't be the first time John had heard. Their boss had seen the trick in action once and had shaken his head at them, looking as if he might have liked to have been reaching for a crucifix. Michael drew a breath to calm himself and tried.

Nothing. Worse than nothing—a pain in his head as if the reaching summons had hit a wall and backlashed inside him. He choked, fighting back the tiny sound it would have made. How fucking stupid of him. Those previous times had been dumb luck, coincidences. In the alleyway below, Eddie Harvey poked the gun muzzle into John's chest and said, "Do you know how often I got fucked up against a wall in that place, pig? How many big ugly pricks got shoved down my throat?"

John shrugged. Michael saw the tiny, casual move of his shoulders, unconcerned as if he had been in the pub with Harvey, answering the question over a pint. "I'm sure you did your share of the fucking and shoving, Ed."

"Bastard! I'm not a faggot, not like you and your pansy-arse partner. Did I see him in there as well? I'll sort him out too, once I've finished with—"

"Don't waste your time. He's not here."

"Lying little shit." Harvey raised the gun muzzle till it was an inch off John's brow. "Get down on your knees, pig. I'll show you what it's like to have to suck cock or choke on it."

John broke into laughter. Michael, who knew the sound and loved it like fresh water and sunshine, heard the genuine amusement in it and shuddered. "You have to be kidding. I saw a stray bulldog knockin' round here might have done the job for you, but—"

"I said on your knees!"

"Fuck you, Eddie. Not in a million years."

"Not even to save your life?"

John shrugged again. "No," he said tiredly. "Not even to save that precious bloody commodity. No."

Harvey snapped the safety off the gun. Michael, scanning desperately along the line of the rooftops for any route to a better position, caught—briefly, impossibly—a flash of bright blond hair. A moment later—yes, again. Anzhel Mattvei gracefully broaching the crest of a wall, taking up a good sniper's position on the flat roof behind it. He had what Michael would have sold his soul for—a line of fire to Harvey—but...

Anzhel, no! It's too far. You'll hit John!

A whistling pop tore the night, a silenced gunshot. Down in the alley, Eddie Harvey jerked as if pushed hard in the back. His eyes went wide. Then his knees buckled, and he dropped neatly to the cobbles.

Michael slithered down the wall on John's side. This time, unprepared, he landed awkwardly. John turned at the crash. "Mikey? What are you doing out here? Did you..." He looked back at Harvey, clearly trying to calculate angles. "Did you knock him off?"

"Nn-nn." Michael rubbed at his knee. Pain was slicing through it, but it didn't feel like his own. "I couldn't get a line to him. I couldn't..."

"Evening, gentlemen." Anzhel swung easily down from his refuge and dropped into the alleyway. Tucking the weapon into the back of his jeans, he nodded at John. "All right, zaichik?"

"You know, I'm almost getting used to that," John said calmly. "Still gonna thump you when I find out what it means. Yes, I'm fine. That was"—he looked up, examining the rooftops, working out where Anzhel must have fired from—"that was a neat shot."

Michael gasped. It was half outrage, half the pain of trying to lurch to his feet. John put out a hand to help him, and he grasped it tight. "A neat shot?" he demanded, trying not to fold back down again, aware that John took hold of him and propped him. "Half an inch and he'd have fucking killed you. What the hell were you doing, Anzhel? I told you not to—"

"I know, I know," Anzhel interrupted him. "I heard you. Looked to me like we had nothing to lose."

"Oh great. What if he'd spasmed on the trigger? What if—"

"Mike, shut up," John said wearily. "He's right. Harvey was gonna do it." He waited until Michael was steady, then let him go. "Thanks, Mattvei. I owe you. Look, we'd better get back inside."

"Not for the sake of information," Anzhel said. "I'll let Mikhaili catch you up on that, but you're right. Dmitri thinks I'm just out here having a piss. I'll go in ahead." He glanced at Harvey's corpse. "You can leave that there. Dmitri takes a body or two as a compliment at these soirées of his."

He turned to go, but Michael called him back. The pain was subsiding from his knee with surprising thoroughness. He'd thought he'd broken something. "Tell me one thing. How did you get a silenced H and K in here past Dmitri's security?"

"Didn't. Might have borrowed it from one of his heavies. I'd better put it back before he notices it's gone." He flashed a bright grin and jogged off soundlessly.

"Mike?"

John's voice called him back from abstracted distance. "Yes," he said, focusing with difficulty on his partner's face. John looked exhausted, bleached out in the lamplight. "Are you okay? You must've been scared."

"Not especially. Are you?"

"What? Yeah, I'm all right. Why would I not be?"

"There's so many answers to that I don't know where to start. I… I know you'd have done it if you could."

Michael closed his eyes for a moment. He hadn't yet worked out for himself that the acid burning up his throat was bitter failure, cold horror at the thought of John's life in Anzhel's hands. "The important thing is that somebody did. Come on."

"Give me my catch-up first. Did you get something useful in there?"

"Yeah. Anzhel provoked one of Sergeyev's foot soldiers into a bit of an outburst. He reckons Oriel's gone to ground in a church in Hounslow."

"Isn't that one parish down from—"

"The place where we found Piotr. Yes. I don't know what's going on, mate, but I don't like it."

"Well, like you always say, we don't have to." John eased his foot out from under Harvey's body. "Poor Eddie," he said dispassionately. "We really left him in the shit. I'm not surprised he wanted a go. What do we do now?"

"Head to Hounslow, I suppose, and dig in. After... after we've sold our drugs, of course. No choice there."

"No, I know. Dmitri will have tabs on all the runners. Great job, isn't it?" John stole a glance at Michael. "You don't have to remind me how much I get paid."

"I wasn't going to." No. Michael had been thinking of an exchange in an empty office—could it only have been four days ago? A moment when he'd said to his partner, *we could get out*. And John had said s*ay the word*. When not in Anzhel's immediate physical presence, Michael couldn't imagine for the life of him how he had come to do the things he had to throw all that away. "We'd better go," he said, a rough little crack breaking the words.

"In a second. I'm sorry I've been cold-shouldering you. Didn't mean to be a kid. Or a... a bad loser, for that matter."

You haven't lost me. Oh, Griff, don't let me be lost. "You've been fine. You've got no reason to be speaking to me now."

"Well, I'm speaking." John smiled faintly and put out a hand to steady Michael as he crouched to tuck the Colt away. "We still doing our tacky little hotel routine tonight?"

"Yeah. We'd better."

"Then come and talk to me there, will you?" John's brow creased. "Unless you're gonna be with—"

"No. No, I'm not. I don't even think he'll come to the same place."

Chapter Twelve

The shabby room was oddly peaceful. On either side, and above and below him too, John could hear the other tenants of the house going about their business, but the door was shut and he was alone. He was used to the music of the unceasing traffic outside; it had become a type of silence to him.

Nothing like the peace that reigned in Glastonbury under the stars.

John got up from the narrow bunk where he'd been sitting and padded over to the window, as if he could physically avoid the comparison. He wasn't even sure he'd ever see the farmhouse again, and he wasn't ready for the wash of homesickness that had accompanied the thought. It hadn't been his home. It was Mike's, a place John had visited while he and his partner had been on visiting terms.

Well, things changed. Hitching absently at the towel round his waist—no need to scare passersby, even in this wasteland, half-derelict street—John knew there was nothing he could be sure of. Not about the world, not about himself. Had there ever been? Maybe not, but so far it had never bothered him. He'd welcomed his fluid universe, his freedom within it, a powerful swimmer in his element. He'd pushed off from his family home and spent most of his time since on the move. His only experience of peace—a foothold, a place to stop and breathe—had been the farmhouse.

And Michael. It was weird how you could go through life and never need a thing until you fell across it. Then you couldn't live without it, though of course you never found that out until it was taken away. There were plenty more drugs than the ones he'd hawked around South London tonight, a watcher from Dmitri's camp close on his tail all the way. If he hadn't been numbed out anyway, John reckoned he might have felt marginally less sick about that—all those shaking hands, sweat-beaded faces—given his own state of hopeless addiction.

He swung round at a light, cautious tap on the door. It should have been locked. As a responsible agent for Last Line, John should have been standing here with a gun in his hand as well as a towel round his waist, but it didn't seem crucial anymore, and anyway he knew who it was. Had felt the little inner tug for the last five minutes, another luxury he'd taken for granted till now. He leaned his back against the window frame. "Mike? It's open."

Michael came in cautiously, checking the corridor behind him. "You should lock this," he said, snapping the elderly Yale latch shut for himself. "I got tailed all the way to the front steps."

"Me too. I wouldn't worry. I'm fairly sure we've been convincing."

"Yeah, horribly. But still."

John surveyed him. Michael didn't look as if he'd enjoyed his evening's pushing any more than he had done himself. He looked as rough as he ever could—merely mortal, shadowed and made gaunt by his acts. In their old shared world, John would have gone to him. Thrown an arm round his shoulders, delivered a bruising, comforting squeeze, and made him sit down. But now his joints felt full of ice and rust. "Is he worth it, then?" he asked, not moving. "This Oriel?"

"I don't know much more about him than Mattvei told you. But—yes, I suppose so. If you think war criminals are worth the hunt."

"You know I do." Last Line had been instrumental in bringing in Conrad Eber, one-time SS commandant, then almost ninety years old and minding his business on his Lambeth allotment, another job no one else had wanted to do. A dirtier one than this, though John had never flinched from it. "I want to know what he means to you, Mike. What catching him would mean."

"I don't understand."

"Okay. Let's start lower. What does Anzhel Mattvei mean?"

"Jesus. You—you *saw* what he means. Wasn't that enough?"

John looked at the faded carpet. He was dripping on it, still wet from the shower he'd taken in the B&B's sordid facilities down the corridor. If he didn't comb his hair through soon, it would tangle irretrievably. "I *saw*," he said carefully, "someone you hadn't seen for years fucking you bareback. Cutting you. I saw you letting him. I saw him make you think you were tied up, and there was—nothing."

"What?"

"Shut up for a second. I know there can't be anything between us, Mikey, but there used to be a hell of a lot that had nothing to do with sex. We looked out for one another. Tell me why Mattvei can do that to you."

"Why… I don't even know what you're talking about." Michael sat on the bed and looked up with an expression half disgusted, half comical John would normally have found irresistible. "*Bareback*, Griff?"

"Without a condom," John clarified for him coldly. "Like you don't know."

"He didn't. That is… I wouldn't have let him. I'm sorry you burst in on us, but you couldn't have seen that clearly. And as for the tying and cutting…" Michael's shadow of a smile faded out. "Okay. Yes. I need that. I haven't hidden that from you."

"You're missing the point."

"For God's sake," Michael breathed. He got up with feverish energy and came to stand in front of John. "It was a rope. Not much, just a…a symbol. You mustn't have seen it, that's all."

"Where did it come from? Your odds-and-sods drawer? Or did Mattvei have one handy in his pocket?"

"John, *stop*."

"I will. I'll back off and leave the pair of you alone the second you tell me he's not harming you."

"The pair of… There isn't any *pair of us*. It's sex, that's all. It doesn't mean anything."

"Then what the hell did it mean with me?"

John hadn't meant that demand to escape him at all, let alone with such passion. He was relieved when Michael looked down, as if he hadn't heard—and an instant later horrified when the strong fist fastened on the knot of the towel round his hips. "If I was to try and tell you that," Michael said softly, "we'd be here all night. Griff, come on. If I've hurt you, let me make it up."

"And how are you planning to do that?"

"Any way you like. But starting here."

Michael sank to his knees. For a moment—long enough for Michael to jerk open the towel and dispense with it—John allowed it. In some skewed way, it felt quite normal. Most of his encounters with other men began like this, and Mike was so familiar to him. His solid grace, his warmth. The inside of his mouth, familiar too, the culmination of a hundred erotic reveries.

John grabbed his shoulders. "Pack it in."

"Why? You're ready for it."

"Technicality." Easing away, evading Michael's restraining grip on his backside, John made a grab for the towel. "All you have to do is look at me to give me a hard-on. You know that. You must've known for years. And God knows, if you're doling out meaningless sex, I don't see why I shouldn't"—his throat seized up—"I don't see why I shouldn't benefit. But this isn't you, Mikey. It hasn't been you for a fortnight, not—not even when you were fucking me." John stumbled away from him. His discarded clothes were on the bed. He scrambled into them, frail shields as they were. Michael had subsided against the wall and was sitting staring at him, his eyes bleak and lost. "Now, are you going to talk to me, or..."

He froze. A single whistle had threaded up from the street. A summons, at once plaintive and challenging—like a bloody owl, John thought, declaring its territory over a springtime hill. Not that he'd ever heard such a thing until Michael had taken him out to walk through the moonlit fields by the Teal. "You said he wouldn't come here."

"I didn't think... Oh God."

"Mike, stay here. You don't have to go to him."

But Michael was already hauling himself to his feet. He leaned his hands on the windowsill and looked out into the dark. "I do. Just to find out what he wants. I'll come back, John."

* * *

Half an hour later, John heard the door of the room next to his click open and shut. The walls were paper-thin. He heard not only that but every word of the developing argument between his partner and Anzhel Mattvei.

Which, if it had been conducted in English, would probably have been quite enlightening to him. John lay on his back on the narrow bunk and tried not to listen in any case, because he could hear—from Michael, anyway—that they were trying to keep it down. The complex sibilants and rasping, purring consonants drew his attention against his will. The language had a music of its own. Weary, despite everything beginning to drift toward sleep, John draped an arm over his eyes. This was how his unknown Michael spoke, the stranger he'd first encountered the night after the Piotr Milosz op, the night after John had fallen and fallen and should have died, he knew, though his collision with the stranger had driven all that from his mind. It hadn't occurred to John then that there was any aspect of Michael he couldn't handle, not even in the cold morning, waking up to memories of scars and blood and pain. Letting the last few days melt from his mind, he imagined himself back to that state of innocence, imagined that Michael was speaking this beautiful impassioned language to him as they lay on a sunny hillside, their bodies moving in synchrony.

No. Too much distress in it. John had heard a lot of notes in Michael's voice but never fear, never, thank God, that scrape of revulsion, not when Mike was talking to him. Waking, John rolled onto one elbow and lay poised, listening. He hadn't undressed. He knew better now than to try to stage an intervention between his partner and Anzhel, but he'd wanted to be ready if Michael came to him.

It sounded as if Michael was about to walk out anyway. His volume had pitched up as he forgot the thin walls in his anger. The door handle rattled.

John shook his head. For a moment he thought his ears had started to sing. There was a sense of pressure in them, as if he'd forgotten to balance before a scuba dive, and then that cleared, and then he was somehow listening to music. No, not listening— immersed. Nothing like the thud of bass that had boomed all night in conflicting rhythms from up and down the street. Slowly he identified it as a human voice.

Then he questioned the word *human*. Rolling onto his stomach, clutching the flat little excuse of a pillow, John tried to free his mind from the unearthly bloody beauty of the sound. It seemed to come into him through his skin. He shuddered, tears stinging to his eyes. It filled up the space between this sordid room and the patch of moonlit sky he could see beyond the rooftops. He wanted it at once to stop and to go on forever.

Then his ears popped, and the spell broke. The symphony dropped away. It was nothing more or less than Anzhel Mattvei, softly singing and—weirdly—John knew the song. He had heard it a hundred times. Never in full, just passing fragments as Mike went about his business in his flat or the office. He sang it when he was distracted, contented, and John had loved to hear it, associating it in his mind with the pleasant routines of their day or... yes, food. Mike often sang it to himself while he was cooking.

John let go a huge pent-up breath and subsided onto the pillow. Other noises were beginning now, but they didn't bother him. The bed on the far side of the wall thumped against it, but not hard, as if someone had gone down onto it gently, gone down without a fight. The vibration went through the bed where John lay—went through the marrow of his bones, it felt like—came again and again and settled into a delicate rhythm.

Whatever the hell Anzhel Mattvei was doing to Mike, it wasn't hurting him now. That was enough for John. He buried his face in the crook of his elbow, trying not to listen, unable not to hear. But even his involuntary witnessing didn't seem wrong. A whisper of Russian came through the wall, close and intimate as if it were at his own ear—as if he were there in the room by invitation, watching, or…

No. As if he and Michael were one flesh. That wasn't new to him. He'd felt it on the streets, in moments of great fear or exaltation. A barrier would melt, and there he would be, burning with Michael's fires, feeling in the same instant how Michael opened to welcome his own cool rush. From the outside it was nothing but one shared look or a hand closing tight on a shoulder. There was nothing strange, nothing alien to John, in the experience.

Nothing to stop him. No alarm bells rang when Mike began to moan in pleasure and the sensation of lift-off wrapped round John too. As if a big hand were under him, scooping him up. Arousal flooded him. His cock stiffened against the mattress, and he shifted awkwardly to accommodate its rise before remembering he was still trapped in his jeans. He thought about unbuttoning— fleetingly, about thrusting down, getting friction and a focus for the starry, glittering cloud of excitement—but somehow there wasn't time. Somehow it wasn't necessary, as if it were all being done for him, and all he had to do was lie there and let it happen. He had been so tired. Becoming so sick of the world, his heartbreak a disease he couldn't have fought off for much longer, draining him. He needed this, needed exactly what he was getting—an escape, a wild ride on Anzhel's wings.

The wrongness of it hit him too late. He was on the brink of a come so big he thought it might register on seismographs, but still he would have scrambled back. He was about to get off, like some kind of perv, on the sound of someone else's sex. But suddenly the broken moaning from next door became words, became English, or one word of it anyway, hot and clear: "John! John, John…"

The lightning struck. Flat on his belly, hands convulsing on the pillow, John burned and fought and flashed to climax. He had an instant to recall that he had used to come like this when he was a kid—untouched, hitting the heights out of a dream, when the world was still new to him and his body a fantastic toy, capable of anything. Too much. His throat was too tight for a scream, but the sound he would have made ripped round inside him, scouring his lungs.

Then he began to fall. He choked in fright. It was such a long drop, and he wouldn't survive this time, that was for sure.

But he was worn to the bone. The cold ground—the dirty mattress, the floorboards and ragged carpets of this place—wouldn't stop him now. A deeper pit opened, his exhaustion coming to his rescue. He cried out softly in relief and let his fall become a dive, stretching out to meet the dark. He split the waters painlessly, shot down deep and deeper and was gone.

* * *

Daylight hadn't made it to the hostel at seven the next morning. John was fairly sure it never would. He strode down the neon-lit corridor that led to the bathrooms. There were two, both communal, on this floor. Michael had just disappeared into the one on the right. An elderly gentleman in ragged dressing gown was shuffling the same way. Catching him up, John took him gently by the shoulders and steered him toward the door opposite. He went without a murmur, and John pulled open the other one.

Michael was splashing water into his face. He flinched and knocked his toothbrush and glass into the sink with a clatter. John saw at once that he was a mass of raw-nerved reflex, and tried not to care. "It's just me," he said, letting the door bang shut behind him. "Why? Will he follow you in here?"

"Morning to you too," Michael responded, trying for a smile.

John looked him over. He had got dressed as far as his T-shirt and jeans from the day before—from the three days before, John reflected, skin twitching with distaste inside his own soiled clothes, in which he'd additionally spent a bizarre night, waking bewildered and stiff, glad his shirt was long enough to hide some of the damage. "You look like a panda," he observed.

"Is it the… penchant for bamboo? Or the nonexistent sex life, because I thought I was getting away—"

"It's certainly not the sex life." John stepped up close to him, grieved that to do so felt like an effort of daring. He lifted a hand and brushed his fingertips over the shadows beneath Michael's eyes—the briefest caress. "It's these."

"You've got them too."

John bit back a moan. Michael's attention was on him, as tenderly and diagnostically as if the last few days had never happened. It wasn't real. John had to end it. "Never mind me," he said. "Why didn't you come back last night? Mike—tell me you *remember* that you didn't come back."

"Of course I do. I—"

"Don't try and explain. Will you just listen for a minute?"

"Well, I need a pee and a shower, but…"

"Mike."

"Okay. What's up?"

And now John hardly knew how to tell him. But overnight his fear had hardened to a certainty. "You got hurt on that mission in Zemelya, right? Tortured. And as far as you remember, Anzhel was… just a comrade, another one of Oriel's soldiers."

Michael had gone pale. "I can't imagine why we're discussing it in a bathroom at seven in the morning," he said. "But yes."

"I think he was more than that. I think he was part of whatever hurt you. I think you were conditioned—programmed, whatever—and he had a hand in it."

Michael actually grinned. He looked so ordinary that for a moment John was reassured. "Don't be so daft," he said, as if John had been trying to get some kind of April Fool's gag over on him. "I've been picked apart by experts. You think they'd just... miss something like that?"

"I don't know. Maybe it wasn't going to show up until Anzhel did. *I* can't miss it."

The smile disappeared. Michael turned away and ran his fingers through his hair, looking past himself in the mirror to some unknowable distance. "You sure you're reading this right, Griff?"

"What is that supposed to mean?"

"It's gonna be hard on you, isn't it? I didn't mean for us... for you and me to start a thing together, and then for Anzhel to turn up. That must've been rough."

John stared at his elegant, clear-cut profile. His lips were pressed together, his brow as smooth as if he'd never known a moment's uncertainty in his life. "Wait a minute. You think I'm putting us both through this because I—I'm jealous?"

"No. Not you—not like that. But I know it's screwed you over. I'm sorry."

Nice work, Agent South. John pulled himself back from his anger, seeing how neatly Mike had diverted him. He would trip up a witness like that during interrogation. "Thanks for the apology," John said carefully. "You give me too much credit, though. I *am* bloody jealous. But I can manage that. What I can't stand is watching you turn into a puppet every time Anzhel walks into the room. He controls you. As a matter of fact, he..." John stopped short. He knew how it would sound. But this was the thing that had terrified him most, that had made him aware he had strings of his own and that these could be tugged just as deftly as Michael's. "He sings to you. To calm you down or to stop you from walking away. Why the fuck does he sing to you?"

"What?" Michael, who had picked up his toothbrush as if about to go on with his morning's ablutions, laid it down.

John saw it gather on his face—the same look of fear that had haunted it that morning in the Acton church, after John's fall and all the way into the hospital until it was established he wasn't hiding any broken bones or internal bleeding.

"What are you talking about? Are... are you okay?"

Any second now he would put out a hand and feel John's brow for a fever. "Of course I'm not," John snarled, fierce in proportion with his longing for the touch. "He sings to you, and you obey him. There's something not right about it. Oh, obviously, but it's worse than... It's fucking unearthly, okay? I heard him last night myself. It got to me too."

"Bloody hell." Michael's pale mask of amazement was genuine; John could see that. And now the fear was definite. "Listen to yourself, Griff."

And here came the hand—reaching not for his face but his shoulder, where it would fasten with a grip that could melt everything else in John's world to dust and shadows. John jerked away, colliding hard with the tiled wall behind him. "Don't."

"I want you to knock off, okay? Go back to HQ and tell Webb you're not well. Anzhel and I can manage for—"

"Oh, I'm going." Hot tears of frustration stung John's eyes. If they fell, so be it. He couldn't risk the gesture of wiping them away. His stupid voice was cracking as it was, betraying him. "I know you two can manage. All I've done so far on this one is need to be translated for and rescued. But I've got to warn you, sunbeam. When I do see Webb, I'm going to tell him what I think."

"What? That I'm playing out some kind of programming, and Anzhel's controlling it?"

"Yeah. In those words exactly."

"Don't waste your time, mate. If he thinks it'll get him Oriel, he won't care."

"Will it? Is that what all this is about?"

"John, get out of here. I don't care why you're going or what you tell Webb as long as you're off the scene. Especially if you think I'm some sort of ticking bloody time bomb. Go."

They stood for a moment, locked in silent confrontation. For a moment John felt as if the barricade between them was nothing—a thin film, the skin of a bubble. Something they'd dreamed up together out of fear, and one good shake would bring them out of it. John knew what he'd say. *Come home. This is stupid; we've got better things to do with our lives. I love you.*

The bathroom door swung wide. A skinny kid with track marks wandered in, bestowed on them a look consistent with his neo-Nazi tattoos, and shouldered past them toward the showers. The bubble skin became a wire fence. "I'm not abandoning you," John said hoarsely. "I'll stay in touch. Do what I can from HQ."

"I know that. Just… just go."

* * *

The Kennington B&B and John's loft apartment existed in two different worlds. Catching sight of himself in the silver-framed mirror he'd hung in the living room to gather and amplify the morning light, John checked the impulse to reach for his gun. It looked as though a tramp had broken into his starkly elegant home. He stripped off his clothing where he stood and walked, oblivious to the people who paid an equal fortune for an equal lack of privacy in the lofts all around him, into the shower.

Emerging, scrubbing his hair with a towel, he looked for a place where he could curl up and consider his wounds, if not actively lick them. Mike's flat—the farmhouse too—had an abundance of such corners. Sofas you could sink into, thick-walled rooms where you could close the curtains and sleep off a night's excesses in peace. John had seldom been around here much during the day. His bed, behind its Japanese-paper partition, lay bathed in dazzling June light, impossible to block out. All the expensive surfaces John had chosen with such care gave back the brilliance too.

He had no idea why he'd chosen the place or what had charmed him about it. He got dressed quickly, skin scrubbed clean now but crawling with the sense of exposure. He glanced at the kettle, but it gave a warning crackle at the very sight of him, and he boiled up the water in a pan on the gas hob instead.

He took his coffee into the living... space, really; it didn't qualify as a room. He perched on the edge of the chilly, gorgeous Krefeld chair Mike had bought him last Christmas, not understanding his tastes but always happy to indulge them. It came as an odd comfort to him to reflect that, in his new circumstances, he wouldn't have to worry about the loft or its contents for very much longer at all. He'd never saved a penny out of his salary and could coast here for a fortnight tops until his next rent payment fell due.

John supposed he shouldn't have been surprised at the view his boss had taken. Webb hadn't let him get as far as his concerns about Michael, and in the familiar office, facing the hurricane of the old man's wrath, hypnotic songs and mysterious conditioning had begun to seem like a fairytale to John too. Webb hadn't given a damn about his agent's reasons for abandoning the op. The fact that he had done so—that he had broken Last Line's first law and abandoned his partner—had been enough. John was suspended, indefinitely and without pay, and could consider himself lucky he hadn't been sacked outright, though Webb would arrange for this as soon as he could coordinate the paperwork.

John's hands shook. He splashed black coffee onto the pale merino rug and didn't care. He'd been stupid ever to mistake the old man's willingness to sacrifice his men for a lack of care about them. The usual terms applied to the Oriel op, he had reminded John ferociously, and if Michael South ended up as the price, so be it. But until and unless such desperate circumstances arose, Agent South's life was precious to Webb as a son's. As all his agents' lives were precious, even that of the errant one in front of him. You never abandoned your partner.

Drawing a breath, John sat up straight. He knew that. He *knew* that. He'd put it into practice every single working day for the last three years. What did it matter if Mike was screwing someone else, or if that someone had some fucked-up gift for turning the man John loved into a stranger? He was John's partner still, and John had shattered the first law.

He jumped to his feet, knocking the coffee over. He couldn't take time to resume his street disguise, and simply threw on the threadbare old coat over his clean clothes. And he sure as hell couldn't take the Jag roaring into the middle of Mike's undercover, much as he might have wanted to, the modern equivalent of riding his charger onto the battlefield and snatching his partner up out of the fight. On the street, he settled for a taxi instead, tersely informing the cabbie he'd pay double for silence and a record-breaking ride back to Kennington.

But Michael was gone. Anzhel too, and the tired-looking hostel clerk had somehow missed the exit of a six-foot, fair-haired demigod when they checked out. John ran up the stairs to be sure, but Mike's room was standing empty, the bunk stripped down.

He made his way blindly back out into the sunlight. Halfway down the hostel's steps, his legs folded and he sank down. No one gave him a second glance. Worn-out junkies and men of the road wound up here all the time, he supposed, too lost to make the journey between their night and daytime worlds.

He tried Michael's phone. No answer, of course. Mike took his undercovers seriously, and for all John knew might have left it in his locker together with his badge. Propping his brow on one hand, John let his own phone dangle from the other and allowed himself one of those dangerous human moments of reflecting that at least things couldn't get any worse.

The phone buzzed. John snatched it up, hope flaring. *Prince William*, the screen said, and for a moment it meant nothing to him except a vague apprehension that he'd somehow pissed off the nation's heir. Then he remembered. Swallowing a scald of bitter laughter—*Quin, of course! Why the hell not?*—he picked up the call.

Chapter Thirteen

"Hello? Uncle Mike?"

Pressing the phone to his ear in the noisy Hounslow cafe, Michael smiled. *Uncle* had gone out the window a long time ago, together with other childish failings. The kid must really want something. "Morning, Quin. Where are you?"

"Um... On a train to London."

"On a school trip, right? Off to see the crocodiles in Regents Park Zoo?"

A pause, during which Michael could hear distinctly the silvery hiss of a speeding Intercity. "You know it's not that."

The exact echo of his brother, when John was caught short and about to confess. Mike's smile broadened. This was very serious, he knew, but at the moment he couldn't seem to worry about it. It was just nice to hear from the boy he'd grown to think of as more of a son than a borrowed nephew. Across the table, nursing his coffee, Anzhel Mattvei smiled too, as if he understood. "What's up, then?"

"Please don't tell John yet. Please don't tell the school."

That was a tall order. Not about the school; if they couldn't find a way to contain their rebellious inmates, that was their own lookout. But the one thing Michael had never done was allow Quin to divide and conquer as far as he and John were concerned. "No promises about your brother, sunbeam. Still, I don't know what I'm not meant to be telling him yet, do I?"

"I can't face another bloody day there. They got a bloody doctor in. Told me I was bloody autistic."

"Really? I'd never have said that. Tourette's, maybe, but—"

"They've got me counting grains of rice and playing the piano to see what kind of idiot I am."

Mike snorted. He laid a hand over the receiver until he could steady his voice. "Do you maybe mean what kind of savant?"

"Whatever. I can't cope with it anymore. Can I come and stay with you for a few days? Please?"

Please was an echo from the past, as well, at least delivered with that kind of sincerity. A right little pain in the arse, Quin had been over the past year or so, adolescence knocking out his sweet childhood manners. The answer was still no. Michael and John had stood shoulder to shoulder in their efforts to deal with him. No way would Michael ever give him refuge, hide him from poor John's unwilling efforts at parental authority. "Don't ask me that. You know the answer."

"I can stay if John says so. Shit." A brief silence, broken by the rattle of a drinks trolley, then Quin's voice returned, ragged with the edge of rare tears. "I know why you do that. I do. But it doesn't always *help* me."

"No, I know. Look, I'll talk to him if I get the…"

Michael broke off. Anzhel's hand had come down on his. He was a fearless sod, Michael would give him that. Even he and John would hardly sit caressing one another's hands in the middle of a café full of building-site workers and truck drivers. But no one seemed to be taking any notice. Maybe times were changing. A gentler world. Even the music thudding out of the radio seemed to have changed from Capital FM to some kind of instrumental. Like nothing so much as a Russian melody he had once known...

"Uncle Mike? Are you still there?"

Michael glanced up. Anhzel's hand was still on his, an undemanding caress. His smile was very sweet. *Kids*, it said. Helplessly Michael returned it.

"Yes, I'm here. You don't have to call me uncle, you know."

"No, I know! But I will if you like it. I—"

"Quin, stop trying to *bribe* me. Is it really that bad?"

"I think they want to dissect me. I know John paid a lot for it, but this school's worse than—"

"All right, all right. God knows I don't want you going to live in the forest again. But I'm not at home at the moment. I..."

"Oh. Are you out on an op?"

Michael bit his lip at the breathless excitement. Not too old to be blasé about everything, then. "No. It's surveillance, that's all. You're going to have to come and meet me."

"I can join you on an op?"

"Not a bloody chance. You can come and get my keys and go home to my flat. Tell me, do you look like a little rich kid today?"

"Of course not!"

Quin sounded offended. But he was very like his brother in some ways, and Michael knew his intentionally faded jeans and cut-off little surfer-style Ts cost a fortune. "Well, do something for me anyway. Stick your expensive bag into a plastic carrier and mess up your hair. And if you can pick up a scabby parka from a charity shop on your way, we'll be sorted."

* * *

Michael watched him approach from the window of the rent-by-the-week flat he and Anzhel had taken on Lampton Road. Quin had obeyed his instructions to the letter. The sight of him made Michael want to cry with laughter—or just cry; his throat felt strange and tight, and his sinuses hurt.

"Is that our boy?"

Michael nodded without turning. He didn't want to see Anzhel just now, didn't want to know how he was leaning over his shoulder and staring out into the street.

"He's very like the other one."

Yes. The resemblance was strong. Michael had seen photos of the Griffin parents and wondered how they'd managed to produce such striking sons, but Quin was as like his brother as if God had been unable to get John's melody out of his head. And every line of Quin—his skinny, long-limbed frame, his tumble of otter brown hair curling out from under the dreadful woolly hat he'd acquired from somewhere—reminded Michael of how much he loved his partner.

A faint moan escaped him, and he leaned his brow on the window frame. Anzhel's fingers pressed into the back of his neck, rubbing, insinuating. "It's all right. You know everything's going to be all right now. You'd better go and let him in."

Slowly Michael went down the stairs and opened the crumbling redbrick's front door. He stepped outside and leaned on the wall, folding his arms. Quin didn't notice. He was too busy ducking into a doorway to check that he wasn't being followed, and once more Michael fought laughter. Now the kid was reminding him of John by contrasts. John, if he wanted, could pull down invisible veils of anonymity and stroll down the middle of a street like this unseen, but Quin was behaving exactly like his own romantic idea of a secret agent—hugging the shadows, constantly checking over his shoulder. He stopped on the far side of the road, scanning the terrace for the number Michael had given him.

Michael stayed quite still until Quin was standing three feet away from him, clearly debating whether or not to go in uninvited. Not shifting a muscle or raising his head, he said, "Let us have a ciggy, then, son."

Quin blinked. "Sorry. I don't... Oh my *God*. Mike!"

"Ssh. Don't tell the whole street." Unfolding himself, Michael directed the startled kid into the shadowy hall and closed the door behind them. "You okay?"

"Yeah, but..." Quin turned, surveying him. "How do you do that? You're really good at it. I never even saw you. How do you—"

"Hush," Michael told him again, voice unsteady with laughter. Once Quin had new knowledge in his sights, some talent or gift he hadn't yet mastered, he would pursue it without mercy, suck its possessor dry. "You just think yourself into the brickwork. I'll teach you, but not now. This coat is very good. The hat too."

"Oh." Quin gave a half-pleased, half-embarrassed glance downward at the horrible brown parka. "Is that the kind of thing?"

"Exactly. But, um... you'd be London's most intellectual little tramp this afternoon, then?"

"What?"

"The accessories."

Quin frowned. He'd done as he was bidden and concealed his satchel in a plastic bag, but the bag came from Oxford's leading academic bookstore. He lifted it and looked at it. "Shit," he said. "I had it in my satchel, and I just..."

"Maybe they *should* be testing to see what kind of idiot you are."

Quin looked up. He was at that stage of youth where straight-faced adult jokes could pass him by—then his smile flashed out, a great incandescent grin just like John's, and Michael knew he'd got over it. That somehow, despite all the rigid schooling and lack of family life, he'd grown into a sense of the ridiculous. He put his head back and burst into laughter. "I'm sorry!"

"No. Don't be. I'm glad you're not entirely a natural at this. Come on upstairs and—"

"Uncle Mike, I…"

What is it, Michael would have asked, but he didn't get time. And then he was too breathless with astonishment. The stiff-necked, awkward kid had walked into his arms. He stayed there just long enough for Michael to return his fierce squeeze, then stepped back, plainly bewildered at himself. Michael too was thrown—by a mile. Quin never hugged. Frowning to disguise the pang the gesture had sent through him, Michael let him go. "What's that about?"

"I don't… I don't bloody know." Quin looked at his feet, blushing. "I'm just sick of being at boarding schools. Of being by myself or just with other kids and teachers, not having anybody to…"

"It's okay," Michael said gently. "I know, all right? Maybe things will be different from now."

"How can they be? John—"

"John just wants the best for you. Have you contacted him?"

"What do you think?"

"I think the school will have told him you're on the run again by now, and he'll be driving round the countryside in a panic looking for you."

Quin halted, his hand on the banister. He gave an incredulous snort. "John doesn't panic."

"Not on the surface, no. But you'd be surprised." Michael gave him a little push ahead of him up the stairs. "The first thing we do is call him, okay? Then I'll give you my keys and—"

"Oh, Mikhaili, give the kid a break."

Michael stopped dead. Automatically he wrapped a shielding arm around Quin. Anzhel was at the top of the stairs, beaming down at them. He was in his full glory. His voice seemed to open up the sordid walls around them and let in sweet summer air. He held out a hand, jogging down to meet them. "Quintus, I presume?"

"Quin," the boy corrected him, but with none of his usual disgust at the sound of his full name. He was too busy staring.

Just for a moment, Michael almost breached surface. Paper chains of thought ran through his head, fragile and swift. *I brought my nephew here. I brought him to Anzhel. Dear God, get him out, get him out...* But Anzhel's summer breezes blew the links away like confetti, and instead Michael watched Quin break into a charmed and charming smile and hold out a hand in return.

"Not going to perform the introduction, Mikhaili?"

"Oh. Sorry. Quin, this is Anzhel, my partner."

A shadow crossed Quin's face. But Michael was too lost to read it, and it was Anzhel who answered it, gently, smiling. "Not forever. Just for this one job, while your brother's busy on another case. I tell you what; you should come with us today. You can stay in the background and see how things are done."

Quin swallowed audibly. His hostility to John had never hidden—was perhaps based in—his desire to be as like him as possible. John, afraid for him, had kept the door shut too tight, forbidding Michael any shoptalk during the kid's visits, evading his questions. He said faintly, "Are you kidding?"

"No, not at all," Anzhel assured him, guiding him into the rented room with a comradely pat to the shoulder. "You should learn. You might be really good at this. You're dressed the part, anyway."

"Anzhel," Michael whispered. His own voice wouldn't come to him. His throat and skull felt packed with cotton wool, and he couldn't remember when the hell he had told Anzhel the boy's full name. "It's not a good idea. He'll be a liability."

Quin heard. He broke off his curious inspection of the room and gave Michael a look of undisguised pain. "You—you asked me to come here."

"I know. To collect my keys and go home, not—"

"You know, I'm not surprised you and John have trouble with him," Anzhel interrupted. He put an easy hand on Quin's shoulder. "A liability? He could be an asset. And all we're doing today is hanging around talking to people, trying to pick up a scent. Don't you even trust him to cope with that?"

It was strange. Michael could see exactly what Anzhel was doing. The mechanics of it were hardly subtle. Flattery, a soothing of the kid's sore spots. Divide and conquer. Everything Michael and John had scrupulously avoided in their shared dealings with Quin. No, not subtle at all, and Quin was too bright to buy it wholesale either. He glanced up at his new advocate, suspicious, one eyebrow on the rise.

Anzhel shrugged. It was a leave-it-up-to-you gesture, and he strolled to the window and looked out, hands in his pockets, softly whistling.

Michael knew the tune. It put a kind of peace inside him— settled all his doubts. It left one channel only for his thoughts, and they ran down it smoothly. He ceased to notice that Anzhel was whistling at all, knew only that he loved him for taking away the noise and the struggle in his head. He loved Quin too. "Listen," he said. "Come with us today. You—you're an asset, not a liability, Quin, and we're only talking to people. You can cope with that."

"Mike, are you okay?"

Michael rubbed his eyes. Through their cobwebby blur, Quin could be John, asking him the question with his brother's exact intonation. A longing to see him went through Michael, followed by intense relief that he was gone. *Far away from what I've become. Far away and safe.* "I'm fine," he said and watched the anxiety clear from Quin's face, replaced by the beaming grin of a kid hearing the answer to a prayer.

* * *

There were fourteen parish churches in Hounslow. Anzhel rejected all but the Catholic ones on grounds of Oriel's messianic tendencies and love of showmanship, but that still left eight to be investigated, approached from the street by inconspicuous men whose questions, in local shops and parks, would set off no alarms. If the magic was wearing off for Quin by the time warm summer dark began to fall, he gave no sign. Michael had told him to stay in the background, to listen and remember, and that was exactly what he was doing. He was even, Michael noted with amusement, trying to blend with the brickwork and beginning to succeed. They had left his Oxford carrier bag behind. He looked like a street kid, hanging around with two older men for God knew what dire reasons. In the West London dusk, streetlights just beginning to flicker and glow, no one looked at him twice.

On the fifth try, Michael got them their lead. A tired, unshaven tramp looking out for a bed for the night, he settled on a park bench and pulled out a quart-sized bottle of scotch and opened it, waiting for its raw cheap fumes to alert the seat's other occupant. In the distance, he could just make out Anzhel and

Quin. Fear stirred in him. There were times and places in London's parks where flesh was bought and sold, a silent network that shot out invisible tendrils to bring custom in. Looking at the boy and the man, Michael could see the possibilities. A pimp with his merchandise: it would be a good key, a good way in.

His stomach turned over, and he concentrated fiercely on his own chances. The lump beside him on the bench had stirred and reached out a hairy hand. Michael knocked it away and drew deeply on the bottle himself, grimly aware that he needed it. "Not a chance, mate," he said hoarsely afterward. "Tell me where around here I can doss for the night, then maybe."

"There's a shelter on King Street. Costs a tenner, but—"

"Spent my tenner." Michael swirled the contents of the bottle temptingly in the streetlight. "What about the church? Does the parish house take people in?" He gave his companion a leer. "Good Catholic, aren't I?"

The tramp actually edged away from him. "Yeah, but there's only one place and it's taken." Biting back his questions, Michael handed over the bottle and waited. The tramp took a pull, courteously wiped the bottle's neck with one end of his scarf. "Priest's a soft touch. Took in an illegal three months ago. He's hiding him. Won't let anyone else in.'

"Whatever. Where's the church?"

The tramp looked at him oddly. And suddenly a shape resolved out of the fractal of tree branches Michael had been watching: a bulk, a looming triangle. The church was there. He had been sitting in its shadow.

Carefully he got to his feet. Automatically he stayed in character, letting his disorientation feed into the move, letting it be clumsy and tired. What he wanted was to kneel in front of this homeless stranger and ask for his mercy, for help, on the grounds of their shared humanity. *The church is waiting. For God's sake, don't let me go. Take this money and call my partner, call John.*

"What the fuck is the matter with you?"

"Nothing." The tramp was holding out the bottle, trying to offer it back. The fear reached its peak inside Michael and died away. Now he wished he could give help, not receive it. He glanced across at Anzhel, waiting like a statue in the trees. Anzhel would wait forever. Michael could never wear out his implacable patience. Could never escape.

A wave of pity went through him. The night was warm, but still no one should have to sleep outdoors in it, not on city streets. "Keep the rest of that," he said, shoving his hands into his pockets. He wanted to be human in a human world, with all its griefs and sharp humiliations. Behind him, waiting under the trees, was something else. Something other than bloody human. He knew that now, but the revelation didn't free him. It made him turn, as surely as if Anzhel had reached out and grabbed his shoulder.

Passively he crossed the expanse of grass between them. It was a beautiful night, he noted from great distance. He thought of the Glastonbury farmhouse, dreaming under the stars. Would he be free in its shelter? Or would he find himself a string-jerked puppet there too, on his own land, with Anzhel moving his limbs for him, bidding the very air when to move into and out of his lungs?

The boy was lost too. He didn't react when Michael approached. His eyes were wide and fixed on some far horizon. He looked like a beautiful sketch of himself, poised at Anzhel's side. Michael came to a halt in front of them. "The church is here," he said. "Oriel's here. He's waiting."

* * *

John, booting the XKR down a long straight road near the Prince William Academy in Hampshire, felt a sudden wave of vertigo. He shook his head, but the sensation persisted. His wheels hit the rumble strip, then the central cat's eyes as he veered. Cold sweat broke on him, and he pulled off sharply into the next layby.

Briefly he thought he was going to puke or black out. But once the car was stationary, the dizziness ebbed. He put his hands on top of the wheel and rested his brow on their knuckles. He was tired, that was all, and his last meal had been a burger with Michael on the South Bank promenade.

He tried the two numbers again, the ones he had been keying on speed dial all the way from London. Once more both went straight to voice mail, as if the phones were out of range or dead.

A cold terror took him, so big it seemed to come from the darkness beyond the lurid Hampshire sunset. In his life so far, Quin had been first a nuisance, then an unknown quantity, and then a painful, unwanted weight. Michael he'd loved from the start. In this moment of conviction that he'd somehow lost both of them, John knew he loved his brother too. He called the school again. In the background, he could hear what he imagined headless chickens might sound like. The academy had never lost a child, the headmaster assured him. Police had been called, tracker dogs too.

Lost a child. It echoed in John's head as he cut the connection. *Lost child.* An anonymous baby when John left home, a stroppy teen by the time he came back, he had never thought of him as a child at all. John told himself that sixteen wasn't a child—that it was way too late for the surge of protective anxiety trying to overwhelm him now.

But Quin—naive, sheltered, hothoused in his fancy schools—was a bloody young sixteen. John started the car and revved her engine, letting her roar carry off some of his fear. He had chosen the damn schools himself, hadn't he? More or less ensured that Quin, bewildered by his own burgeoning intellect, wouldn't know how to function in the world. No wonder the kid made a run for Michael whenever he could. Mike just treated him with ordinary love.

And sent him home with the imprint of his boot on his arse if he thought Quin was there without John's permission. No, he'd have heard from Mike by now if...

John turned the car in the road and pointed her south. He'd been going to help with the search in the academy's grounds, up trees and at the bottom of dragged lakes if necessary. But when he felt around the edges of his sickening terror for Mike, he found Quin's image there too.

Go now, or you'll lose them both. John, who had never had a psychic flash in his life and would have laughed at the suggestion he was having one now, jammed his foot down and sent the Jag flying back in the direction of London.

Chapter Fourteen

The church lay deep underground. Michael was buried alive the second he stepped into it.

He swung round. Behind him the door stood open. Beyond it he could see the street—headlights, taillights, lights in shop windows. He could see men and women and a patch of tired city sky. Life went on out there. All Michael had to do was walk back into it.

High time he did. This op was over, their quarry run to earth. He knew how it should end. He should call for reinforcements—for Shaw and Skelton, anyway, his fellow assassins. He should call Webb, check there was no stay of execution, and go about his business. His mind found a grip on these rules and procedures and was briefly his own again. He took a step toward the door.

Anzhel was blocking his path. He pushed Quin gently ahead of him into the church and closed the door behind them.

Candlelight and the crush of tons of earth above Michael's head. His memory of the ordinary street was snuffed out the instant he could no longer see it. This was the underground church. This was his end point, his destination. The place he had been heading for during all his three years of illusory freedom. He was a murderer, wasn't he? In John's presence, he had forgotten. John was the cleansing rush of salt sea waves, bearing Michael's sins away. John would have absolved him, but Michael was suddenly glad there was no need. His corruption had no place in the upper world. His only absolution lay here. It would finish him, and John could grieve for the man he thought he had known. Not the killer, not the stone-hearted MI5 cat's paw who had somehow believed his mission and his cover precious enough to have joined in with a genocide.

No one else needed to die. In the shadows round the altar, the priest was going back and forth, preparing for mass. It was a peaceful scene. An old man dressed in clerical black, the verger, perhaps, or a brother priest, was sitting quietly in the fifth pew back. Michael could get both of them out of here before the endgame began. Anzhel—standing in the middle of the aisle, his hand on Quin's shoulder, surveying the church as if he'd created it—would prevent anyone else from coming in.

Michael went to sit beside the old man in the pew. His boots made no sound on the tiles, and the priest—yes, from here Michael could see the pale gleam of the dog collar—didn't move at his approach. Michael waited for a moment, letting his eyes adjust, making sure there was no one else in the church and that the old man would have a clear exit route. "Father," he said gently. "I'm a police officer." That was the official line, the way he and John always broke the ice with their civilians. People understood, and it was a hell of a lot shorter and simpler than the truth. "Don't be scared, but the man living here as a refugee isn't who he says he is. He's dangerous. So I need you to get up and just leave quietly by the nearest door. Do you understand?"

No response. The old man's eyes were fixed unblinkingly on the altar. "It's all right," Michael told him, reaching to touch his hand. "I'll go to the other priest in a moment and get him out too. You'll be okay."

Wide eyes. Bulging slightly, Michael saw. A thyroid problem? The hand beneath his was clammy. "Father?"

The tongue protruding between the teeth. Michael, too hard-trained to cry out, reached and caught on instinct as the old man slumped sideways and into his lap.

The candlelight dimmed. Human-shaped shadows fell across the pew: Anzhel and the other priest, who had come down from the altar and was gazing serenely at his dead colleague. "Anzhel," Michael whispered. "Oriel's killed him. Get the other one out, and I'll go after him."

He fell silent. This was terribly familiar, wasn't it? A church and candlelight and two men looking down on him as if he amused them.

These two men.

Lukas Oriel, unchanged, thin and tall in his stolen priest's robes, leaned over him. He put a knee on the pew next to Michael and stilled his escape reflex, the muscle-tearing jerk that would have carried him out of range, with a touch to his cheek. He was smiling. He examined Michael, gently turning his head to one side then the other, and Michael sat for the inspection as if his bones had turned to lead.

Oriel straightened. "Undamaged," he said. "You've done well, Anzhel. Is the programming intact?"

"Almost. He responds instantly to the music cue, and if you tell him he's chained up or bound, he is. He only resists when the other one's there."

"Yes. Griffin. Is that why you didn't bring him?"

"I had to drive him off." Anzhel made a face of rueful apology at Michael. "Believe me, it wasn't easy. But he's too strong when Griffin's with him. He's complete."

Oriel was nodding. "Good. Yes, that's good. We'll need that, and Griffin, soon enough. But this is best for now. I need to know I can use the fire. Michael!"

Michael flinched. He came to attention with painful force, letting the old man tumble off his lap and crash down between the pews. What had John said to him? *I can't stand watching you turn into a puppet.* But John was a dream from another world. Michael hadn't met him in the days of the underground church. John didn't exist. "Yes?"

"You came here of your free will?"

A puppet, strings being tugged from impossible distance. There had never been one on his jaw. Michael, who now remembered Lukas Oriel and every second of his torture, felt a faint, fierce satisfaction: he had never talked. He wouldn't now.

A hand cracked hard across the side of his face. "Prisoner! I asked you a question!"

"Don't," Anzhel said mildly, and when Oriel turned on him, his expression savage, only shrugged. "I just mean there's no point. I can control him physically—make him dance for you—but he won't say much. Yes, he came freely. It was hard to stop him once he knew who he was hunting. He was amnesiac about you, but clearly he remembered something."

"And you, Anzhel? What does he remember about you?"

"What I taught him to. It came as quite a shock. He and Griffin were fucking each other."

Oriel emitted a rumble of laughter. "Oh, you arrived just in time. We don't want anyone becoming as strong as that, not yet. We don't need anyone"—he leaned back in, shoving his face close to Michael's—"anyone becoming invincible. Now, prisoner—you, not Anzhel, unless you want me to ask the pretty lad myself—tell me about this boy you've brought me. Tell me about Quintus."

Quin. Quin belonged to the upper world, the world of Michael's last three years. He'd dropped out of Michael's memory along with John and all the sweet, ordinary griefs and joys belonging to that other life. Now he leaped back, burning. Michael jolted galvanically and surged upright. Anzhel made a gesture he had never been in time to see before—a circling index finger, as if pointing out a bracelet around Michael's wrist—but somehow he evaded the thick black ropes that snaked out of the pews to restrain him. He shouldered past Anzhel and Oriel and crashed to his knees in the aisle. "Quin!"

"I'm here, Mike."

Michael jerked his head up. The ropes found him—coiled across the aisle and pinned his hands behind his back—but from here he could see the boy, sitting calmly in a pew across the aisle. He was in his usual attitude of lax irreverence, one knee tucked under him, his elbow resting on the hymnal rail, but he was very still. "Quin. Are you all right?"

"Yes. But I just want to do what the angel tells me."

"Oh, son. That's not an angel. That's…"

What? If Michael turned, what would he see? His ears were full of implanted lies. No one was sitting at the old church organ at the far end of the aisle; its keys and stops were quite still, and yet the air was reverberant with music, dear and deep to Michael as blood. If he turned, would he see Anzhel blazing light, shining from under his skin as he had the night before in the tawdry B&B, melting the walls and lifting him up on incomprehensible wings that had turned—oh God, as he had soared to climax—that had turned into John's? He shook his head, but the music was inside it. The vision too, unbearably beautiful. "It's okay," he choked out. "Quin, it's okay. Just do as he tells you for now."

"That's right."

Michael gasped. He hadn't seen Oriel move, let alone come to kneel familiarly in front of him. "What do you... what do you want of me?"

Oriel folded his hands in his lap. "Your nose is bleeding," he observed, and Michael felt a hot splash on his jeans. "Don't fight your programming, and it will stop. First of all, I want the boy. We'll take it that you've given him to me. Now, do you know what he is?"

"I haven't a... bloody clue what you're talking about. He's John's brother, just a kid. Let him go."

"Oh no. He's something much better than that. I'll tell you truthfully, Michael, that I don't yet know myself, but it's a great concern to all of us—isn't it?—that he should be protected. I need him; I need you. Eventually, when you're under better control, I need your partner too. In the meantime, the child can be a simple hostage, and that's all you'll remember when I send you about your business tonight, my messenger." Oriel reached out and stroked the place he had slapped. He smiled. "My angel of the fire. Now, can you attend me?"

Silence had been Michael's ally before. Oriel could get him to do anything but talk. Silence, apparent submission, would serve him now, long enough to work out his escape. He nodded.

"Good." Oriel settled more comfortably on the strip of carpet that ran up the aisle. It was an attitude of storytelling, and Michael, who didn't want to hear, tried to shrink back from him, finding behind him instantly the iron grip of Anzhel's hands on his shoulders, holding him in place. "You know that I tried to help my people, don't you?" Oriel asked, pushing back a strand of hair from Michael's eyes. "That I used my science, my gifts, to bring out the things in the earth that would avenge them? Plutonium, uranium, immortal things that would burn on forever, just as Zemelya burned. I made bombs. Warheads. I was ready. Then the balance shifted. NATO forces found my refuge, my church, my factories. They took from me almost everything I'd made, including you, and that was a shame, considering the pain that went into your creation."

"I'm not yours." The words came out in a whisper. Michael hadn't meant to say them at all. But he *had* talked, hadn't he? In the other church, in a white-tiled cell? Had found a litany of survival. "My name is Michael South. I work for MI5. They'll come and find me. My name—"

"Oh, I remember that." Oriel nodded and smiled, as if he'd heard again a well-loved song. "But they won't. They didn't, and nor will this band of hired murderers you work for now. Listen to me. It's time for you to prove who you really are, to me and to yourself. Somewhere in this city of yours—this beautiful London, which survived a blitz—I've concealed a weapon. You would call it—what?—a *dirty bomb*, the nightmare the Western world didn't hesitate to visit on others as a means of ending its arguments. It's a small nuclear device—"

"Christ, Oriel! Where?" The effort of the question made Michael's nose bleed harder. He wanted to wipe his face but the ropes round his wrists snapped tight.

"Where doesn't matter. It detonates remotely. You will take the trigger mechanism, drive it into range—three miles east of here should serve—and detonate it. The explosion will take out a few blocks. The fallout, depending on where the wind blows, will turn the whole city to a desert. As it was in Dorva."

He got up. Anzhel hoisted Michael upright too and held him there. The warmth of his chest and belly pressed against Michael's back. His lips brushed the side of Michael's neck, and on them Michael heard and suddenly knew the song that controlled him. "My mother," he said. "She used to sing that."

Oriel stopped with his hand inside the stolen priest's jacket he wore. He looked sharply at Anzhel. "Should he remember that?"

Michael felt Anzhel shrug. He ceased singing, and a silence fell in Michael's heart like the end of creation—or the beginning. "It doesn't matter. He's yours to command. Use him."

But it did matter. Oriel was holding something out to him. Anzhel tapped him on the wrists and told him he was free, and so he was, and he reached out and took the small, heavy box without looking at it. It did matter. He was looking through the door of the Glastonbury farmhouse three decades before. His schoolbag was over his shoulder. He came into the kitchen, where his mother was waiting for him. For the first time in all his childhood's memory, she didn't get up smiling at the sight of him.

Men emerged from the shadows around her. They were like Easter Island statues, like the rocks of Stonehenge. Michael couldn't see how his mother meant to stop them, but she was his goddess, and he stood faithfully, jacket trailing on the ground, while she darted in front of them, her beautiful long hair swinging. She put her slender body between him and the men.

He didn't see what they did to her. It left no marks, and when they picked her up and carried her away, she looked only asleep. The men came to seize him.

They backed off, looking at their hands. Michael smelled charred flesh and felt sick, but it was no good. If they touched him, they would burn. He couldn't help it. He looked up, past their wide-stretched eyes and into their brains, and made the fire start there. Then they were gone. Michael heard the scatter of gravel, the roar of an engine. He picked up his jacket and his satchel. He went through to his mother's room and stood by the side of her bed. He was just home from school. She was asleep.

No. She'd died to save him. John would die to save him too—had shown him that a dozen times over during their time on the streets. Thirty years later, Michael entered the kitchen again, and there he was, straightening up from the fridge, smelling of fresh come and river-water, smiling like holy redemption. *John.*

"Mikhaili," Anzhel said. "It's time for you to go to work."

Michael nodded. He dispensed carefully with Anzhel's support, sliding the box into his pocket. His hands were free. He put them to use, hooking out Anzhel's gun from the belt under his jacket where he had concealed it. He took three fluid steps away, just enough to get distance, and he grabbed Quin blindly by the shoulder. "Get up. Come with me."

"I-I can't!"

"Can." Michael hauled him upright by the fabric of his coat. "Get behind me. Behind!" Pain was beginning to slice through his head. Soon it would be unbearable. He had perhaps a minute in which he could act. He took aim on his demons. "You two bastards stay back." Shielding Quin with his body, he began an unsteady track toward the door.

"Ah, Mikhaili. Don't." Anzhel held out a hand to him. For the first time since Michael had known him, his serene brow had a crease in it, his eyes a shadow of fear. "You'll hurt... you'll destroy yourself. You don't understand."

"I understand enough. Either you or this fucking psychopath moves, I'll drop you cold."

No. Not a minute. The plates of his skull tried to tear apart. The candlelight blurred, and the human shapes in front of him morphed into shimmering ghosts. He couldn't hold them in his sights. And already they were moving—floating toward him, extending ropes of light to haul him back. "No!" he yelled, and felt behind him Quin's wiry strength, so like his brother's that it could have been John there, sweet and real at his back. Quin, who should have cut and run the second he had the chance, holding him tight. "Quin, go! Get out!"

"Not a fucking chance. What do I do?"

"Just… stay behind me." The lights were merging. Anzhel and Oriel, drifting off into the candles. Jerking up his free hand to steady his grip on the gun, Michael took his first wild shot. Another and another, counting down through the clip. He didn't know how many he had, couldn't tell by the feel of it what Anzhel's concealed weapon had been. Something compact— probably no more than six. He fired again, straight into one pillar of light, but it didn't fall.

The fifth shot was no more than a convulsion of his fist on the gun. The bullet flew wide and ricocheted off metal somewhere in the dark. There was a hissing and a dull thud, like the ignition on the farmhouse cooker, the gas one he'd had installed because John was visiting regularly and liked to be cooked for.

"Mike! Mike, it's on fire!"

Michael's vision cleared. Now Quin was trying to drag him away. For an instant Michael saw, in detailed tableau, Anzhel and Oriel turning to look at the rose of fire that had burst in the air. He must have nicked a gas pipe. Nearby candle flames had done the rest. The church would burn.

Not fast enough. Michael took Quin into an arm that felt like a shielding wing and shoved him out into the porch, then turned back and stood in the middle of the aisle. He loved fire. Fire came easy to him. Even now, blood streaming from his nose, his skull splitting into two, he loved it. He put out a hand toward the rose of fire and watched it bloom. He made it into a roiling sphere. Shuddering in pain and joy, he lifted it high over the altar and made it burst. He waited long enough to see Lukas Oriel's hair and clothes ignite.

Then he fell out into the porch, merely human, bleeding and sick from the agony in his head. Quin caught him and began to go through his pockets.

"What... what are you doing?"

"Where's your phone? I'll get John. I'll get an ambulance, the fire brigade—"

"Left my phone behind."

"Where the hell's mine?"

Quin scrabbled frantically in the pockets of his jeans and the scruffy parka. Michael wanted to tell him that, if Anzhel had taken it from him, he'd never find it and never remember the theft, but he couldn't speak. The pain surged unbearably, and he struggled out of Quin's grasp, retching. "Get away from me. Go!"

"I'm not gonna leave you." With distant surprise, Michael felt the boy take hold of him. He was awkward, a scared kid suddenly forced to deal with a sick grownup, but he was there—squeamish Quin, who recoiled from human illness like a cat. "What do I do?"

"Just... go. Find John and get out of the city. Go far away."

"Mike, you're not gonna do this." Quin's voice shook with an edge of crazy laughter. "You're not gonna bloody well nuke London. I won't let you."

Michael threw up. There was hardly anything left inside him, and his throat burned with acid. "Can't stop me," he rasped. "I'll hurt you if you try. Sorry, Quin. I can't fight it anymore."

And it worked. Despite winning the point—despite his relief at being obeyed—Michael felt pure desolation as Quin's grip vanished and the church door banged shut. He curled up, pressing his brow to his knees. Maybe Oriel had overplayed the game with him—maybe the strain of resistance would disable him in time, keep him here on his knees till fire burst through the doors of the porch and consumed him.

A short fierce roar. Michael flinched and looked up. How much time had passed? If this was the end, he was glad. He couldn't so much as stand up, let alone run away to go and unleash hell on the city. He was so tired. And his soul wouldn't bear the weight of any more sin—all those lives in the bleak Zemel forest and John's life too, tearing apart in his hands. He wished he could have seen him, that was all. Spoken to him long enough to tell him what a prisoner Michael had been, what a slave, since he had entered the Acton church and seen Piotr Milosz. To tell him he loved him.

Quin burst back into the porch. He threw open the door so hard that it jammed. Beyond it Michael saw the street, the ordinary night somehow unfolding still. He saw a little VW Golf, pulled right up on the pavement and purring, its headlights ablaze. "Get up!" Quin yelled, grabbing him and starting to pull. He had about a quarter of his brother's heft but all his determination. "Get the fuck up, Mike. We're going!"

"No. No car. I'll take us into range and use this thing."

"Yeah, if you were driving." Quin ducked under Michael's arm, draped it round his shoulder and lurched up. "Come on. I'm taking you home."

"Quin, I've got a gun."

"You won't use it on me."

The boy dragged him out. He pulled open the car door and dumped Michael into the passenger seat, then ran round the front and got behind the wheel. The car was bumping onto the road before Michael could get air enough into his lungs to protest. "Stop. You can't drive."

"Oh, you reckon?" Quin's jaw was set and grim. He crunched gears and made the Golf roar like a rally car, but indicated properly before pulling out into the traffic. "Posh schools mean posh friends. Weekends in their country homes and miles of countryside to tank around in with Daddy's spare Range Rover."

Unclenching one hand, Michael reached across and took the straining VW's handbrake off. Quin gasped as she shot forward. Then he caught up and eased off the gas. He wasn't bad, Michael thought through a fresh surge of pain. "Quin, *stop*! Where have you got a car from? What have you done?"

"Broke into the priest's house and stole his keys." Signs for the M3 westbound appeared on their right. Quin lurched across two lanes and a small traffic island to make the turn. "Don't say anything. You're the one running errands for the bastard who murdered him."

The words hit Michael like whiplash. But Quin was right. He did have an errand—a mission, if you wanted a more dignified word for it. Thinking about its accomplishment brought the pain down to a level he could almost see through, breathe through. He put a hand beside Quin's on the steering wheel. "This way."

"No. That's east, like…like Oriel said."

"Do as you're told, damn it!" Michael yanked the wheel, sending the car off in a squeal of rubber down the next left turn. It took them into an alleyway. Good. This would connect to the main route back into London, and no witnesses for whatever he was about to do to this impossible brat who had come between him and his destiny.

Quin veered up onto the pavement, narrowly missed a parked lorry, and jammed the brakes on. "No!" he yelled as they jounced to a halt. "I'm not letting you do it!"

Michael uncoiled out of the car. For the first time, he could feel what a lovely night it was. Even in the city's outskirts, scents of rural summer made it through on evenings like this—an occasional breath of distant fields, of soil gently cooling in the dusk. The Tor would be beautiful tonight, rising numinous and vast from the mist. His nose was bleeding still, but it was letting up, and at last his head was clear. He took a deep breath of the good air, strode round the front of the car, and hauled Quin out of the driver's seat. So skinny and light—like lifting a cat out of the way. Michael could snap him into pieces. Common sense dictated that he do so. Break his neck and dump him. "Get in the passenger seat and shut up." Quin twisted to look at him. His face was a blank of incomprehension, tears sticking his eyelashes together. Michael repeated the command, loud and harsh. "Do it now!"

"Mike, if you're going to bark orders at me... do it in English, will you?"

Michael swallowed. That *had* been English, hadn't it? His tongue knew no other words. There was no other language in his brain. Afraid to try again, he took Quin by the shoulder and the scruff of his neck and marched him round the car's bonnet. Getting in behind the wheel, he put the Golf into gear. Eastbound, eastbound. Michael breathed and felt the clearness in his head, the sweet light. He had fought—one way or another, he had fought—for three years. It was over.

He drove through Isleworth and stopped on the edge of Syon Park. He wanted to see trees and open spaces while he was doing this. Quin watched in silence, huddled against the door, while Mike extracted from his pocket the heavy little device. He could hear himself sobbing, which was odd, because other than relief at this final surrender, he felt nothing. He was glad he had Anzhel's gun with him, though. He was sure it had one more round left in the clip. Once he was done here, he could go.

Quin said faintly, "I was trying to take you home, you know. Not to your flat—to Glastonbury."

Michael turned the detonator over in his hands. It was so tiny. He could hardly believe in its potential. Maybe it had none—

maybe Oriel was testing him, checking the strength of his strings. He could hear the boy speaking, but the sound was distant, a transmission through static from his old lost life.

"You're different there. I am too. I stop wanting to run away, and I stop hating John for not wanting me to live with him. He's different too. He stops thinking about his car and his clothes and the job. I feel like I *know* him."

Michael nodded. There were joggers running through the park, women pushing buggies on the pavement. There were seven million people within thirty miles of him. Maybe the device was a dud. "Yes," he said. "We're all different there. Better."

"Look, I don't think I'm the language type of idiot savant. I don't understand."

Michael made a huge effort. He'd never had trouble learning languages, but the rediscovery of his English now felt like an anguished rewiring of his brain. Blood ran down the back of his throat. Pain began to sledgehammer into his skull. He put the detonator back into his pocket. "Quin, can you take me there? Can you take me home?"

Chapter Fifteen

Out on the dual carriageway, the Jaguar coasting at ninety, John pressed the hands-free button and sat back. Silence fell in the car. Inside his head, he knew he would hear forever the voice of his boss, informing him coldly that his partner and Anzhel Mattvei had failed to report in. That they were missing, and a church in West London was burning to the ground.

Unthinkingly John went through the moves to get past the next lorry. The old man had wanted him to come back to town. He should. It made sense. If he had ditched out on Michael, abandoned and lost him, he had to trace him sensibly, to work from the point last seen, even if that trail led to a charred corpse in a church. He would turn back, leave the motorway at the next junction.

The phone buzzed again. John saw Quin's name appear on the screen and almost burst into laughter. Trust the little sod to turn up now, when John's hands and heart were too full for him to give a damn.

But that wasn't true anymore. Relief swept through John, and he punched the pickup button. "Quin. You all right?" Not his usual first line of inquiry on these occasions, he remembered with shame. He usually opened with *where the hell are you* and *what have you done.*

"No! John, help me!"

"What?" John got the Jag out of the fast lane and steadied her against his own astonishment. Quin would sooner die in a homemade forest shelter than ask for his help. "I will. I will, okay? What's the matter?"

"It's Mike." A pause, as if Quin couldn't think of a way to express the enormity of his situation. John listened to the background sounds. They were very like his own—the roar of an engine being pushed hard, the swish of overtaking traffic. "I'm with Mike. He's... I don't think he's well."

John drew a breath against the surging thud of his heart. Not well and inexplicably with Quin... but alive. "Okay. Get him to pull over and talk to me."

"He's not driving. I am."

"You're kidding me. Bloody well stop!"

"I can't. I've got to take him back to Glastonbury. We found that man, that Russian you were looking for. He gave Mike a box—a thing, a detonator. There's a bomb in London. If I don't get Mike home, he's going to set it off."

"Who is? You found Oriel?"

"Yeah. He made Mike different. Made him do stuff. And Mike's gonna use this bloody detonator if I don't get him away!"

"All right. Calm down. Give the phone to Mike."

"I don't think he can talk. He's bleeding, John. And his head hurts, and he's speaking Russian."

Well, that's never a good sign. John set aside flashing memories of his last night in the Glastonbury farmhouse and struggled to concentrate. His kid brother was driving. Mike was in the grip of whatever hellish programming Oriel had laid into him, and there was a… "Quin. What sort of bomb?"

"A bad one. Nuclear. It's in the city."

"Christ almighty. Can you get the detonator away from him?" John envisaged the attempt and shook his head. "Second thoughts, don't try that. Where are you now?"

"I dunno. Been on the road about an hour, and I left London from Hounslow, so…"

"You're on the M3? I'm near you. I'm near you, okay? I'm coming in from the south, but I can find you if you just pull over and wait."

"I don't dare. He's in too much pain, John. He can't hold on unless I get him home. He'll—"

Quin's frightened voice broke off. John braced for the sound of crunching metal, but a moment later Michael spoke, fractured by distance and static. John could have cried with joy to hear him, but he wasn't getting a word. "Mike," he interrupted him. "Mike! If you're buggering about the country with my kid brother in tow, don't tell me about it in Russian. All right?"

A silence. It was somehow raw, tense with struggle. Then Michael said clearly, "Call backup. Get them to the house. If I can't fight this, they can't let me leave. Not alive. Do you understand?"

"Mike, no."

"You have to. I'm losing. Oh, John—if it comes down to it, don't let it be some half-assed police marksman who takes me out. Let it be one of our own people, or…"

"Yes. I'll take care of you." Tearing down the motorway, his soul going ice-cold inside him, John made the impossible commitment. "Comes to that, I'll take you down myself."

"All… all the way?"

"You know it. But it's not gonna happen like that, sunbeam. We're going to live. I'm on my—"

The line cut out. John hit callback but got dead air. He kept his fingertips pressed to the phone, steering blind and deft with his free hand. "I'm on my way. I'm on my way."

* * *

Michael stood alone in the farmhouse kitchen. He hadn't put the lights on—didn't want to dismiss the ghosts he could see without them. He remembered so much now. There was his mother, slender and beautiful, struggling to cook for her boy and her father-in-law in an antiquated English kitchen. She was always busy. Always watchful too. She paused often to glance out of the windows. She flinched and held Michael close to her when the outer door clicked, but it was only the old man. He came in stiffly, the sheepdog Alice by his side. He grunted at Michael's mother's kiss and made a gesture of warding her off. It was for form's sake only, Michael knew. He'd soon learned to love her affectionate ways and had wept like a child on that day when Michael, fugued out by shock, had only been able to sit on the bedroom floor and stare.

He went to fetch the kettle. It was a prosaic gesture in this dreamworld, but real life went on, and he no longer wished to thrust a divide between the two. Quin had driven him all the way home, swearing his head off when they first hit the narrow Somerset lanes, then lapsing into a grim silence. He would be exhausted, wanting a cup of tea. Michael filled the kettle, set it to boil, then leaned over the sink and carefully washed the blood off his face. He smiled as he did so. Always such a bloody pantomime when John tried to fix tea or coffee for either of them. His fingertips were permanently scarred from all the electric shocks.

Michael would have given anything to hold his wrist and kiss the little marks, one by one. To explore his body and love it inch by inch, as he should have done. They had started at the wrong end, at passion's far extreme. John had said—Michael remembered now, with painful acuity—*this gonna be it, then? Here in the kitchen?* And Michael had closed his heart to the grief in the question, shoved him down and screwed him over the table, as if he had been a one-nighter, a fling. Had done so much worse to him here in this house that he wanted to die of shame.

A faint metallic ping brought him back. It was quite distinctive. Straightening, Michael dried his face on a tea towel, then went to pull open the back door.

It was strange. Every time he decided he would never smile again, never feel anything but sorrow, Quin's varying efforts at cunning made him want to break into laughter. He restrained himself. Quin, having very clearly just let down the VW's bonnet, was now attempting to pocket something unseen. He threw Michael a too-bright smile. "Are you all right? I was just coming in."

Michael nodded. He leaned on the door frame. "Not bad. What is it, then? The spark plugs?"

Quin's shoulders sagged. "Shit."

"It's okay. Pulling the rotor from under the distributor works better." Michael held out a hand, and Quin surrendered the oily, still-hot plugs into his palm. "Don't try it tonight, son, please. Or anything else. I don't want to hurt you."

"You won't."

Quin sounded weary. But his head was high, and he met Michael's gaze squarely. Michael wondered what it would take to replace the trust in his eyes with betrayal. He steered him gently into the kitchen, pulled out a chair for him at the table. "Still like your PG Tips with sugar? Or have they converted you to ginseng at those fancy schools of yours?"

"Mineral water," the boy said tiredly. "Tea and coffee are toxins. They might set off my attention deficit disorder. Or my hyperactivity syndrome. I can't remember which I'm meant to have."

"Shall we take our chances?"

"I will if you will."

Michael poured tea for both of them and sat opposite Quin. He rested his elbows on the table and pushed his fingers into his hair. His hands smelled charred, as if he'd been rearranging furniture in hell. "I'm sorry to have brought you here."

Quin stirred his tea. "It's okay. That Anzhel bloke could… make you do anything, couldn't he?" He shot Michael a wry look, the exact equivalent of John's. "Anyway, I think I brought *you*."

"Yes, you did. Thank you."

"Do you think it'll work? Being here, I mean… Do you think it'll stop you?"

"I don't know." Michael lifted the mug to his lips, but it was a gesture only. His throat was tightly sealed. He wouldn't eat or drink until this was over. "It hurts less here. But I don't know."

"Do you want me to put the lights on?"

"No. I need the ghosts." Michael shook his head. "Sorry. I know I sound like a nutcase. I mean I just want to be able to see out of the windows properly. For when somebody comes."

A shadow of fear brushed Quin's face. "Who do you think will come? Apart from John?"

"John?" Michael's voice quivered on the word. "He won't come here."

"He will. He will, Mike. He said to me in the car—he's on his way."

"No. You don't understand. There's some things you're too young to worry about, but me and your brother... I've screwed all that up."

"With John? Hang on. Which part am I not meant to understand?"

"Well... any of it, I'd hoped." Michael rubbed his eyes. "Sorry. Don't mean to treat you like a kid. It's just when I met you, you were only twelve, and you're kind of frozen in time for me."

"Rubbish. You're the only one who's noticed I'm *not* twelve anymore. I know John's gay. And I know he had a boyfriend a week, but whenever he came to see me, he never shut up about you. It was Michael this, Michael that. What you said, what you did, what you thought about things."

Michael quirked a smile. "I'm sorry he bored you so."

"No. I wanted to hear. Better than listening to him bang on about whichever brilliant school he'd discovered for me next. And when we all came down here, I just assumed... you'd sorted out your differences. That you were together."

"We were sleeping in separate rooms, Quin."

The boy shook his head, as if in appeal not to be teased with technicalities. "I don't mean like that. Well, maybe I do, but that's not the important part. I'd see you both outside, working on the walls or arguing over whose turn it was to go and get more pig manure for the garden, and—"

"I know. We're all about the romance."

"And I knew he loved you."

"Quin. Don't."

"No matter who he was running around with. Just you."

Michael had covered his face with his hands. He was trying not to see his world as Quin evoked it. Because there it had been—in the domestic trivia, the ordinary business of life here with John. A look across the table, across a half-dug trench in the garden, that told him he was loved. And he had taken that and broken it.

His ghosts shifted. His grandfather turned and dissolved into the stonework in the place where a door had used to be. All around him, Michael felt the house the old man had built crouch down, like a beast at bay, defensive and waiting. His mother flickered to the window and stood glancing out of it and back to him, her eyes bright as stars. And a moment later, Quin heard it too—the distant purr of an engine. He jumped to his feet. "It's John! I told you, didn't I? I knew he'd come."

"Sit down and be quiet."

"No. The lights are out. He might not know we're here. Let me go and let him in!"

Michael pushed wearily upright. His head was throbbing. He couldn't bear much more, and it was with gentle thoroughness that he took hold of Quin and lifted him away from the door. "If I told you to run, would you do it?"

"Not a chance."

"If I begged you. Let yourself out through the living room window and run. Don't stop, don't look back."

"I'm not leaving you."

"Oh God, Quin. If I had a kid, I'd give almost anything for him to be like you. But that's not John."

* * *

A cold wind was blowing. It came from unknown spaces to the east and curled itself round the farmhouse, testing the windows. Michael heard it cut through the sultry, airless night, and he took up position in front of the door. He'd never had a proper lock put on it, to John's disgust. He'd learned very young that there was little point, that trouble would find you regardless. He waited.

The door swung wide. Beyond it there was only empty dark. From the corner of his eye, he saw Quin huddle back into a corner, truly frightened at last. Cold air filled the kitchen, dank and heavy with ozone.

Between one blink and the next, Anzhel was there. He filled the doorway, a darkness on darkness. All his lights were out. His hair was slicked back and thick with soot, and Michael could see that one side of his face was charred. He stepped into the room. "Not bad," he said. "Not a bad run for it at all, though it's a shame you didn't get time to train junior here to notice when he'd picked up a tail. I'm tired now, Mikhaili. It's all over. Come with me."

Michael was glad to. Resistance had become a fingertip grasp on the edge of a cliff. Painful, pointless. To let go and fall at last, a deadly relief. He reached into his pocket and took out the detonator. Anzhel examined it briefly, then handed it back. "All right. You have to do it yourself. You understand that? Then you can rest." He smiled, an uneasy flicker in the shadows. "I'll take care of you then. You're mine once this is over. Oriel promised you to me."

"Oriel burned. You should have burned."

"You should know by now it takes more than that. Come on."

Somewhere far off in the house, glass shattered and fell. The sound was tiny. On any other night, any night other than this pin-drop, heartbeat silence, Michael might not have heard it. He tried not to show that he had. It had been liquid somehow, a trickle of water to arid lips in a desert. He and John had reglazed the big west-facing windows themselves, only a few weeks ago. The large sheets of glass had been hard to source. They'd spent an afternoon hunting round reclamation yards in Shepton Mallet and joked with one another about the penalties for getting locked out and breaking in that way. No, each big sash had a grid of little panes above it. Break one of those, they had agreed. Small and easy to replace, and then it was only a matter of reaching in and unlocking the lower frame.

Michael tried to keep Anzhel walking. For a moment he thought it had worked. Anzhel looked diminished, tarnished somehow, as if their encounter in the church had drained him. He and Michael could fall together now, carry out Oriel's bidding, burn up and disappear. "Come on," Michael said in his turn. "I'm ready. I want this to be over too."

But Quin had struggled to his feet and was staring in the direction of the sound. He was bright as a star, Michael thought, but he had used up all his store of grownup resourcefulness and calm. He was a kid again, shaking with relief at the prospect of rescue. "It's John," he whispered, ignoring Michael's warning glance. "Mike, it is. He's come."

"What? Your poor zaichik of a partner?" Anzhel wheeled round, dragging Michael with him. "You're kidding me. After all the trouble we took to get rid of him? How have you done it, Mikhaili? How have you made these people—John, this boy— love you so much that they won't let you go?"

"I haven't. They don't know what I am." Michael tore his arm out of Anzhel's grasp and stood in front of him, blocking his path. "John doesn't know. You're not going to hurt him anymore."

Anzhel nodded. There was a kind of weary pain in his eyes, a loss. He took out the gun from his belt and handed it to Michael with a gesture that was almost a shrug. "No. You're right. Not me."

Michael frowned. He couldn't hear his partner's approach beyond the door—how silently John would move, threading the familiar dark!—but he knew he was coming as surely as Quin did. Michael didn't know or care why Anzhel had surrendered. It didn't matter. To set eyes on John would be enough. He'd never expected to see him again. His heart gave a painful lurch of joy. John would be in the hallway by now. He would take three catlike paces, four. A pause before the next one—listening, assessing—then a graceful step back to press his spine against the wall. He was virtually ambidextrous but preferred to lead into an unknown scene from the left. Michael would come automatically to cover his right.

To cover the blind spot he now moved into, raising Anzhel's gun. He glanced reassuringly at Quin, whose face was a mask of horror. *Everything's okay. Stay still.* The door from the hallway swung half an inch open, then another. Then John stepped through, took one look at his brother and Anzhel, and snapped up his weapon. "Quin! You all right? Where's Mike?"

"I'm here."

John froze. Michael was so close behind him, he felt it: the sudden stilling of every muscle. He was close enough to inhale the scent of John's hair, and he did so, eyes stinging with tears of pleasure. John must have been home. He'd showered. Beneath the curling, still-damp strands was the place where a bullet would cause such devastation that not even an instant of pain would be felt, not even a flicker of surprise. Michael ran the snout of his Glock up the delicate vertebrae of John's neck, counting. There. Right between the occipital bones at his nape, the exquisite hollow that seemed designed to take the shot. He put his arm around John's shoulders and drew him gently back against him. "Griff, you'd better give Anzhel your weapon."

"Okay." John sounded calm. He clicked the safety back into place and extended the PPK to Anzhel in a steady hand. "You…you've got your gun to my head. You do know that, right?"

"Yes."

"All right. Just checking. Because…you've been a bit shaky lately."

"I'm sorry. It won't be for long."

"Uncle Mike!"

Oh God, that was Quin. Michael had half forgotten about him, and wholly forgotten how the kid looked when he cried. He'd only seen it once or twice, in the early days before Quin had grown his stiff upper lip and his shields. He was huddled in a corner by the fridge, sobbing unashamedly in fright. "Is it a trick? Are you gonna do something?"

"Yeah, he is. Don't you worry, kiddo. I tell you what, Mikey… Whatever it is you *are* gonna do, you might be decent and not make my little brother watch."

"Of course." Mortification swept through Michael, as if he'd forgotten Quin's birthday or left him at a station somewhere. "Sorry. Quin, you can go."

"No! I told you I wouldn't leave!"

"Idi v svayu komnatu!"

Anzhel shrugged as Quin and John unwillingly looked to him for translation. "Er—that's *go to your room*, more or less. Might be best if you did, *boychik*. I won't stop you."

"Fuck you! I don't have to do anything you tell me, you mind-bending bloody lunatic!"

"Quin!" John snapped, and Michael heard the ripple of laughter in it even now, and loved him and loved the boy so intensely he thought his heart would burst, and eased the gun a little deeper against John's skull. "*Not* helping. Do as you're told. It'll be okay. I promise."

"That's right." Anzhel nodded encouragingly. He didn't seem to mind being called names, and his expression as he held the door for Quin was almost benevolent. "Don't try to leave or call anyone. It's good, you know, Griffin, that he has this spirit. He'll need it."

"What's he to you? All he needs at the moment—all I need—is for you to quit screwing with Michael's head and let him go."

"That's just it." Anzhel closed the door and came to lean on the kitchen cabinets facing John. "It's like the ropes now, with your Mikhaili. You don't have to tie him. The idea's enough. And I don't need to sing to him anymore. A glance will do, a suggestion."

"Oh God. Tell me what you did to him. So if we ever get out of here...so I can help him."

"Well, that's academic now for you. But there are things I want *him* to know, just so he understands whose creature he is, how completely he's owned. Mikhaili!"

Michael stirred. He had begun to feel sleepy, and John felt so good in his arms. They had never simply slept together. He'd never had the chance to hold him from behind, bury his nose in the crook of his shoulder and neck and fall asleep under Glastonbury stars. "Yes, Anzhel?"

"Three years ago—nearly four, now that you've had your time on the run with your *lyubovnik* here—Lukas Oriel handed me an MI5 agent he'd captured and tried to break. You were a novelty to him, Mikhaili. You were his first failure. He gave me strictest orders to pick up where he'd left off. You were terribly special to him."

"*Pochyemu?*"

"Why? That's something you'll have to work out for yourself, as the years go by. And you will. You'll have to, or the world will always be a nonsense to you—random, a kaleidoscope. For now, what I've hidden from your memory is this. There was no Russian forest. No undercover work with me, no Ashkeloi gypsies, no massacre."

"No Piotr, Piotr Milosz…"

"Oh, he was real. And he was an Ashkeloi leader, an uncommonly brave one. But the closest you got to those firesides, those dark forest nights, was the inside of a cell under Oriel's fortress. Deep, deep underground."

Michael drew a breath. It came out as a sob, shaming him, and to his astonishment he felt John reach up and take a comforting hold of his wrist. "Anzhel, pochyemu? *Ya nye veryu.*"

"You do believe me. These are our first truths. Piotr Milosz was your fellow prisoner. You identified with him, wanted to help him, so I used his story to set up a scenario I could use to control you. He assisted, with a good deal of persuasion. He hadn't the benefit of your training or nerve, and by the end of it he was broken. Very much our puppet, our man. When Oriel wanted to call you home, he sent Milosz. He knew the sight of him would begin to trigger your conditioning. And then you would be ready for me."

"But you had to hunt down Oriel just as much as I did."

"Yes. The fall of the fortress scattered us. It had been so long since I stood at his side. He had to test me again, and my task was to find you, then use you to help me locate him. To bring you to him. Your test…" Anzhel lowered his head. All traces of triumph were stripped from him, as if someone had plucked his wings. As if he were sick of the game. "You know your test. You have to come with me and complete the mission he set you. You have to kill your partner first."

Michael stared down the tunnel of the years. He saw a white-tiled cell. In it, a perfectly beautiful man walked about. Sometimes he wore a white coat. Sometimes he was in camouflage fatigues, like a rebel soldier, and he had propped up beside him a weary, skeletal Russian Michael knew as Piotr Milosz. Anzhel was telling Milosz what to say. The scene changed, and Anzhel sat on the edge of a narrow bunk. He said, *"Sing me the song your mother taught you,"* and Michael obeyed. Michael was strapped to the bunk. It could be moved—set almost upright so you thought you could take your weight but not quite, or it could be tipped back so your head would be lower than your feet, and when the water came—just a little; Anzhel hadn't always blindfolded him, and he could see how little it took—it would run straight up into your sinus cavities. Michael drowned, over and over again, and the song his mother had taught him played through speakers in the cell, and Anzhel talked.

Anzhel had been his torturer. The impact of this glanced off Michael's mind and disappeared. He could see into the forest now, and he understood that all those people, all that darkness, frost, fire, and blood, all those lives, had existed only in the white-tiled confines of the cell. He said, clearly and in English, "I never killed anybody."

"That's right. I wanted you to know. To make you free of the guilt of it, and to show you that despite this recall, this revelation, you belong to Oriel still. You will still complete your mission. Mikhaili, do it now."

Michael gathered John against his body. He could feel his breathing, low and tense: the controlled heave of his ribs that meant he was most frightened and most determined not to let it show. Unable to help the caress anymore than he could the tightening of his gun hand, Michael held him. "John, I never killed anyone."

"I know."

"Why doesn't it make any difference? Why can't I stop this?"

"Because of how hurt you were. In a way…" John tailed off, then drew a shuddering breath and continued, lifting his head in desperate, last-ditch pride. The movement made tears spill down his face, though his voice remained steady and calm. "In a way it doesn't matter. I'm glad you didn't kill those people, but it's academic—to me, anyway—because I loved you even when I thought you had."

"Griff—"

"Shut up and listen. I loved you then. I love you now, and I'm going to love you even when you pull that trigger. Even afterward, Mikey. Always. So go on and finish what you're doing here, but when it's over—when you're sane again—you just bloody remember that, okay? *Remember.*"

Michael tasted water on his lips. He couldn't account for it. Fear seized him, but the sensation wasn't the suffocating rush of the waterboard. No—holy water, a cold clean ocean through his burned-out heart. His vision dimmed, then cleared to sudden acuity. The chains of his conditioning snapped and fell away. He was nothing but light, light in sun-shafted water.

Holding a pistol to the head of the man he loved. Who loved *him*. Michael jerked the gun away and pushed John to one side. He stepped around him quickly and interposed himself, his own flesh and bone, between him and Anzhel, who was straightening, astounded, snapping the catch off the weapon he'd taken from John. "Why?" Michael whispered. "Why the hell did you try to make me kill him?"

"I could try to make you understand. But it would take time, and it's late, Mikhaili. So much later than you think, for all of us."

"Put the gun down."

"I can't. You're free, and that's too dangerous. Oriel—"

"Oh, screw Oriel! He used you the same way he used me!"

A terrible smile contorted Anzhel's face. "Are you saying you...*forgive* me?"

Michael drew a shaky breath. John, who would never settle for being human-shielded, was coming to his side. Michael could forgive anything. "Yes, if it matters to you. Drop the gun. If the bastard's not dead already, help us hunt him down."

"No. You know I can't leave you alive. Not either of you."

Michael shook his head. It was hard for him to be frightened of anything now, and Anzhel sounded barely convincing. Resigned, maybe. Tired. Nevertheless, he steadied the PPK, seemed to focus with an effort—and pulled the trigger.

He couldn't have missed. Not Anzhel, who had shot John's little nark like a goldfish in a barrel down a dark alley from impossible range. Michael registered the thud of the bullet driving into the door frame behind him. But time was moving for him at distorted crisis-speed. Comprehension came after the fact. Too late for Anzhel. *Too late for all of us*, resounded in Michael's head as his hands came up almost without his volition and closed tight round the Glock, squeezing. *So much later than you think.* The shot rang out before the echo of Anzhel's had died, and Anzhel jerked and fell.

* * *

John cradled the matted blond head in his lap. He hardly knew why he did so, except that, whatever this man had been to his partner, he wasn't someone to be left dying alone on the floor. Michael, kneeling by his side, had wadded up tea towels and was making competent but hopeless efforts at wound pressure. The bullet had caught Anzhel square in the heart. John couldn't understand why he was still alive, much less why now he looked more his old self than he had in the fraught half hour before. His debonair grin was back, and he was watching Michael's desperate first aid with a kind of indulgence. "Mikhaili."

Michael glanced up. "What?"

"Leave it."

Michael glanced at his hands. They were bloodstained to the wrist. After a moment, he nodded and eased back. "My name is Michael."

"I know. You insisted on that all the way through. No matter what I did to you." His breath rattled. John lifted him a bit to try to ease it, and he managed a brief scarlet laugh. "And you, Agent Griffin—you didn't like the names I called you either. A zaichik's a lover-boy. A little soft one, perhaps: a bit of fluff."

John met Michael's eyes for a moment and brushed a strand of hair off Anzhel's brow. "Oh, ta. Thanks for letting me know."

"Turned out not to suit you after all. I'm sorry. Michael, I'm sorry I tortured you."

"I told you before. It's forgiven."

"I don't see how it can be, but… Listen. There's no bomb. Oriel told me in the church before he gave you the detonator. He wanted to give your strings the hardest pull he could, that was all. There isn't anything else I need to tell you, is there… Wait. One more thing. Look after the boy. He's important, maybe more important than…"

His voice faded out. His skull became heavy in John's lap, and his eyes fixed on an unknowable point beyond the farmhouse roof. John pressed a finger to the artery in his neck. "Mike, he's gone."

Michael swallowed audibly. "You're sure?"

"Yes. I'm sorry."

"Look, you'd better… Will you go and find Quin?"

John lowered Anzhel's head gently onto the kitchen's stone flags. He stood. He didn't want to let Michael out of his sight for a second. But Michael was motionless, his gaze as fixed and unblinking as Anzhel's, and Quin would be frightened.

The hallway was empty. John followed sounds of frantic searching into the living room. He found his brother flat on his back beneath the table, trainers sticking out, apparently checking the underside of a bookcase. At the creak of the door, he sat bolt upright, banging his head. "John! I thought...I thought you or Mike might have an extra gun somewhere." He scrambled to his feet. "I heard two shots. I thought it was you and Mike. I thought—"

"You think too much," John interrupted him gently. "Still, I suppose that's mostly my fault, isn't it?"

"Is Mike all right?"

"He will be."

"But somebody got shot. Somebody died."

"Yes. Anzhel. Were you going to come blasting in to save us?"

"Yes. Well, no, because I couldn't find a sodding gun."

Quin's voice broke over the last words. John put out an arm to him, but the kid just stared. John couldn't blame him. They never touched. He'd left all that to Michael, watching with admiring envy how his partner hugged, chivvied and shoulder-punched the brat into smiling humanity. It took an effort, didn't it? It took not expecting a shy teenager to make the first move. "Come here a second."

Quin obeyed. He didn't exactly sink into his brother's arms, but he came to stand close by his side, trembling and chilly. John asked, "Are you cold?"

"I don't know."

"You're probably in shock. You drove all the way here?"

"Mm-hm. I'm sorry."

"No. It was the right thing. Look, I've got to go and see to Mike, and—well, there's a corpse in the kitchen. I know you can cope, but I don't want that in your memories. Do you understand?"

Quin nodded. "Yeah. Okay, I'll make myself scarce."

"Not too scarce. Just for a few minutes."

"I'll go and have a wash."

"That would be good."

John gave him a squeeze and let him go. Halfway through the door, he paused and looked back. "Quin, you're okay, right? Anzhel didn't hurt you?"

"No. He...pushed me around, like he does, but it didn't hurt."

"And—did Mike?"

Quin frowned while he worked out what his brother meant. Then his brow cleared, and he gave him a look that made John search all the way down to find undamaged roots for his own deeply shaken faith. "Of course not! He tried to help me. He wouldn't let them take me hostage. And it was Anzhel that made him do all that stuff. It wasn't him."

"No." John gave him what he hoped was a reassuring smile. He could still feel the impress of Mike's gun muzzle at the back of his head. Something worse was still trying to gnaw into his heart. "It wasn't. Thanks for helping him. Everything will be all right now."

In the kitchen, he found Michael kneeling still at Anzhel's side. The room was dark, only a faint blue trace of summer dawn beginning to gather in the windows. *Anzhel made him do all that stuff...* Yes, John believed it. But for three weeks now, all he had seen were the things Anzhel had made Michael do. And, unseen,

Michael had called or allowed Quin to come to him: Michael, who would kill anyone who hurt a hair on the boy's head.

It wasn't him. John believed that. He wished he could be certain how much of Michael was left, now that Anzhel was subtracted from him, torn out of him and left dead on the kitchen floor. Michael in the pale dawn light was beautiful, a graveyard angel and about as human. About as much in need of human comfort. John began to turn away.

"Griff?"

It was nothing, a bare rasp. Blackbirds skittering on the roof would make more noise. But when John looked again, Michael was staring up at him. "Griff? What've I done?"

John had never seen anything so lonely. He went to him, dropped down and knelt at his side. "You had to kill him."

"Not to him. To you."

John put out a hand. He brushed a fingertip touch to the side of Michael's face, turning him to the light. Hungrily he examined him. Michael returned his gaze, and there was nothing in the wide dark eyes John hadn't seen a thousand times before, seen and loved. It was just Mike. "I'm okay," he said softly. "We'll get over it."

"I don't even know why you're still here."

"Didn't you hear me back there?"

Tears brimmed suddenly. "Yes. But you can't love—"

"Shut up." John took hold of Michael's shoulders, tugging gently. Michael resisted for a second, then gave a choked, incredulous cry and surrendered. "Don't tell me what I can't bloody do," John told him, catching him, gladly losing breath as Michael seized him, hands clenching so tight in the fabric of his shirt that the contact burned. He put a hand round the back of Michael's skull as the first sob tore through him. The next was muffled on his shoulder, hot breath coming and going, a scald of tears. "It's all right, love. It's all right."

Somewhere off at very far distance, the sound of an engine. John filtered it out, then recalled that he was not in London. No vehicle but the odd tractor came near the farmhouse at this hour. He had to struggle to make himself care. Mike was in his arms, and despite the hot tang of blood in the air, he felt as if he'd just stepped out of hell into sunlight.

The engine purr increased. It doubled itself, then trebled. In the gap between one racking sob and the next, Michael heard it too and stopped himself, choking. "John…"

"Yes. It'll be Diane and Nick and whatever army they've brought to round you up. Come on. Better let them see you're okay."

He was hoisting Mike to his feet when the first set of wheels hit gravel. A fierce crunch, then a sweeping grind as if the lead car had barely stopped in time and skidded broadside to the house. He frowned. "That one came in hot, even for Diane."

"Yeah. They think I'm still about to go bomb London." Michael's voice was raw. He let go of John with a visible effort and grabbed a handful of kitchen roll. "How much of a mess?"

"Carnage," John confirmed for him, smiling. "Here, give me that and I'll—"

Something rattled. A faint metallic clatter, off beyond the hallway. In the living room, John thought, meeting Michael's eyes. He'd left the window open behind him, hadn't he?

An explosion rocked the house. The wall between the kitchen and the living room held, but dust burst from the mortar, and a crack went across the kitchen ceiling like a lightning bolt. John seized Mike, who was already reaching for him, and together they dived for the shelter of the massive, ancient table. "Mike, what the fuck—"

"Dunno." Michael unshipped his pistol and grimly checked the clip. "Where's Quin?"

"In the…" Sick terror twisted John's gut. "In the bathroom. Please God."

"Go find him. What have you got?"

"Not much. Couple of rounds."

"Right." Michael didn't flinch when the next blast came. He pushed a hand under Anzhel's body and extracted the weapon from the holster at his back. "Take this. Look after Quin and yourself."

"What? Where are you going?"

"To surrender. John, let me go."

John didn't relax the grip he'd fastened round Michael's arm. "No! I don't know who these fuckers are, but if they just wanted your white flag, they wouldn't be lobbing grenades."

"Whatever." Michael suddenly smiled and, to John's astonishment, leaned in and planted a rough, tender kiss to his mouth. "I love you too. Now go get Quin."

* * *

John couldn't find him—not in the bathroom or bedrooms, or any of the places where he might have taken cover. The air was thick with smoke and dust. How long did it take a teenage kid to wash? How long since John had left him on his own? Time was on his side in that this was Quin, sufficiently like him to have made Mike put a second bathroom on his list of building priorities for the occasions when both of them stayed in his house, but John was kidding himself, wasn't he, if he thought the kid had stayed safely out of harm's reach, away from the…

Away from the living room, whose outer wall was down. John crashed to a halt in the doorway, choking on airborne plaster. Half the ceiling had come in, vast oak beams stark like whalebones crossing the dawn sky on weird diagonals. No. Quin would have finished his wash, come back to the kitchen to find him and Mike, and then with his odd new tact, as if he not only wasn't fazed by their relationship but wanted to encourage it, he would have veered off. The house wasn't all that big. He would have come back here.

John had an instant to reflect on all the times he'd have given his arm and a month's pay to be rid of him. Then the wall behind him burst as a third grenade detonated, the shockwave throwing him just clear of its collapse. He scrambled halfway to his feet, blast-deafened and sick. The sound of gunfire came to him like distant fireworks. "Mike!"

Strong arms closed round him. He felt himself lifted and hauled into the remains of the porch. The oldest part of the house, Mike had told him, the lintel so ancient it bore cup-and-ring marks, enigmatic musings of a forgotten race. He and Mike kept coats and outdoor boots there, like most country families coming and going through the back kitchen door. The front was for weddings and coffins, Mike had said.

He dragged himself into the present. Mike had set him down against the last intact wall and was crouched behind the ruined one opposite, shielding him, returning fire. John couldn't allow that. He felt around and located Anzhel's weapon tucked inside his belt. His hands were numb, but they obeyed him. He pushed off the wall and dropped into place beside his partner. "Mike. Who are they?"

"No idea. Balaclavas. And you were right. They didn't like my white flag. Where's Quin?"

"Couldn't find him." John shuddered, his experienced, deadly hands remaining steady on the gun. It was hard to see in the half-light, but he could just about make out the direction of incoming fire, a human head lifting and ducking down behind a car. That was too tough a target. He took an optimistic shot anyway, put another two neatly into the vehicle's wheels out of habit. "I can't find him!"

"Shit. We will, okay?"

John didn't think so. He had whatever was left in Anzhel's clip and maybe two in his own. Their assailants were pumping lead at them with the freedom of abundance. It suddenly came to him that he and Mike were at last stand. Fear flashed through him, then an unexpected wash of peace. *By your side, anyway.* His shoulder touched Mike's. He drew a deep breath and took aim.

Movement on the edge of his field of vision. He snapped round to face it. But Michael grabbed his wrist with bruising force and bore his weapon down. "No!"

Because it was Quin. It was Quin, and yet it wasn't. John dragged a hand over his eyes, trying to clear them of dust. Quin was walking calmly across the garden. He had lost the dreadful filthy parka he had for some reason been wearing when John arrived. He was in his jeans and the white Shoreline T-shirt Michael had bought him last Christmas. He was just Quin, but John could barely look at him. His eyes streamed and burned when he tried. Some effect of the dawn light was putting a veil between them, making the air iridesce—

Quin, he tried to shout, but his mouth and throat were numb too. The boy came to a halt in the direct line of fire between the porch and the cars.

The hail of bullets continued for a second, then stopped. A voice John knew well but briefly couldn't place broke the echoing silence. "What the hell are you doing? Take him out!"

"You can do what you like, mate. I'm not about to shoot a teenage kid!"

And John did know *that* voice. At his side, he saw Michael too coming to astonished attention. "Diane?"

She emerged from behind the car. John thought he could see a glimmer of tears in her eyes behind the balaclava mask. "I'm sorry!" she yelled. "I'm sorry, okay? Fuck this, Nick. You're on your own."

She bolted for the second car, parked in the shelter of the first one and intact. There was a moment when John could have taken her out—several when he could have disabled the vehicle. Both, he noted from shocked distance, were anonymous, not from the Last Line car pool, their number plates conveniently splashed with mud. John could have put a round into her skull in the time it took her to roar down the driveway and out into the lane.

Instead he knelt frozen in the ruins of Michael's house, staring at Nick Skelton. Nick in his turn seemed transfixed by Quin, who for some reason was heading straight for him, smiling serenely. *Walking on water.* John felt dazed. Skelton raised his pistol and took aim.

John's PPK clicked empty on the kill shot. Before dismay could find him, Michael was a blur at his side, a pissed-off puma clearing the wall. Skelton never saw him coming, went down with a yelp under the force of his flying tackle and crashed to the turf. Mike flipped him over, pinned, disarmed and straddled him. He grabbed the balaclava and ripped it away. "You bastard, Nick! What the hell is this?"

Skelton coughed. "What's it look like?"

"It looks like a hit."

"Right. You should know."

"On me? You didn't see me in the driveway with my hands up?"

"Yeah, I did. That wasn't an option."

"What, then—take me out at all costs?"

"Yes. He said you were compromised, too far gone. You know what he's like. He said to make sure."

"Webb. Okay. Fair enough. Did he send you to kill John too? And—Christ, Nick. You sat and ate pizza at Quin's last birthday party!"

"You and any witnesses."

Michael sat back, breathing hard. Then he got up, hauling Skelton upright with him. "Get out of here."

"What?"

"Go. I don't want you or anything to do with you anywhere near my partner or that lad. You go tell Webb what'll happen to the next bastard who comes within a ten-mile radius of any of us."

Skelton found a sickly smile. "Come on, Mike. You know how this goes. He sent me and Di out independently. He'll tell you we were working on our own."

"I know. Plausible deniability. We all signed up to it. Well, John and I have paid for that. Everybody's bloody accountable sometime." He turned Skelton round and began to march him toward the gate. "Get out of here."

"Er... Diane took the car, Mike."

"Right. Keep going in that direction about six miles. If you're lucky, you might get the nine o'clock bus."

Skelton set off. He took the first few steps unsteadily, staring back incredulously over his shoulder. Michael closed the gate, and for John it wasn't hard to equip him with wings and a fiery sword. First sunlight poured over the hills to the east, casting him in bronze and gold—a sentinel finding his post at last, the home ground he wanted to guard.

Skelton stopped in the lane. "If he wants you dead," he said harshly, "somebody'll come for you. You know that."

"We'll deal with it. If you miss the nine o'clock, there's one at four. Sometimes."

John watched him retreat into green shadows. The lane was an old one, what the locals called a holloway, sunk so deep between its banks that the elders and hawthorns in their summer abundance almost made a tunnel of it. Skelton broke into a jog. After a moment, he vaulted a fence, or John thought he had. Skelton was hard-trained to disappear, as they all had been. To melt like ghosts into a landscape of fields or city streets. To emerge again as suddenly.

Somebody'll come for you. They would never be safe, would they? Not if Webb had cut them loose. John took hold of what was left of the porch wall and used it to lurch to his feet. He looked at his partner, who was still calmly watching the lane—and then at his brother, who had walked through a hail of gunfire to shield both of them.

He stumbled across the lawn. Quin didn't respond to his name, remained motionless, his dust-smeared face abstracted and empty. John shook him gently. He pulled him hard into his arms. "Quin! What the hell are you doing out here?"

Quin stood rigid, chilly as marble. John had long enough to wonder if, having somehow retrieved him physically, he had lost him in every way that counted. But suddenly the boy relaxed so completely that John had to make a grab to catch him. He rested his brow on John's shoulder, his expression as peaceful as if he were settling to sleep in his own bed. Then he looked up, frowning, and met John's eyes. "John? What the hell am I doing out here?"

"It's all right." John forced back a tremor of laughter at the just-woken confusion in his voice. "You'll be all right now." He held out a hand to Michael, who had turned at last in the gateway and was coming to them across the sun-diamond grass, staring at

Quin like a phoenix who had risen from his rubble-strewn vegetable patch. "Mike, he's okay."

"I don't see how." Mike took John's hand and reached with his free one for Quin's tangled hair. "Where was he?"

"No idea. Quin, I couldn't find you. Where were you when they started chucking grenades?"

"In the…in the living room."

John glanced at the wreckage of the walls he and Michael had built. "He couldn't have been," he said to Mike, who was also surveying the ruins. "There's not a mark on him."

Quin straightened. He didn't dispense with his brother's support or try to avoid Michael's hand on his skull, caressing, checking for damage. "I was. I went in to get a book. Then I heard the cars. I went to the window, and…something came in. Something metal. And then I don't remember, not until—" He broke off. "Oh, Mike. The farmhouse!"

Mike's grip tightened around John's. Their fingers interlaced strongly. "It's okay," he said. "I was rebuilding it wrong anyway. We need two decent-sized bedrooms, not three little cubes." A dawn breeze had risen, carrying off some of the smoke and dust. Summer daylight was falling on earth held in darkness for three hundred years, sweet cleansing fire. For the first time in all those years, there was a view of the Tor. "Everything's going to change."

Chapter Sixteen

John climbed the hill to the north of the farm. The last of a glorious sunset was lingering still, painting green-gold fires from horizon to zenith. The night would remain luminous for hours to come. John took the grassy track slowly, breathing the cooling air deep into his lungs. There was no hurry. No need to be afraid.

This was the first place Michael had shown him on his first weekend visit. They had both been so awkward, their easy workday bond dissolving in the silences, trying to weave back together, unsure of the new design. Disconcerting for both of them, that first voluntary sharing of free time. The odd hour at the pub at the end of shift had been one thing, but what did it mean when one apparently straight but unattached man invited an openly gay one to stay with him in the country? John smiled. They had both striven so hard to make it mean no more than that. They were friends. Michael had a nice place and needed help sorting it out. And, on that first Friday night, they had come up here under a full springtime moon, tides of yearning rushing in silence between them. They'd listened to the owls, and John had seen strange lights shimmering over the Tor and known better than to mention them to his pragmatic partner, who'd told him over dinner what a nightmare the constant influx of New Agers and UFO nutcases had become.

He came to the crest of the hill. The breeze was fresher up here, a relief after a hard hot day's work. The close-cropped turf was still warm when he settled on it. He pressed his palms to it, feeling for the solidity of earth, aware of the slope beneath him slowly exhaling stored heat. Flank of an unimaginable beast laid out across the Somerset countryside, falling into vast sleep... John, not prone to flights of imagination even if he did see lights on the Tor, shook himself. He was reaching for distraction. Beginning to be scared. Mike had been gone for such a long time.

From here he could see the farmhouse, stripped down now almost to its foundations. That had been Mike's one concession over the last fortnight, while they closed up their places in London and sorted out their affairs—to have a professional building team come in and take down those parts of the house not already blown apart. The structural damage had been too great. His city flat was on the market to pay for the third-time-lucky creation of the farm. All John had been able to contribute to the project was the sale of his Jag, which he'd part-exchanged against a massive Toyota 4x4, better suited to lugging masonry back and forth and dealing with the potholed Somerset lanes. He'd done it without consulting Mike, who'd been duly horrified, but John hadn't minded. There'd been a moment two weeks before, tearing down the Hampshire roads, convinced that the objects of his pursuit were already lost to him, when the car had turned into a toy around him, its charm evaporating like a dream. They'd driven the truck down to Glastonbury early that morning. The caravan Mike had ordered had been delivered, a place to live while they worked on the build.

They would be in close quarters, their accommodations far from luxurious. Which was fine with John, who had discovered that he could after all survive without a power shower, but in many ways he still felt as unsure of himself as he had during that first weekend.

Especially after today. John got up restlessly and began to gather stones together for a fire. He wondered if there was any way he could have kept his mouth shut. He'd tried, as an experiment, working shoulder to shoulder with Mike all that morning. Their first task had been to sort through the demolished masonry, looking for pieces still good enough to use again. There had been plenty, despite the blasts, as if you could rip the old house apart to her bones yet never quite kill her. They had got as far as the remains of the kitchen area, and Mike had stopped work suddenly, staring at the place where Anzhel had fallen.

"I wish they'd let us know about the inquest. I'd feel like this was really over then."

"Mike, there isn't going to be one. Anzhel's body wasn't found here. And Oriel's never turned up in that church in Hounslow."

John had had to tell him, he supposed. He packed his hearthstones into a neat ring and added a handful of the kindling he'd gathered on the way up. There his Boy Scout skills failed him, and he fell back on matches, swearing softly as one after the other sparked and burned without catching. They'd gone to see Webb as soon as they had got back to London. He'd greeted them with gruff pleasure and every ounce of the feigned innocence Nick Skelton had predicted. Shaw and Skelton had gone rogue, he'd declared, or perhaps had been working the other side all along. A terrible betrayal and beyond reparation now, since neither Nick nor Diane had been seen since and couldn't be found. Webb would be willing to compensate the damage to Agent South's property. The old sod had got as far as taking out his chequebook and a pen.

He'd heard their resignations with an outraged dismay John could almost—almost—believe to have been genuine. Mike, nerves still raw, emotions near the surface, had slammed out of the office straight away afterward. And John had moved to follow, but Webb had called him back. The theatrics had vanished. He had looked like himself again—a tired old wolf watching the antics of the forest life around him with weary contempt. *"If you're going to cast off the support of this agency, Griffin, you should know we have no proof that Mattvei and Oriel are dead."*

Mike had taken the news calmly. They had discovered the old kitchen table somehow intact in the ruins, and John had helped him dust it off and carry it out to the barn. Then Mike had leaned both hands on its silky, time-scarred surface and said that he needed to go out for a while. Errands he was better off doing on his own, if John didn't mind carrying on here. He'd stop off and get groceries. He wouldn't be long.

That had been eight hours ago. John checked his mobile, but the signal was coming and going with the breeze or the ley lines or whatever other weird forces swirled around this place. John didn't want to phone him and intrude on his solitude. For the past two weeks they had been gentle and chaste with one another, respectful, both treading softly on uncertain ground. On the other hand, night was falling. John would give him half an hour more, and then he would grab his gun and the 4x4 and tear off after him into the lanes.

His phone beeped, as if somewhere the thought had been received and understood. *Sorry I'm late*, the text said. *On my way home.*

John's stomach unclenched. It looked as if Mike wouldn't be far behind on his promise. Familiar headlights appeared briefly on the rise of land a couple of miles away. Now he could enjoy the night, and his own attempts to get a fire going, which, even if he was ridiculously bad at it, was still a satisfying activity. The twigs spat and crackled as if they were damp, although he'd been careful to pick up only the driest forage on the track through the woods. Still, it seemed to be taking. He settled down beside it cautiously. He wouldn't permit himself to watch for Mike's approach. Nor would he allow the paranoid fantasy to surface that it wasn't Mike at all but whichever unkillable ghost from his past who had murdered him and stolen his car. If he jumped at every shadow, he would never know a minute's peace again. He had lit a beacon on the hill. He would let the night unfold.

A car engine whispered in the valley. A door closed softly, and then after a time John couldn't measure, a long stride began to stir the grass. A rhythmic crunch on the small stones of the track, and then only a sense of oncoming presence, silent on the rich turf.

"Griff."

He let himself at last look up. Michael in the dusk was a sight worth waiting for. He was still in his work clothes and his jeans and T-shirt contoured him lovingly. Was his hair quite black? John had thought so, but in certain lights—this mixture of sunset and flame—there was a sable brown to it, almost a bronze. John wanted to devote a long while to the study. All the attention he had once directed at the mirror seemed to have turned outward and fastened on his partner. John could barely look away. "Hiya," he said, flatly in proportion to the leap at his heart. "You okay?"

"Yeah. Sorry I ran out on you." Michael crossed the last few yards of ground between them and crouched by the fire. He had a leather satchel slung over one shoulder and a big carrier bag in his hand. "Could you manage some dinner?"

The enticing scents drifting John's way were more than woodsmoke. Incongruously in the rural English night, he could smell Oriental food. "That's never a takeaway."

"Believe it or not. Some enterprising kid's opened a Szechuan in Teal village, close enough to get it home hot."

"I love Szechuan."

"I know. They must've known you were moving in."

John kept his eyes down and concentrated on helping Mike untangle from the satchel strap and start to unpack the fragrant cardboard boxes from the bag. Somehow, despite all their preparations—clearing John's flat, putting his things into storage—neither of them had gone so far as to express this great change in words. Yet Mike said it easily now, as if it were the most natural thing in the world. Something blossomed in John's chest—pleasure of a kind he'd never felt before. Not his usual reflexive enjoyment of a moment, but enduring, golden, real. "Very nice." He sat up and made an expansive townie's gesture at the rolling countryside around them. "Shouldn't we be living off the land or something, though? Catching rabbits and cooking them?"

"What, on this poor little fire? Be lucky to warm up their fleas."

Mike leaned forward and gave the fire an encouraging poke. John couldn't see that he'd done anything all that special, but the struggling flames leaped high, became a blaze to ward off wolves. They sat and watched in silence. Then Mike said, helplessly, as if the words were being shaken out of him, "I like fire. I think I like it a bit too much."

"Just as well I like water," John responded absently. He wasn't sure what he meant, except that the coolness of the river below them had suddenly suggested itself to him. The river and dewfall and the cure for Mike's fevers. At this moment, he felt as if he could stretch out his hands and make it rain.

"We should destroy one another, technically."

"Or generate a hell of a lot of steam."

Mike snorted. John hadn't meant to make it sound suggestive. But he had, absurdly so, and Mike was laughing, blushing like a kid, eyes brilliant. "At least let's have dinner first," he said, reaching into the bag and ceremoniously handing John a plastic fork.

They ate peacefully. Mike asked if he'd heard from Quin, and that was no longer the appetite-killer it had been. John talked to him every day now. The daily calls had started as a safety measure, a twenty-four-hour check-in to ensure that whatever dangers the boy had encountered hadn't followed him back to his school. But John had discovered that Quin unshielded and happy had plenty to say for himself—ordinary, diamond-sharp observations of the world around him, his days, and school routines. That he could pick up the phone and greet John with shy affection, bid him good-bye with a curiously adult injunction to take care. John had begun to look forward to the calls. "He's fine," he said, passing Mike the chicken and snagging a bit more of the delicious spiced veg for himself. "Perfectly happy to stick out a few more weeks of summer school, if he can have his August here when the place is a bit more habitable. I heard from the head of Glasto secondary while you were out. They'll be happy to take him from the start of the September term."

"Good. No problems with the next-of-kin paperwork?"

"Because his brother's shacked up with his uncle Mike *in loco parentis*?" John asked happily. "No, I think they have to be open-minded these days."

"And they're not concerned that he's a hopeless runaway?"

"Well, since he's been trying to run home, and it's day school, they're not bothered. They reckon he's our problem." Their eyes met in rueful acceptance of the changes to an already transformed lifestyle Quin's arrival would bring. "Mike. One last time. Are you sure about this?"

"Never more sure of anything. In fact"—Mike wiped his fingers and unbuckled the satchel—"that was one of the things I did this afternoon. Saw my lawyer in Glasto. He gave me some stuff to read if I was thinking about becoming Quin's legal guardian."

John almost swallowed a green bean whole. He gratefully took the bottle of Somerset ale Mike held out to him. "What? You mean *adopt* him?"

"I suppose so. Is that too much of a head-fuck?"

"No. I should think he'd die of joy. But you're already doing everything a parent would. You don't have to set it in stone."

"No, I know. It'll just make it easier if… Well, that was another thing. Something I should've done ages ago, and I don't know why I didn't. I'm sorry."

He stretched out an arm. John couldn't read the anxiety in his face, then understood with a shiver that he wasn't sure his gesture would work. They'd barely touched lately, old fears and injuries stiffening. Unhesitatingly John set aside the carton and went to him, closing his eyes in pleasure and relief as Mike's embrace tightened, putting an arm round his waist in return. "Sorry, mate. I don't think they're gonna let you adopt me too."

"Highly improper in the circumstances. No, I mean about the house. I've got the papers here. I had them drawn up a couple of years ago, and then I got…scared, I suppose, that you'd think it was weird or something, so I never asked you to sign."

"In a minute I'll work out what you're on about, won't I?"

"The house and the land. I want to put it in joint names. Then if anything happens to me, it'll be simpler. No homophobic panic while they try to find my nonexistent missus."

John stared at the sheaf of documents Mike had pulled out of the satchel. Between the firelight and the embers of the day, there was just enough light to read the top sheet. It was straightforward, and—yes—dated back in 2009. He and Mike had barely known one another then, he'd thought He'd been down to the farmhouse for a visit or two. John remembered—oh, he'd never forget, would he—the half delicious, half dreadful sense of beginning to fall in love, chastising himself all the while because this new partner, hospitable and kind as he was, could surely never return the feeling. "No," he whispered, unable to trust his voice. "If I lose you, I don't want your house or your bloody land. Anyway, whatever happens to you..." He pulled Mike closer until he felt ribs crackle under his arm. "It's going to happen to me too. Isn't it?"

"All the more reason we should sort this out now. So it can all go straight to Quin, in trust until he's eighteen. That's this sheet here. I've got a pen."

So John sat up and signed where Mike showed him. Questions died on his lips about why it had to be now, why Mike had brought these papers up a hill to be signed by firelight instead of waiting for morning, a flat surface, the caravan's little fold-down table. He already knew. "I'm sorry," he said, folding up the document carefully and handing it back to Mike. "I tried to think of every possible way I could get round telling you."

Mike nodded. For a moment he looked as stern and distant as he had that morning when John had broken the news; then the mask dissolved, leaving only a worried man behind. "Can't have been easy for you. But I put a bullet into Anzhel Mattvei from close range. If he got up and walked away, I need to know."

"Mike, come on. If someone took his body—if Webb's playing that deep a game or somebody else is screwing with us—that's bad enough. But I felt him die. If there's anybody creeping around in the shadows out there, it's not him." John was close enough to feel Mike's shiver as if it had been his own, and he shifted to kneel behind him, caressing his arms. Shielding his back from the night and whatever monsters it contained. "It's someone as human and killable as we are. And we can deal with that."

"Well, that's another point." Mike's hand closed warmly round John's wrist. He glanced up at him sidelong, his expression odd. "I went to see a couple of other people this afternoon. That's why I was so late. The first was the builder, to pick up some papers he'd rescued from the house while they were working. He gave me a whole load of stuff, some photographs that... Oh God, no. It's too crazy. I might try that one on you after another couple of beers. Anyway, I got those, and then I decided—I don't know why—to go and look up the police inspector who dealt with my mother's death. I remembered something, Griff. Breaking the programming must have shaken it loose."

"Something about your mother?"

"The way she died. I didn't come back and find her. She was alive when I got home. And...men were with her, three or four of them."

"Jesus. They hurt her? Why?"

"They weren't after her. It was me. She got in their way, and they just..."

He faded out. John remembered the easy, almost flippant way he'd related her death to him before. "What did they do?"

"I don't know. Something that didn't leave any marks. But I fucking hated them so much. It was like my brain caught fire. They came for me, and I put the fire in my hands. And then I reached out and put it in them. I'm aware, by the way, that I sound like a total nut job here."

To John he sounded newly and completely sane. But he nodded agreement, brushing a kiss to his cheek. "Yes. But go on."

"I've lost months of my memory after that. Years, maybe. I think my granddad just picked up the pieces and carried on as best he could. I do recall him"—he paused and gave a brief, unexpected smile—"standing on the doorstep, giving what-for to some social worker who'd come to try and take me into care. I don't think there was much of a police investigation, but this afternoon, standing in the bloody cereal aisle at Sainsbury's, I suddenly remembered the name of the guy who carried it out. Jim Ford, our village bobby. Retired years ago, but I knew where he lived, so..."

"Was he there? Did you see him?"

"Yeah. He's old, but he's still pretty sharp. His missus gave me tea and about five of the most horrendous home-baked cupcakes. Anyway, Jim said they looked into my mother's death as far as they could, but once the coroner's report came back, there was no reason to go on. He said there was only one other weird thing about that day. The ambulance crew who were checking my mum over got suddenly called away. There'd been a crash on the Drove Road. You know the long straight stretch where you like to see if a car can fly..."

"Yeah. Sorry."

"No. I am. God, I can't believe you sold her. I'll buy you a new one, I promise, something even stupider—"

"Ssh. Don't be daft. Go on."

"Okay. It was one car, no other vehicle involved. No marks of a skid. More like they'd just pulled over, you know? But the car was on fire. It was so fierce and hot they couldn't get near it, and when it finally died back, there was nothing left. Bones and teeth.

Jim said they could just about tell there'd been three male passengers. There were no matching dental records, and the numbers were burned off the car chassis. It was like they'd dropped out of the sky."

John held him. The night was warm, but even so he'd felt waves of fever heat coming off him as he'd unfolded his story. His T-shirt was damp. "What happened?"

"They gave it up eventually. There was nothing to connect it to my mother. But Jim said he'd always felt uneasy about it, as if there *was* something, some link. He said the Drove is the road he'd take if…"

"If he wanted to get away from here as fast as possible."

"Right. If he was running for his life."

"And you think what happened to them was something to do with you?"

"Tell me it sounds crazy."

All right, if that's what you need. John closed his eyes. He dismissed the visions that instantly leaped up of the impossibilities surrounding the last few weeks of his life—and further back than that, if he dared to look. "Okay," he said. "You were just a little kid, and you were in shock. Kids imagine all sorts of things."

"Oh, John." Mike turned in his arms. There were tears on his face, but he was smiling, as if he very much appreciated John's effort, or appreciated something about him. "Thank you. Nice try."

"You're welcome. It's good practice for all the other stuff I'm gonna have to explain away before I feel like I'm living on planet Earth again."

"I know. I'll help you, unless we go completely nuts and decide to tell each other—oh my God. Look."

John jerked round in the direction of his gaze. Webb hadn't asked them to turn in their weapons—a final courtesy, perhaps, an adjustment of the playing field—and his PPK was within a short sharp reach. As for Mike, he might not have worn his harness for a shopping trip, but he'd be tooled up somewhere. They both would be, for the rest of their lives.

But it was just the moon. John grabbed a breath in shock just as Mike had done. She'd sprung up in sudden completeness, huge and honey-gold, her lower arc poised impossibly on the crest of Teal hill. "I know it's just refraction or something makes her look so big on the horizon like that, but…"

"Yeah. Or I heard it's because you can see trees and things right next to her, so you get an idea of the scale for once. I reckon we could explain away all our disasters and miracles if we wanted."

"I don't want." John swallowed. His throat hurt. "I want us to tell each other the truth, even if it's crazy. Even if it sucks."

Mike closed his hands on John's shoulders. His grip was uncertain, clumsy with hesitation, but he turned him back to face him, and John went willingly, aware of the change in the dynamic of their touch—that, suddenly, he wasn't the one doing the comforting. Mike had touched him so often like that before all this shit had hit the fan—strong, reassuring, and John, who had looked after himself for so long he'd forgotten how to do anything else, had melted in silence beneath his caress. God, he'd missed it! "Okay," Mike said softly, drawing him close. "The truth. Where do you want me to start?"

You know where. "That first time—that first fuck. Was that just your programming kicking in?"

Mike flinched. He put a hand round the back of John's skull as if he could shield him from the past as well as the future. "It was part of it. I'd seen Piotr, and things were coming apart. But it started because I thought I'd lost you."

"Okay." John could take that. It was bitter, but it was clean. "So it would've happened anyway, but—"

"It would've been different. It would've been so different, love."

Mike drew his hand from the hair at John's nape and placed it on his jaw, gently lifting. John obeyed the encouraging move and met his kiss halfway. Memories of the wrong place where they'd started—that open-mouthed thrusting—boiled up in him, generating heat and appalling shyness. He broke away, laughing. "Sorry. Give me a second."

"You're scared."

"No, I just—"

"First time we tried this I threw you down and screwed you over a table. Time after that I tried to rape you."

"Don't say that!" John grabbed him as if he could shove the word into a box and slam the lid on it. He bore him down onto the turf. "Don't. Not you."

"Griff, I did."

"Well, don't. Don't *cry* over it, love, not now. It's forgiven."

"How can it be?"

"Listen. That time I belted you in the face, if you recall. I can handle you. And the time before that"—he kissed the salt off Michael's face—"time before that, you made me come like holy hell. Twice."

"Twice?"

"Yeah. You just didn't notice the first one. You're remembering all this stuff now, aren't you?"

"I did before. I'm not gonna take refuge in amnesia—"

"I mean remembering properly. Like you were there, not just..."

"Not just watching. Yes. Oh God. Makes me want to die."

John leaned over him. The aching place in his heart—the hollow where the word *rape* had banged around for him, as well—

was closing, its pain washing out in Mike's tears. "Don't die, handsome. Not now."

"Why not? I can't think of a better time, before you work out what a git I am. John, stop that. I don't deserve—"

John captured and silenced the protest. He covered Mike's mouth with his own. Both went briefly still, earthquake victims braced for the next shock, the impulse of violence that had come hard on the heels of their previous attempts at a kiss. Then Mike moaned. A shiver ran through his whole body. His lips parted under John's. He put an arm round John's neck and pulled him down, the gesture at once tender and urgent. The three weeks just past closed up in John's head and vanished. They were at the beginning of their time together, he and Mike, exchanging the kiss they should have done. "Can we?" Mike gasped, as if hearing the thought. He snatched another kiss, heated and velvety, tongue brushing tongue. "Can we start it again?"

Fire and water cleans this slate. "Yes. I will if you will."

"Lie down. Let me touch you. Let me show you what I should've done before."

John thudded down onto the turf. His dignity was gone, but he didn't give a stuff. The full moon lurched off the horizon and shone straight down into his eyes, her ancient pockmarked face amused. "Yes," he said, reaching to grab whichever parts of Mike came to hand first. "Show me."

"I want to take it back to the start. Kiss you, roll around in the grass, do everything we missed—"

"Well, are you going to show me? Or…" Delicious laughter rippled through John, twin sensation to the lift of his cock. He'd been so thrown by Michael's silence the first time around. "Or just *tell* me about it, because…"

"Oh. Sorry. God, now we've come this far, I hardly know where to start…"

"Here." John guided his hand to the top button of his shirt. He arched in pleasure as Mike deftly undid it, pushing the fabric aside to expose one hardening nipple. "Yes. And here…" He fell back gasping. Mike had the idea now. His tongue was trailing a line of sweet fire up John's breastbone, his hand on an exploratory mission round the waistband of his jeans. His mouth closed hotly on one nipple then the other, bestowing tongue-flicker blessings. At the same instant, he found his zip. John surged up into the moment of his release. "Mike, yes!"

"You're so hard. Do I do that to you?"

"The *thought* of you does that. Touch me."

Mike did. He drew John's rigid shaft from its trap of underwear and jeans, blindly shoving clothes out of the way. John cried out as his grip closed, loudly enough to make sheep scatter in the darkness downhill. "Sorry!"

"What the hell for?"

"I should be quiet. We should be careful. We should listen out for—"

"Ssh. Nothing can hurt you when I'm with you."

Briefly John considered this large claim. Nothing felt wrong about it. The warm earth under him seemed to confirm it, the vibrant light of sunset singing to the moon. Then he couldn't think about that or anything else anymore. Mike was jerking him off, his movements tentative but strong. "Oh, that's it. Please. Harder."

"Do I do it right for you?"

"Perfect. Bloody beautiful. But I tell you what, love. Come here."

"What is it?"

"You've been to hell and back. In Russia and with Anzhel. I want you here in my arms when this happens. Right here."

Mike made a faint sound, as if he'd been hit in the lungs. "I'm okay. I can do this. I want to.. I want to suck you off, make it good for you."

"You will. Mike, this is *you*. You can look at me sideways and make it good for me. This time, though... Just come here."

He thought Mike wouldn't obey him. His movements were stiff, reluctant, as if he'd lost the links between sex and everyday affection. Nonetheless John took his chances, deftly undoing his jeans before easing him down to lie beside him. Poor bastard had only been half-erect for all the talk, anxiety rolling off him in waves. John slid his hands down over his backside, pulling him close, and suddenly Mike gave it up and fell against him, struggling into his embrace. "That's it," John whispered. "Can feel you now. Get hard all the way for me. Oh, there you are." They grappled and thrust in the firelight, finding the beat, the deep perfect rhythm at last. John rolled on top, Mike's grasp closing on him to hoist him there. He rose up strongly, bracing on his arms. Mike's shaft drove hard into the space between his thighs, and he writhed to accommodate him. "Are you gonna come for me?"

"Yes. So hard. Griff..."

"Yes. I'm there. Let go, let go!"

* * *

In the night's deepest stillness, Mike sat watching strange lights over Glastonbury Tor. John was stretched out beside him. In deference to his phobia concerning ticks, Mike had spread out a blanket for him, and he was profoundly asleep.

Out cold and smiling, but he stirred immediately at Mike's gentlest caress of his hair. His eyes opened wide. "Is everything all right?"

"Yeah. I didn't mean to wake you. Look at these, though."

John rolled onto his stomach. He propped himself on his elbows and watched the display for a while. "I didn't think you ever saw those."

"No, I...I saw them. My life felt weird enough without going looking for trouble, that's all."

Pulsating sapphire globes, melting and reforming, flickering impossibly fast from one side of the Tor to the other. "What do you think they are?"

"Interactions of human consciousness with the earth's magnetic field, changing according to shifting cultural perceptions?" Mike caught the glimmer of his partner's incredulous glance and smiled. "Or marsh gas. Aliens."

"*You're* a bloody alien," John accused him comfortably, and they settled back down on the blanket together, leaving the mysteries of the universe to their own devices. "You all right, then?"

"Never better. You hit me like a beautiful truck. I slept like the dead." Mike pillowed John's head on his shoulder, holding him close to keep off the dewfall chill. "That first time..."

"More you talk about it, the less of a bugbear it'll be."

"I'm not sure about that, but God, you just wiped me out. That first time, how the hell did I make you come twice?"

John chuckled. "No one else ever managed, not two on the trot like that. I was pretty excited, I suppose. And I'd wanted you forever."

"You'll think I'm stupid. I didn't know."

"Well, I wasn't parading it."

"No. All those boyfriends! I sometimes thought, the way you looked at me or... Then I told myself no one as gorgeous as you could—"

"Oh please." John waved a deprecating hand and shifted in the firelight, doing nothing to diminish Mike's impression of his beauty. "Anyway, if we're talking about gorgeous, don't you ever look in a mirror?

"I used to. After Zemelya, I didn't like to. If I looked good, even my own reflection seemed to be mocking me. I'd hear his voice—Anzhel's—calling me his *krasavcheg*, his handsome one, which in Zemel is more what you'd call your best horse or dog."

"Oh, Mike."

"I'm sorry. I made my mind up I'd never even say his name in front of you again."

"What? Why?"

"I betrayed you with him. I wouldn't insult you."

John looked into the passionate dark eyes fixed on him, hot with indignation on his behalf. "You really are very Russian at times," he said, daring a small smile. "Very Tolstoy. It's all right. You may speak his name in my presence." He sobered. "You're going to have to. Anzhel Mattvei won't fit into some tiny box you want to lock up inside, not after everything that happened. Talk to me."

"Okay. Okay, love, I will. But just now all I can think about is how I wish you'd…"

His voice had faded to a whisper. John pressed close, kissing the side of his neck. "What? Anything."

"Fuck the feel of him out of me forever."

The silence that fell was deep, even for the heart of a Somerset night. Only the murmur of their campfire disturbed it, that tiny blaze somehow still bright after hours consuming one handful of fuel. John pushed up onto an elbow. He examined Mike's face, stroking back his hair. "That's a serious one."

"I know."

"You've been hurt. Not just by Anzhel. In the jail, right? You got screwed over by the guards, the other prisoners?"

"Not them. They never got a chance. But the guards, yeah. In a way it was easier once Anzhel took me over. None of the others dared go near me then."

"Great." John kissed his brow, the gesture full of sorrow. "I asked you to tell me this, didn't I, but it's bloody hard to hear. Mike, all that left you damaged. Like I said back then, I've been with plenty of blokes who liked to be tied to the bedposts and roughed up a bit, but..."

"But not one that wanted to be cut."

"Not one I loved."

"Oh, Griff."

They clung together, grip to savage grip. Struggled and fought until John almost rolled into the fire, saved at the last instant by Mike's laughing, alarmed catch. Within seconds they were hard and ready, shuddering with need. "Was that all Anzhel?" John gasped. "You having to be hurt?"

"Not all. He brought something out in me, and when I thought I'd been part of Oriel's genocide—the pain did help. It felt like expiation. But I don't think I need it now, love. Not with you. Not—not tonight."

"Okay. Listen, though. You know where I've been, what I've done. I've been careful." He broke off, grinning. "Especially after you started worrying about me, telling me to watch myself. Felt like a prince then, didn't I? But I'm not about to tackle you in all my naked glory, so..."

"You think I'd expect that? I remember what I let Anzhel do to me, and Christ only knows where *he's* been knocking around." He ruffled John's hair and found spare blood supply for a blush. "You know how I went to the lawyer and the builder today?"

"Yeah. Oh, the butcher, the baker..."

"Right."

"Don't tell me you found time for the candlestick maker, as well."

"I don't know why. I wasn't sure you'd ever let me near you again. But—yeah. Pass me that bag."

They dispensed with the rest of their clothes, the fire blazing up at Mike's admonitory glance to keep them both warm. They spent a minute dealing with the marks Anzhel had left on him, healing scars that lost the last of their pain under John's mouth, the unfazed kisses he pressed to each one. Then John lay down close behind him and waited. He was big, stretching still farther in John's caressing hand, but he was scared, and all the condoms and KY in the world weren't going to ease that. John ran an expert finger down the length of his cock, pushed it into the suede, tender dip between his balls. Mike arched his neck back and John met him with a full, fearless kiss. "We don't have to do this, you know."

"We do. I do. Please."

John reached round him, keeping one arm tucked under his head, a steadying, cradling embrace. He squeezed nearly half a tube of lubricant onto his fingers—the rest was already soaking his sheathed cock—and took the slippery touch up and in between Mike's buttocks, smiling at the muscular twitch that promptly tried to close him out. "Is that reflex or a no?"

"Reflex. John."

"Yes. I'm with you, okay? We'll get you there." He ran a thumb down his cleft, gauging. "Oh, mate, you're so beautiful. Open up a bit for me, just a… Yes. There." His thumb slipped in, meeting brief resistance then powerful, squeezing surrender. John rode the wave and withdrew quickly once Mike was lubed up inside, meeting his anxious moan with the first push of his cock. "There. You want it?"

"Please. Before I have a fucking heart attack. Now."

John pushed into him. Wild heat shot through him, a moment when he could have burned to unthinking conclusion in Mike's flesh, but he clawed back, a wail bottling up in his throat. *You can want someone too much.* He took hold of Mike's shaft again, but Mike impatiently batted his hand away, thrusting back against him. "Don't need that," he rasped. "Just—inside. All the way."

So John let him have it. *So gentle,* a faint voice spoke in his head. *Meant to be so gentle with him.* But it was no bloody good. Mike was bucking in his grasp, fighting for more of him, and when John hooked an arm round the back of one knee to draw it up and spread him, he cried out in ferocious joy and helped, heaving over onto his front. John slammed into him, thrusting to his length, nearly all the way out again, then back, great strokes that neither would withstand for long. Mike convulsed, fingers driving into the turf. John grabbed his hips and lifted him, feeling the force of his climax in hot muscle spasms round his cock. Somehow he hung on long enough to wring it all out of him, and then when Mike was folding down—when the setting moon turned red with the blood-haze of his desperation—he heaved in to the root one last time and went still. His hands clenched on Mike's hips. Briefly he thought something was blocked—he wouldn't make it and would die here of unanswerable need—then the knots dissolved, and he was coming, hard and long.

Mike caught him as he fell. John crashed into his lover's arms, eyes closing, darkness coming down. He stayed conscious long enough to feel Mike's arms going round him, to register his breathless kisses. His fractured enquiries as to his health. "Yes," he managed. "Yes, I'm fine. Don't leave me."

"Never leave you, angel."

* * *

The morning sun was high when they broke camp, the ashes still glowing deep ruby pink in the brilliance. A fresh breeze was sweeping up off the river. Cars swept by on the Glastonbury road, tiny silent jewels at this distance but visible, and the Tor was just a strange terraced hill. An ordinary summer's day.

Michael shook out the blanket and folded it. John was clearing up boxes and bottles. They hadn't spoken much since waking—shy with one again for new reasons—but they looked at one another often, muted glances full of merriment and fire. Promise too. Skin tingling, the deep parts of his flesh deliciously aching, Michael tried to concentrate on the simple job of packing the blanket into his bag. Papers rustled, and he pulled them aside to make room. "Oh. I forgot about these."

"What?"

"Come here for a second and tell me I'm just being weird. These photographs."

John crouched beside him. "Those are… God, are they our first ever staff party at Last Line?"

"Yeah. Our intake group, just after the old man decided we might be good enough to keep."

There they all were, around a table in a Baker Street restaurant. Webb himself, glowering upon his new recruits as if he bitterly regretted every one of them. Diane Shaw perched playfully on Michael's lap. Nick Skelton, hoisting an unsteady toast with an over-full glass. The handful of others who had made it too, all of them gone now, some killed on the job, others wasted, thrown to the wolves and the wind. John, resting his chin on one hand, watching his partner, his smile no disguise for his yearning. "God," he said. "Heart on my sleeve even then. I didn't know you'd kept these."

"Well, mine wasn't on my sleeve. Not sure where it was, but that was the only shot I had of you. And I could hardly ask you for another, so yes, I kept them."

The kiss they exchanged was light, cautious of mutual bruising. So much love in it that tears prickled up into John's eyes. "I think I'm meant to be telling you what a freak you are."

"Yeah. Look at these. How long ago was it?"

"Oh, I dunno. Three years. More now. Nearly four. Why?"

"Not a huge amount of time, I suppose, but…"

"It is a long time in this bloody job. Look at this. Nick hasn't got a white hair on his head."

"That's what I mean. It's long enough to change people, a little bit anyway. Diane looks like a kid, and even Webb has a few less…well, on anyone else I'd call them laugh lines."

"Yeah. People changed."

"Apart from us."

John looked at him. He took the photo gently from his hands and turned it into the sunlight. He examined the faces of his colleagues and his boss. "What? Don't be daft."

"I'm serious, Griff. Look at us. Not a mark."

Silently John gave the photo back. His heart was beating too hard, and he felt as if he were catching distant music, a symphony he had known all his life and somehow lost. "You're a freak," he informed his partner lovingly. "Weird doesn't even start to cover it."

"You can see it too. I know you can."

"Shut up." John cupped Mike's face in his hands. He stroked back the hair from his temples, beautiful sable hair as rich and dark as the day he'd first met him. "You and me, we don't have any business worrying about life's mysteries. We've got enough on our plates just getting from day to day."

Mike nodded. He closed his eyes as John kissed him, blindly folded the photo up and pushed it into the bag. "A house to build," he said.

"Yes. An irritating kid to raise. And I don't know what to believe about Nick and Diane, or Anzhel and Oriel for that matter, but we're going to have to keep the watch, sweetheart, every day."

"One day at a time?"

"That's right."

"With you. All I ever wanted."

About the Author

Harper Fox is the author of many critically acclaimed M/M romance novels, including Stonewall Book Award-nominated *Scrap Metal* and *Brothers of the Wild North Sea*, Publishers Weekly Best Book 2013. To find out more about Harper and see updates on her current writing projects, please visit www.harperfox.net.

www.ingramcontent.com/pod-product-compliance
Lightning Source LLC
Chambersburg PA
CBHW031719170626
46808CB00005B/1806